How the Lady Was Won

The Survivors: Book VII

Shana Galen

Also by Shana Galen

Acknowledgments

Thank you to Abby Saul for editing and formatting and to Kim Killion for the cover design. Thank you to Sarah Rosenbarker for proofreading. Any and all mistakes are the sole responsibility of the author.

Special thanks to Gayle Cochrane for her help with graphics and promotion.

One

London, 1810

He wasn't supposed to be nervous. He was supposed to be confident and self-assured, to soothe his bride's frayed nerves.

But Colin had never done this before.

He paced his bed chamber and glanced at the bracket clock. The hour grew late. If he waited much longer, Lady Daphne would think he didn't want her.

He *did* want her.

He didn't really know her, but he found her attractive enough. Still, just because she had stunning blue eyes and long, silvery blond hair didn't mean he wanted to take all of his clothes off and go to bed with her. He didn't so much mind the part where she took off her clothes…

Except that seemed an awkward thing too.

Was he expected to make some comment on her body? Was he supposed to be overcome by passion at the sight of her naked flesh? How was he to know what the right thing to

7

say might be? When he lay beside her, was he supposed to whisper words of love? He didn't love her. He knew almost nothing about her. And he was not a man given to strong emotions. He didn't want to be overcome by passion or tortured by love. His schoolmates had always called him The Poet, but that was because he had dark, curly hair and a perpetually brooding expression. He wasn't very good with words.

And he was an absolute failure when it came to emotions.

The clock chimed midnight, and Colin knew he could not wait any longer. Trying not to think too much about what he should or shouldn't do, he opened his bed chamber door and crossed the corridor to tap on his wife's door. The sound was muffled, but in the silent house, it seemed to echo like a pistol shot. Her family, all tucked away in their beds, had probably heard the quiet knock and known exactly what it meant. He wished he had thought to suggest they spend their first night together at a hotel. He wished he had his own residence, but it seemed an unnecessary expense when he was leaving in a fortnight to join his regiment in the army.

Still he was nervous enough without having to do the deed under the Duke of Warcliffe's roof. Colin would have to sit across from his father-in-law at breakfast in the morning. The duke would chat about the weather or some such thing, while both of them thought about how Colin had deflowered the duke's youngest daughter the night before.

"Come in!" Lady Daphne's voice was not nearly as quiet as he might have hoped. But she was not a quiet woman. He supposed that when one was the youngest of nine children, one had to fight not to be ignored. Lady Daphne certainly made sure no one ignored her.

Colin opened the door and poked his head in. "I hope I am not disturbing you." She was seated in bed, the pillows behind her propping her up so that her blond hair streamed down her shoulders and over the white linen of her nightclothes. He'd never seen her without her hair piled high and embellished with curls and feathers and jeweled pins. She looked smaller with her hair loose and brushed into soft waves. Her face looked pale, her plump lips starkly red in contrast. A lamp burned on the table beside the bed, and she placed the book she'd been reading near it.

"I've been waiting for you," she said. Her eyes, so blue under dark brows and lashes, met his gaze without hesitation.

Of course, she had. He should not have made her wait.

"I apologize." He closed the door and stood awkwardly in front of it. Did he start undressing now or did he undress her first? Or perhaps he just lifted her skirts and did it that way. That would save both of them the embarrassment of removing clothing. She pushed the coverlet aside and slid out of bed. Colin couldn't help but follow the flash of ankle he saw and then her bare feet as she padded across the carpet to a bottle of wine on the dresser. She had such small, white feet.

"Do you want a glass of wine?" she asked, holding a bottle out to him.

He nodded. He wanted this over, but if she wanted wine, he wouldn't deny her. She poured two glasses and crossed to him. Her night rail was not flimsy, but it was not exactly meant to hide her body. A row of bows lined the front from neck to knee, and there was a gap of about two inches between each, giving him tantalizing glimpses of bare skin. Of course, her nightclothes would have bows. Everything she wore was covered in copious bows. But while those were mainly for show, these seemed functional. If he pulled at the corners of one, the nightrail would open.

Colin drank half his wine.

"I thought we might talk for a while," she said, looking up at him uncertainly. She was nervous as well. He really should say something like, *you have nothing to worry about* or *I won't hurt you*. But what if he did hurt her? He looked down at her. He wished she were a bit taller and not quite so delicate-looking. Her breasts pushed at the bow containing them, and his mouth went dry.

"If you like," he said, sipping more wine. His glass was almost empty.

"We don't know each other very well," she said, stating the obvious. "But I'm certain our mothers would not have wanted us to marry if they hadn't thought we would make a good match."

Colin didn't necessarily agree with that statement. The Duchess of Warcliffe and Viscountess FitzRoy had been friends since girlhood. They always said they were as close as sisters. Colin suspected they wanted their youngest children to marry because it would formally connect the two families, although no one in the families—save the viscountess and the duchess—wanted to be connected. The Warcliffes were loud and proud and given to much entertaining. The FitzRoys were quiet, restrained, and given to much reading. Colin didn't want to contradict his wife of barely sixteen hours, especially not right before he deflowered her, so he gave her a noncommittal nod.

"What do you like to do?" she asked him.

They'd had a handful of conversations, and this was a repeat of one of them, so Colin knew the answer. "I read and go to the theater. You?"

"Oh, I like to go to balls…"

And dance, he thought.

"…and dance," she said. "Do you ever go to balls?"

"Rarely. Do you like horses?"

She wrinkled her nose. Well, that was enough chatter for him. He gestured to the bed. "Perhaps we should get on with the, er, wedding night."

She looked at the bed and swallowed. "I had hoped we would come to know each other a bit better…before. You might tell me your deepest, darkest secret, and then I could tell you mine."

Colin narrowed his eyes at her. She was barely eighteen and had been under the watchful eye of her older brothers and parents since she'd first been placed in her crib. He rather doubted she had any deep, dark secrets. And if she did, what was he supposed to do or say if she told him about them? His own secrets were just that—nothing he wanted to tell her or anyone else for that matter.

A few years before he had fancied himself in love with the older sister of one of his fellows at Eton. He'd written her a poem expressing his sentiments and slipped it to her clandestinely. She'd handed it back to him the next day, patted his cheek, and said he was a silly little boy.

He would not be made a fool of again.

"It's been a long day," he said. "I think we are both tired. Perhaps we can save the conversation until tomorrow.

"Oh." She set her glass down and smoothed her nightgown. "Very well. I've not done this before. What should I do?"

Now might be the time to confess he had not done this either. They could figure it out together. They could laugh together at mistakes or sigh together with pleasure. But Colin was not good at confessions. He'd made them before and been properly ridiculed.

"Lie on the bed," he said.

She walked to the bed as though going to her execution. While she climbed under the covers, he sat on the edge and removed his shoes then his coat and cravat. Finally, he pulled his shirt out of his trousers and turned to face her. She was watching him with those big, blue eyes, even her lips pale now. Colin decided this might be easier if he turned out the lamp.

He lowered the flame until the light sputtered and died, and the two of them became but shadows in the dim light from the hearth. Then he climbed into bed beside her. He fumbled a bit, looking for the hem of her nightclothes. Colin might only have a vague idea of what to do, but his cock was ready. The mere suggestion of touching a woman was enough to excite that appendage.

He found her hem and began to push the garment up.

"Aren't you going to kiss me first?" she asked.

He stilled. She was right. He was supposed to kiss her. He'd kissed women before—well, girls really. He'd been given the odd day off at Eton or Oxford and had gone into the village to have a pint with the other lads. There was usually a pretty girl about, and he'd kissed a few. Even in Oxford there were ladies willing to do more than kiss. He hadn't sought them out because he'd agreed with his father when he'd sat Colin down and said, "Human beings are not commodities to buy and sell. No FitzRoy would ever condone that sort of thing, much less be part of it." His father had been speaking of the slave trade, but Colin knew his father's directive included fallen women as well.

Daphne was trembling. It was a slight movement, which he imagined she tried to hide, but with his body so close to hers, he could feel her quaking. Perhaps kissing her would relax them both. "You're right. I should kiss you." His eyes were adjusting to the dark, and he found her face easily and cupped it. He balanced himself above her and dipped his mouth to hers. Her mouth tasted slightly of peppermint as he brushed his lips over hers. Her lips were soft and plump, the sort of lips made for kissing. He tasted them, suckled them, plundered them. Her arms came around his neck then and she sighed in pleasure. He teased her mouth open and dipped his tongue inside, tasting more peppermint on her tongue. She tensed again, but he coaxed and charmed until she opened to him and even slid her tongue against his.

This was the part of the kiss where he usually had to stop. Sometimes he could manage to sneak a quick touch of a breast, and he moved his hand now, down her shoulder and over the swell of her flesh. She tensed again, and he tried to think of what he should say to relax her, but his palm brushed over her nipple, hard against the thin linen. He couldn't really think with his hand on her like this. He cupped her breast gently, and it more than filled his hand.

She was still trembling, so he kissed her again. But she didn't respond as she had before. His cock strained against his trousers and he longed to free it, but she was so stiff now. "Should I stop?" he asked, breathless.

"No. It's nice. It's just all so new, all these feelings."

No. Not feelings. He did not want her to start talking about feelings. He kissed her again, and she returned the kiss. Her body even arched slightly, pressing against his. That was all the encouragement he needed. He loosed the placket of his trousers, freeing his cock. Drawn to the heat of her body, he pushed her nightrail up and settled between her legs. She was so warm. He touched her curls and she jumped.

"Sorry," she said.

"It will only hurt for a moment." That's what he'd heard anyway. He had no idea if it was true. She nodded, looking up at him with worry creasing her forehead.

He entered her, his cock seeming to have a mind of its own. She was tight, and he had to push to enter. Stars danced before his eyes as pleasure began to build. He moved deeper inside her and heard her gasp of pain. He tried to stop, but the orgasm was on him. One more thrust. He tried to be gentle. He felt his seed spill into her, felt the barest hint of a climax, and then he was looking down at her and feeling completely unfulfilled.

Her face was tensed, her eyes closed and her lips flat. He pulled out, and she opened her eyes and looked at him. "Is that it?" she asked.

He knew she didn't mean it as an insult. He'd given her no pleasure whatsoever. He'd barely had any himself. He would have enjoyed it more if he'd used his own hand. What had he done wrong?

Colin tucked his cock back into his trousers then looked at the wetness on his hand.

Blood.

"That's it," he said. "Are you hurt?"

"It wasn't so bad."

Again, he knew she didn't mean to insult him, but it was difficult not to feel some shame at how poorly he'd performed.

"I'll leave you to your, er, ablutions," he said, rising from the bed.

She pulled her nightrail down and sat. "You're leaving?"

"I wouldn't want to impose on your privacy. Good night, Lady Daphne."

She stared at him. "Good night, Mr. FitzRoy."

He opened her door and crossed the corridor again. When he was back in his room, he slumped against the wall. The clock read twenty past twelve. The whole interlude had taken less than twenty minutes, and the act itself about thirty seconds. He'd hurt her with his clumsiness. He would never forget the way her face looked, scrunched with pain.

Well, he had done his duty. He needn't do it again. His mother, God rest her soul, might not be proud of him, but he'd done as she'd wanted. He'd be on the Continent fighting the French in a month. He'd probably be killed, and he imagined Daphne would be glad to marry again. This time she could marry a man who could give her what she needed—a man who knew how to do more than kiss, a man whose throat didn't lock up every time anyone asked him something more personal than the state of the weather.

If he died, it would be better for everyone.

***

Seven years later

Lady Daphne was in trouble. Again. Trouble seemed to follow her like a hungry puppy, and she could not resist feeding it. Except this puppy had grown into a savage beast and wanted to bite off her arm.

"I see your friend the Earl of Battersea is here," Lady Pavenley said, her gaze directed across the crowded ballroom. Her tone was one of mild indifference, but Daphne knew she was gloating. She'd already seen the earl, and it had taken all of her willpower not to turn and flee. He hadn't seen her yet. She hoped. How many events had she left early in the past few weeks in order to avoid him? She'd stopped counting.

"I do hope he asks someone besides Lady Daphne to dance," Lady Isabella said. "I find the silver at his temples quite dashing."

Daphne found everything about the earl more disturbing than dashing. Of course, she'd thought him dashing at one time too. That had been her mistake. Now she just wished he would leave her alone.

The three ladies stood in a circle at the end of the ballroom. Daphne imagined they looked like a trio of flowers. She wore her signature pink, Lady Pavenley wore violet, and Lady Isabella wore yellow. Daphne was under no illusion that either of her friends—if someone who would just as soon stick a knife in your back as pass you the salt could be called a friend—had any concern for her. Like the rest of the *ton* they were here to watch the show. And that show's fifth and final act would only satisfy if someone was scandalized. No doubt Daphne's companions hoped it would be Daphne.

"I have no interest in dancing with him," Daphne said, hoping she sounded airy and unconcerned. In reality, she was scanning the ballroom, looking for the nearest exit.

"Well, not all of us are married to war heroes," Lady Isabella observed. Her own husband was in his mid-forties with bushy eyebrows and hair that poked out of his ears. Like Daphne, she had married a man of lower rank. Lady Isabella was the daughter of a marquess and her husband was only the heir to a lowly baron.

Lady Pavenley tittered. "Yes, Mr. FitzRoy is quite dashing. He dashes about here and dashes about there. He is forever dashing about." Noting the absence of Daphne's husband was a favorite pastime for Lady Pavenley, who was married to the Earl of Pavenley. He was a notorious drunk who rarely attended a ball without vomiting on the floor or pissing in a corner.

Daphne observed, not for the first time, that the three of them should have been friends. Society liked to call them the Three Suns, ostensibly because the earth revolved around them, but also because they were all considered beauties who outshone other ladies. Daphne was the most conventionally beautiful, being blond and blue-eyed. But though her hair was pale, she had naturally rosy lips and dark brows and lashes. Added to that she had her grandmother's aristocratic cheekbones, her mother's lush figure, and her father's strong straight nose. More than one man stopped and stared when she passed.

Lady Pavenley had dark hair, almost blue black, and deep violet eyes. She was tall and regal and quite voluptuous. Lady Isabella had chestnut hair with tones of red in it that Daphne was never quite sure were actually natural. She had large breasts that always looked like they might spill out of her low-cut gowns. They had done so on more than one occasion, and the result had been poets who wrote sonnets to her ruddy nipples and pale orbs.

But the three were not friends, though they put on a show for the eyes of Society. In reality, they were enemies who had called a truce because if they'd gone to war they would have ruined each other so thoroughly that only a few scraps of hair and a bit of lace would have remained.

Instead, they ruined or elevated others. One nod from the Three Suns toward a debutante and the girl was sure to be a success. One cross word about her dress and she would have to leave Town in disgrace.

Daphne had no thirst for blood. It wasn't until after a Season or two that she realized the power her favor or censure held. She'd ruined a girl's chances at a good match completely by accident. If she'd been in a foul mood and frowned in the direction of an unmarried young lady, the *ton* would follow suit.

These days Daphne tried not to smile or frown at any unmarried ladies, but the other two suns were not so kind. They relished their power and status. Lately, Daphne had grown rather tired of the *ton* and the endless social engagements. She wanted something more than mind-numbing chatter and endless gossip.

"Where is dear Mr. FitzRoy tonight?" Lady Isabella asked. It was the question one or the other of them asked every time they were together. Surely they knew she had no idea, but it was undoubtedly interesting to see how she would justify his absence over and over again. His absence was humiliating, and the other Suns made sure to humiliate her as often as they could.

Daphne knew FitzRoy was back from the war. She'd heard he was living with his sisters and father in the country. But lately he'd been seen in London, so he must have a residence here. As a woman, she couldn't very well search him out.

And he hadn't bothered to search for her, though she was not difficult to find.

Unless she wanted to admit she hadn't seen her own husband in seven years, Lady Daphne had little choice but to play along with the Suns' game. "You know him," she said, though of course none of them knew Colin FitzRoy. "He has important work to do."

"What sort of work?" Lady Pavenley asked with a sneer.

"War hero work," Daphne said, then added, "He mentioned deciphering a document. It's top secret, of course. He cannot even tell me what the coded missive contains."

The two ladies looked interested, despite themselves. Daphne knew they didn't want to believe her, but they were not quite sure if some of what she said could be true. One day she'd be exposed for the liar she was and publicly humiliated.

That night was not tonight.

Unless the Earl of Battersea found her. He was making his way across the ballroom now, and this was her last chance to escape. "I think I shall find the ladies' retiring room," she said, turning to go.

"I'll go with you," Lady Isabella said.

Not wanting to be left alone, Lady Pavenley also moved. "I shall go too."

There was safety in numbers, but it was temporary. She had to escape the ball, and she couldn't do it with the Suns circling her. Walking ahead a bit, she spotted the young son of a peer. He looked as though he'd been scrubbed and shaved within an inch of his life. The still soft flesh of his jaw was ruddy from the razor yet. As she passed him, she grasped his arm and whispered, "Lady Isabella wants to dance with you. Go and ask her."

The lad's eyes widened, but he didn't waste any time stepping before Isabella and bowing almost into her bosom, effectively detaining her. That tactic would not work with Lady Pavenley. She was too tall and imposing to be approached by a man who didn't know her. Instead, Daphne scooted past a woman about her own mother's age. She nodded in greeting then said, "Lady Pavenley is looking for Lord Pavenley. Could you help her?" The matron's nostrils flared with interest, like a hound scenting prey. And she arrowed straight for Lady Pavenley while Daphne slipped out of the ballroom.

Once free of the ballroom, she looked left then right. She couldn't very well walk out the front door. People were still arriving, and she would be seen. It might be a half hour before her carriage could be found, and by that time Battersea would find her. That meant she would need to go out the back, past the mews. Once on the street she could hail a hackney and go home. She'd send one of her father's footmen to tell the coachman to return to the duke's town house.

Most of the town houses in London were quite similar in layout, and it did not take her long to find the servants' back door and exit along a dark path. At the end of it, she saw a gate and, on the other side, the row of mews. Thank God. She was free of Battersea and free of all the whispers and speculation about her absent husband. She started along the path, careful of her footing as it was dark. Too late she saw the man step out before her. He was large and dark, a cloak obscuring his body and a hat pulled low on his forehead.

She gasped and stumbled backward, almost losing her balance. Was he a thief? A murderer?

"Lady Daphne," he said.

The use of her name did little to quell her fear. "How do you know my name?" It couldn't be Battersea. She'd just seen him inside.

"How do you not know mine?" He lifted his head and removed his hat, bowing to her in a sort of mocking way. It might have been dark, but she knew those features.

"FitzRoy," she whispered.

He arched a brow at her. "Let's find somewhere we can talk, wife."

Two

Colin had been watching her for the last hour. He hadn't wanted to see his wife, but the Duchess of Warcliffe had harassed him for weeks. Finally, he had agreed to go to this ball if only his mother-in-law would leave him in peace for a little while. He hadn't intended to speak to Lady Daphne. She need never know he was even in attendance. He was good at blending in. He kept to the edges and the corners and didn't look anyone directly in the eye. He'd stood next to men he'd known at school and ladies he had danced with at other balls, and no one had noticed him.

That was why in the army Colin had been called The Pretender.

He could have contented himself just watching Lady Daphne. Her mother had said she was in trouble, but nothing looked amiss to Colin. As he had observed on several other occasions, she laughed with her friends, she danced with several gentleman, she sipped champagne. Obviously, the Duchess of Warcliffe had lied to him in order to force a meeting between himself and Daphne. Colin should have just gone home as he had other nights. He didn't need to speak to Daphne, and yet, here he was.

Now that she knew who he was, the terror in her eyes had fled, replaced by skepticism. "So now you want to talk, do you?" Her voice was as sharp and cold as ice.

Colin allowed himself a half smile. It was the perfect jab; he would give her that. He could hardly blame her for stabbing at him, considering she'd had nary a word from him since he'd left for the army. "I would like a word, yes. Unless I'm interrupting other plans. A clandestine meeting? There's no one else out here. I looked."

"I'm tired. I want to go home." That wasn't like her. The Daphne he knew always danced until dawn. But the Daphne he knew didn't creep out the back.

"Sneaking out of a ball through the servants' door. Why?"

She put a hand on her waist, probably intending to look stern. But it was difficult to take her too seriously in her pink frothy dress covered in twenty-eight bows. Yes, twenty-eight. He had counted.

"That is not your concern," she said.

One bow on each sleeve.

She frowned. "Honestly, I can't see how *I* am any of your concern."

One bow at her bodice and one at the middle of her back.

"I haven't seen you for seven years," she continued.

Four rows of four bows each down the length of her skirt, two rows in front and two in back.

"And now you pop out of nowhere and have the gall to question me."

Eight bows circling the hem of the dress.

"We have to speak at some point. We're still married," he observed wryly.

"That's not my fault!"

"Nor mine." But they had to confront it at some point. Why not tonight? He offered his arm. "Let's go."

She looked at his arm and then at his face. He wondered what she saw when she looked at him. When he had spotted her tonight, he'd felt as though he'd been punched in the chest. She was so beautiful. She'd been beautiful when he married her, but she'd also been quite young. She hadn't really grown into her mouth or her eyes, and they'd looked almost too big for her face. But she looked absolutely breathtaking now. Her silvery blond hair was piled on her head with a long curl falling over one mostly bare shoulder. Her brows were slightly darker than her hair and perfectly arched, her lashes almost black—something he assumed was helped along by cosmetics—and her eyes were of the deepest blue. It was hard to see anything but those eyes, they were so compelling, so vibrant, but if his gaze strayed to her cheekbones, he could see her face had thinned a bit and looked more sculpted. Her lips were his undoing, though. They were plump and red and such a perfect bow.

He fondly remembered kissing those lips.

"Where are we going?" she asked. "That is, *if* I choose to go with you."

That was a good question. He'd intended to go to the Draven Club after he'd checked in on her at the ball, but he couldn't very well take her there. And he couldn't take her home. They couldn't talk privately with her father, mother, and siblings frowning at him and giving him cutting looks. "Mayne House," he said on a whim.

Her brows came together. "Where?"

"The residence of the Duke of Mayne. I happen to know he's been spending a great deal of time in Berkshire on business"—if one considered a new wife business—"and his door is always open to me." Colin had taken advantage of his friend's generosity on several occasions already this Season. Colin had only returned from the Continent and his army duties about eighteen months ago. He'd gone to his father's country estate to help with various matters there. And then, just as he'd settled in, he'd been summoned to London by his former commander, Lieutenant Colonel Draven, for help with matters pertaining to the remaining Survivors.

He'd known Daphne would be in London, and he'd known he wasn't ready to see her yet. So he'd moved into his own family's town house. Lately, it had been rather crowded as all three of his sisters were in residence.

"Are any of Mayne's servants at his town house?" she asked.

"A small contingent, yes." He wiggled his still extended arm. "Don't worry. You won't have to be alone with me." Not unless she wanted to, and he rather doubted she would ever want to be alone with him again.

"Very well." She took his arm, laying her hand on his sleeve so lightly he couldn't even feel the weight of it. "I haven't called for my carriage."

"We can walk. Mayne House is only a block away." He looked down at her bare arms, the thin muslin of her dress, and whatever that gauzy material was called. It was a mild spring evening but perhaps a bit too cold to walk about so exposed. Already he could see gooseflesh on the bared skin of her chest. He had the urge to put his hands there and warm her. Instead, he removed his coat and draped it over her shoulders.

She gave him a long look then put her hands through the sleeves. The coat looked ridiculously large on her, but he liked seeing her in it. Of course, with her hands tucked in the sleeves, she no longer held onto him. He went ahead and opened the gate, holding it for her as she stepped through it and onto the lane running alongside the mews.

Once they were on their way, she said, "What do you want to talk about?"

He shrugged. He had rather figured she would carry the conversation. "You still haven't told me why you were sneaking away from the ball."

"And you haven't told me why you were at the ball. Did you even have an invitation?"

"I believe your invitation included me."

"Oh," she said, confirming his supposition. "But if you'd mentioned your name, surely all of the guests would have been talking about your presence. Someone would have mentioned it to me. Your absence at every social function I have attended since your return from the war has been noted." Her voice sounded brittle and accusatory. She'd undoubtedly had to deal with the brunt of the curiosity about their estrangement. He was sorry for that now. It would have been much more convenient for her if he'd died in the war.

"And what do you tell people when they ask?" His voice held a note of idle curiosity, but he very much wanted to know the answer.

"This and that." They turned onto a wide street lined with trees, and tucked behind the trees, stone mansions with bright windows and flowers blooming in boxes at the windows. It was quiet enough in Mayfair to hear an owl hoot or an insect chirp. Most of the *ton* was still out for the night.

"Do elaborate," he said, clasping his hands behind his back as they walked. "I might need to know what *this* or *that* refers to if asked."

"Are you mocking me?"

He looked at her. "No." He spoke sincerely. He was not the sort of man to mock anyone but himself.

"Tonight I said you were deciphering a coded document."

"Code breaking?" He stopped in disbelief. "I know nothing of code breaking."

She rounded on him and put her hands on her hips again—or at least where he assumed her hips might be as his coat made her look like an amorphous shape. "And how would I know what you can or cannot do? It sounded like something a war hero would do, and everyone says you are a war hero."

He closed his eyes and rubbed the bridge of his nose where a headache bloomed. "I'm not a war hero." Without pausing to see if she followed, he began walking again.

"But were you not part of that special team?"

"It was a troop, and I would not call it special."

"Well, I once danced with Rafe Beaumont at a ball, and he said you saved his life in France."

That sounded like the sort of thing Rafe would tell her. He would think he was doing Colin a favor and perhaps even playing matchmaker to mend the fences between Colin and Daphne. But Rafe had left for America some months ago and Colin hadn't heard from him since. "When did you dance with Beaumont?" He sounded irritated, though he hadn't meant to. Rafe was a known womanizer, and women couldn't seem to resist throwing themselves at his feet. Colin knew he had no say over who Daphne did or did not throw herself at, but he rather hoped it wasn't his friend and fellow member of the Survivors.

"It was last Season, I think. Early in the Season. He spent a quarter of an hour extolling your virtues. So you needn't be envious."

Colin threw her a disgusted look. "I am not envious."

"No, you wouldn't be."

He wasn't certain what reply he should make to that, but he was saved from having to do so when he saw Mayne House. "It's just there," he said, pointing to it.

"It's dark, and there's no knocker." She slowed, putting a hand to her throat. He remembered that she often did that when she was uncertain about something.

"I told you, he is out of town."

"How do you know the Duke of Mayne?"

"We served together with your friend Rafe."

"He's not my friend. I danced with him. I dance with a lot of men."

"So I gather. And if I'd known Rafe would come back and tell you all sorts of stories about me, I wouldn't have saved his life."

"Ha!" She pointed a finger at him. "You did save his life."

"We all saved each other's lives. Except when we didn't." He started up the steps and tapped on the front door. He had to tap rather loudly as she was right and there was no knocker. Finally, Banks, the butler at Mayne House, opened the door. "Mr. FitzRoy." He stepped back to admit him, his eyes flicking to Lady Daphne but saying nothing. "You are home early, sir."

"You know my wife, Banks," Colin said. "Lady Daphne."

Banks bowed. "I have not had the pleasure, my lady. Welcome."

"Thank you." She allowed the butler to take Colin's coat and Colin was treated to the sight of that pink gown again. The bows were infuriating enough, but the neckline made his jaw clench. It was not scandalous—nothing like her friend Lady Isabella wore—but it was just low enough to hint at the glory that were her breasts beneath it. The half-moons of her pale flesh rose and fell from the lace edging of her bodice every time she breathed.

"Lady Daphne and I would speak in the parlor, if that is acceptable." Colin gestured to a closed door on the right. It was a small chamber with several comfortable chairs and a writing desk.

"Of course. Would you like me to send for tea or other refreshments?"

"No, Banks. We just need a few minutes."

Banks snapped his fingers at a maid who had appeared. "We'll just have the fire lit for you then."

When the maid had finished and scurried out of the parlor, Colin closed the door and turned to Daphne. "So, what sort of trouble *are* you in?"

Daphne paused in the midst of taking a seat on one of the luxurious chairs upholstered in pale green. How could he possibly know? She and Battersea had an agreement.

FitzRoy pointed at her. "Interesting. When your mother came to me saying you were in trouble, I doubted her. You didn't act like a person in trouble. But now I can see the guilt all over your face. You *are* in trouble."

She smoothed her face like she might smooth her dress and sat, arranging her skirts about her. "What you interpret as guilt is actually surprise. Your statement was unexpected."

He leaned against the chair opposite her, studying her face. His eyes, so green under those long, dark lashes assessed her uncomfortably. Fortunately, she had been in the public's eye since she'd been old enough to step out of the nursery. She was used to scrutiny. She should have relaxed the longer he studied her. FitzRoy was no different than most people she knew. If someone knew her secrets, they would have said so by now. His silence was intended to unnerve her so she revealed what he wanted to know. It was a tactic she knew well from years among the *ton*. But his gaze on her had never relaxed her. He was far too compelling.

When ladies said they fancied a man who was tall, dark, and handsome, they envisioned Colin FitzRoy. He had the face of an angel with full lips, a Roman nose, and chiseled cheekbones. His eyes were light green fringed by black lashes and dark brows that slashed above his pale gaze. If he'd pulled his dark curly hair back or cut it short, he would have been a strikingly handsome man, but he wore it full and tousled about his face, giving him an air of mystery.

Daphne's own hair was pinned so tightly that her head ached, and she itched to wrap her hands in his soft curls and brush them from his forehead or tuck them behind his ears. She hadn't ever seen his ears.

"Go on," Colin said.

"Unexpected," she explained, "because I didn't realize you had so much gall. Really, who do you think you are? You left for the war and never wrote me a single letter. Then when you finally returned, you completely ignored me. I had to hear from the gossips that you were back in England. Do you know how humiliating that was for me?"

He lowered his gaze, obviously chastened.

"And now you come here and demand to know intimate details about my life. You have no right to ask me anything. You don't know anything about me."

He looked at his hands, draped over the back of the chair. He had long fingers with lean, square nails. "Does the

Duchess of Warcliffe know anything about you? Why would she tell me you needed help if you did not?"

"My mother? She loves nothing more than a scheme. You know that."

"She has been cornering me throughout London, insisting that I take you in hand."

Daphne jumped to her feet. "Take me in hand! I am not a child, sir."

He shrugged. "Those were her words, not mine."

"I've done quite well without you all these years. I don't need your interference now."

"Interference? What am I interfering in? The trouble you still haven't denied?"

"This is ridiculous." She lifted her skirts and moved around the chair. "I will not stay so you may invent falsehoods about me." She swept past him in a haughty swath of muslin, silk, and organza, but he caught her arm at the last moment, ruining her exit. Slowly, he pulled her back until they were face-to-face.

"I will admit I was shooting arrows into the dark," he said, his voice low, "but I rather think from your reaction that I have hit close to the mark."

"Is that what you think?" She felt warm, too warm. She hadn't been this close to him for so long and her body reacted without her permission. She wanted to melt into him, surrender to his hand on her bare arm, touch him back.

He raised his brows and for a moment she thought perhaps she'd spoken her thoughts aloud, and he was challenging her to touch him. But then she remembered she'd spoken—said something to buy herself time. She needed to remember she was angry at him, furious. He'd hurt her, and she wanted nothing to do with him. She took a shaky breath. "Let me ask you something, Colin."

His eyes seemed to twinkle with amusement, but that couldn't be. The man didn't have emotions. He'd all but said so himself. "What is it, *Daphne*?"

"You haven't cared what I did or did not do for the past seven years. Why do you care now?"

"I was on the Continent for the majority of those years."

"And I suppose all the letters you wrote inquiring after my health were misdirected?"

The amusement left his eyes. "I should have written," he said.

She lifted one shoulder, dismissing the years she had written to him faithfully and hoped without hope he might reply. "It doesn't matter now. You never cared for me, and you needn't start pretending now."

"You never cared for me either. It was an arranged marriage that we were both forced to agree to."

She flinched slightly then quickly tried to cover it, but he'd seen.

His hand on her arm tightened and his eyes seemed to look right through her. "You didn't want this marriage. Did you?"

She looked away. "Of course not."

He released her as though her skin burned him. "Oh, my God."

No. What an idiot she was. How could she let him guess at the truth? She'd never let him know how she'd really felt. How much his dismissal of her had really hurt. "I didn't want this marriage. Not then and not now." To underscore her words, she turned away from him, saw the door, and started for it again. "I'd appreciate it if you would go back to leaving me alone."

She grasped the door handle just as Colin's arm snagged around her waist. She gasped at the feel of his body pressed against her back and his breath on her neck. She shivered. Why did she still feel this way about him? He'd brought her nothing but misery, and still she felt the undeniable pull of attraction when she was near him.

"I don't believe you." His whispered words only further tantalized the tender skin beneath her ear.

"I don't care what you think." Her voice was thin and reedy, uncertain. She did not care. It was not as though he was someone she could trust or count on.

"Tell me the truth, Daphne."

"I…" She couldn't tell him the truth about Battersea and his threats. How could Colin help her? By lecturing her? By lecturing Battersea? Colin would just disappear again, and she'd be in a worse position than she was now.

No, she had made the mistake of trusting Colin FitzRoy once, and she would not do so again. "Let me go," she said, her hand still on the door handle. Colin released her, but before she could open it, the door handle turned on its own. Colin pulled her back just in time for the door to swing open. A very large, very frightening-looking man stepped into the doorway, completely blocking her exit.

The man had long, wild brown hair and three days' growth of beard, and wore a linen shirt with a skirt. Daphne looked up at him, watched his scowl deepen, and stumbled backward. Colin caught her, and she scrambled to pull him away. They had to reach the door on the other side of the room or jump out a window before the lunatic who'd just burst in on them slit both their throats.

But Colin stood still, hands on his hips. "Duncan. What are you doing here?"

"That's the question I was aboot to ask you. Dinnae know it was you, Pretender." He looked over his shoulder. "Why did you nae tell me, Banks?" he yelled.

Daphne immediately recognized his accent as Scottish. As Colin seemed to know the Scot, she gave him another look and realized he wore a kilt, not a skirt. That didn't make him any less fearsome. He was a head taller than her husband, who was not a short man, and the Scot's shoulders filled the doorway. His gaze fell on her, and Daphne tried to look brave, straightening her shoulders and lifting her chin.

"Looks like I'm interrupting."

Colin glanced at her, seemed to consider, then said, "Lady Daphne, may I present Mr. Duncan Murray. We fought together in Draven's troop. Mr. Murray, my wife."

The Scot's eyebrows went up, but he bowed politely and stepped into the parlor, making it feel far too small. "A pleasure, my lady. I've heard a bit aboot you."

This surprised Daphne. She glanced at Colin, whose face held no discernable expression. He was very good at hiding whatever he might be thinking or feeling. "Forgive me, I've heard nothing of you."

The big man shrugged his shoulders. "Your man doesna want to talk about the war any more than the rest of us." His gaze went back to Colin. "What are you doing here?"

"Mayne said I could stay here if my town house felt too crowded. With my sisters there, I haven't a moment's peace."

The Scotsman nodded then walked to a cabinet and opened it. He pulled out a decanter of amber liquid and sniffed. "Brandy. Suppose it was too much to hope for whisky." He closed the cabinet door, obviously preferring nothing over brandy. For Daphne's part, she would not have minded a sip or even a gulp.

"And you?" her husband asked.

"My mother sent me to London to find a lass for a bride. She said not to come home withoot one. I saw Mayne in Berkshire, and he offered me a room here. I just arrived a few hours ago. Scared the butler half to death." He winked at Daphne.

He would scare the ladies of London half to death too. Colin asked his friend about the Duke of Mayne, and though Daphne should have been listening to the conversation as the duke was always a source of much gossip, she could hardly pay attention when she noticed the Scot's gaze strayed to her and stayed.

Daphne took a step back again and almost fell over a chair. Instead, she sat in it, hoping to be as unobtrusive as possible. But the Scot interrupted Colin and pointed at her. "Your wife is a lady."

Colin looked at her. "Her father is a duke," he said, not really answering the question.

"Maybe she can help me."

Daphne tried to swallow the lump in her throat. "How can *I* help you, Mr. Murray?"

"You ken ladies. You can get me a wife."

Daphne shook her head. "No, I cannot."

But the Scot was not deterred by her head shaking or her outright refusal. "It's simple enough, lass. Just introduce me to your friends at the next ball."

"That might be difficult," Colin said, walking toward her. Finally, he was actually being useful. He stopped before her and looked down. "I don't think she has any friends."

"For your information, I have many friends—a fact you would know if you'd bothered to spend any time with me."

Colin gave her a skeptical look.

"I dinnae mean they had to be close friends, my lady. Just any lass who isnae a chore to look upon and has a backbone. My mother eats timid lasses with her tea."

Daphne stood. "You are behaving as though a wife is something you order, like a coat or hat. You have to woo a wife, court her, write poetry."

The Scot looked at Colin. "Is that how he married you?"

She opened her mouth then shut it again, not sure what to say. Colin stepped in. "A pretty woman with some courage is rather impossible to find in the circles Lady Daphne moves in. I ought to know as I was raised in those same circles."

The Scot pointed to her. "You found one."

Colin glanced at her. "She is pretty."

Oh, the nerve of these men. This was what she had always hated about her father. He spoke about her as though she wasn't standing right there. "There are plenty of marriageable women in London who are not merely pretty but beautiful and have more strength and courage than the two of you combined. But you are both overlooking a very important point."

"What's that?" Colin asked, arching a skeptical brow.

"I do not owe Mr. FitzRoy any favors. You will have to find someone else to assist you with your search, Mr. Murray. I'm certain there are women in Scotland. Perhaps you might go back and find one there."

The Scot shook his head. "Willnae work. They all know of my mother."

"What is wrong with your mother?" she asked, against her better judgement.

"Nothing is wrong with her, lass. She's strong-willed." His shoulders slumped, and he looked like a man thoroughly defeated. Daphne tried to push down the compassion she felt for him. She wanted nothing to do with Colin or his friends. The Scot sighed. "I'll just be going now. I've imposed on you too long."

Daphne watched him go then rounded on Colin. "I am not helping him find a wife," she said as much for herself as for him. "And now I think it's best if I go home."

"Shouldn't we discuss"—he gestured between them— "this further?"

"What is there to discuss? I don't want to be married to you any more than you want to be married to me." She raised her brows. "Unless something has changed, and you *do* want to be married to me?"

She heard his intake of breath and watched the way his throat moved when he swallowed. He just could not seem to stop humiliating her. Of course, he did not want to be married to her. This entire evening had been a waste of time.

Daphne brushed past him. "I am leaving."

"You can't go by yourself. It's not safe."

She opened the parlor door. He might think he could control her, but he would soon find otherwise. "My carriage is at the ball. That's just a few streets away." She stalked into the foyer and a footman scrambled to move out of her way.

"I'll walk with you."

"No, thank you." Still, she was not a fool. She shouldn't go out in the middle of the night alone. She pointed to the footman. "You. You can walk me back to the ball."

"My lady?" The footman looked from her to Colin. Colin seemed to consider for a moment then nodded.

"Escort her to Lord Ludlow's ball and see that she's put safely in her carriage. Come back and see me when it's done."

"Yes, sir."

Daphne turned to open the door, but the butler had already opened it for her. She swept out, followed by the footman. She didn't look over her shoulder, but Colin must have come out as well, for she heard him say, "Goodnight, my lady."

She stared straight ahead. "Good-bye."

"Not yet. This isn't finished."

The words sounded like a threat.

Three

Two evenings later, Colin was reminded of why he and Duncan had never spent much time together, either during the war or after. Colin's mission had always been to blend in, to hide, to pretend to be someone who belonged even in the most unlikely places. Duncan Murray did not blend in. Even wearing proper evening clothes, the man drew everyone's attention. At Lady Rosemont's musicale, heads turned, fans were opened, and all conversation was reduced to a murmur as soon as Colin and Duncan entered.

For a long moment, the guests, who were assembled in the drawing room and milling about while waiting for the evening's entertainment to begin, simply stared at the two men. And then, as though Moses had raised his hands to part the Red Sea, the guests moved aside, revealing Lady Daphne at the other end of the room. She paused mid-step, and Colin realized she'd been about to escape through a side door. She closed her eyes as though in agony. Then she straightened her shoulders, a gesture that reminded him of a warrior donning his armor, and gave him a too bright smile. He smiled back. To his surprise, he was genuinely pleased to see her.

She was dressed in pink again tonight, but this evening's concoction was pale pink with nary a bow in sight. The waist was high and the skirts straight. A darker pink sash circled her frame just below her breasts.

Duncan leaned close. "She doesna look happy to see you."

"Shut up."

Colin moved away from Duncan, walking through the parted crowds until he reached his wife. He gave her a bow and she offered her gloved hand—her gloves were pink, he noted.

"Do you mind if we have a word in private?" she murmured, her smile still stuck in place.

"I am your servant," he said.

With a nod, she turned and walked away. Colin had no choice but to follow her. Now he saw the bows. The sash was tied in a bow and the tails of that bow were covered by dark pink bows that trailed down her backside and legs. More bows cascaded between the tails of the bow, making her buttocks and the area between her legs look like a pink and white rose garden. Colin wondered how she managed to sit in such a gown. He wondered if she realized how provocative such a design was to any man who looked. His gaze couldn't help but be drawn to her backside and the space where he would fit nicely if he had her on her knees.

Colin shook his head to clear it of the image.

She led him out of the ballroom and into a small side chamber that must have been utilized as the staff's serving area because several footmen stood about filling wine glasses and placing them on trays. The murmur of conversation ceased as soon as they entered, and the servants all turned to stare.

"Excuse us," Colin said, moving back toward the ballroom.

Daphne held up a hand. "Yes, please excuse us," she repeated but in a very different tone. When the footmen exchanged uncertain glances, she cleared her throat. "Get out."

Within seconds, the chamber was empty but for the two of them. It was not a tactic Colin would have used, but he could admire the confidence she had that her wishes would be obeyed. Daphne walked to the serving table, lifted a champagne glass from a tray, and downed the contents. She coughed a little, lifted another, sipped, then turned to look at him. "Are you trying to cause a scene?"

Colin raised a brow. She was obviously upset. He could feel an emotional outburst gathering in the chamber like a storm. Knowing what was coming only made him calmer, more detached. "No," he answered simply.

"Then why are you doing this to me?" She gesticulated wildly, her cheeks turning pink.

"I'm not doing anything—"

"Do not deny it! No one has seen us together since our wedding, and yet, here you are, unannounced. Worse, you bring that brute of a Scot to Lady Rosemont's musicale. She will have an apoplectic fit. No one will listen to the music now. They'll all be watching you to see if you make a scene."

"I rather think you are the one making the scene, my lady."

That must have been her breaking point because she slammed the glass down, sloshing the contents on the table. She took a deep breath, perhaps to compose herself. "I do not want you here, Mr. FitzRoy. I want you to go back to wherever you were and leave me alone."

"I can't. The other night you all but confirmed you are in trouble, and I'll have no peace until I rescue you from it."

"You never cared if I was in any trouble before."

"Perhaps I've changed."

She gave him a long assessing look, and he felt the skin under his collar heat. Her gaze still intent, she stepped forward. They were quite close now, and he could smell the champagne on her breath and the tart, fruity scent of…something familiar. It was probably her perfume, but he liked to think of it as wafting from the flower-shaped bows on her gown. "You haven't changed."

It unnerved him how easily she saw through him.

"And I do not need you to rescue me. I am perfectly capable of taking care of the problem on my own."

"So you admit there is a problem."

"I do, and that problem is you!" she shouted. The color in her cheeks was high and her eyes bright. Her chest heaved as she gulped in air.

She looked magnificent.

"Why are you so out of sorts?" he drawled.

Her jaw dropped and she all but hissed. "Because I have built a life these past seven years without you. Then here you come, like a toddler who sees a block tower and knocks it down without a thought. You are ruining everything!"

"That's a bit of an exaggeration."

"You would say that. I've known you and your family since childhood. You like everything calm and composed, sterile and emotionless. Well, I am not emotionless, and I am feeling one emotion very strongly right now." She moved even closer, and he had the urge to step back—that or take her into his arms and show her…what? She had described him accurately. "Do you know what emotion I am feeling right now?" she asked. He pretended to study her and contemplate. Her cheeks were pink, her chest heaved, exposing the pale flesh of her breasts, and her blue eyes burned into him. He did not think it was the same emotion he was feeling.

"I'll answer if you do," he said.

She tossed her head. "Ha! Who can ever tell what you are feeling? I don't even think you *have* feelings."

"They may be primitive and embryonic, but I have them. If you can tell me what I am feeling right now, I will defer to your anger"—he paused to make certain she knew he had acknowledged her emotion—"and leave."

Her eyes narrowed. "And you'll take the brute with you?"

"Yes." Colin couldn't really make that promise. Duncan did what he wanted, and Colin certainly didn't have the strength to make him leave if he chose to stay. It didn't matter. She'd never guess what he felt. He'd made a career out of playing a part, schooling his features, remaining dispassionate even while everyone else was panicking.

"And as a gentleman, if I guess you will tell me the truth."

"You have my word."

"Very well." She tilted her head to one side, the silvery curl she'd worn trailing down from her elaborate coiffure sliding over her shoulder and along her arm as she did so. He stood very still as she studied him, but his skin warmed as her gaze slid over it. First his eyes, then his mouth, then his lips; his throat, back to his eyes. Thank God she hadn't looked lower. She would have guessed easily.

She tapped a finger to her rosy lips, and he couldn't drag his gaze from that finger.

"You are feeling…smug." She smiled, quite smugly.

"No."

Her smile dropped, and anger flashed in her eyes. She really couldn't keep anything she felt hidden. He could read her like a child's primer.

"Then what?"

"Shall I show you?"

"You? Show an emotion? By all means."

He didn't wait for another invitation. He snagged her around the waist, pulled her close, and pressed his body against hers. She was warm, as though there really was a fire burning within her, producing all the glorious color infusing her skin. She gasped, and he supposed she had felt his erection. One hand slid up her arm, the silky strands of her curl tickling his skin, until he cupped the back of her neck. He looked down at her, his gaze flicking to her mouth and then her eyes. Her eyes were wide with surprise, but they'd also gone dark with desire. He didn't know when she'd last been kissed—an hour before or seven years ago—but he had not kissed anyone since her, and that was a very, very long time ago.

He lowered his mouth to hers, capturing her lips slowly to allow her time to turn and give him her cheek. She didn't move, and his lips tasted hers without any hesitation. He knew what he wanted, and he took it, opening her mouth and deepening the kiss so he could taste the champagne she'd drank. She was compliant and soft in his arms, her body relaxing against him, as his mouth took hers. Her hands clutched at his bicep, and when he slid his tongue along the roof of her mouth, she gave a small moan.

That moan almost undid him. Except he was not an impatient young man any longer. He had her wanting him as much as he wanted her, and he wanted to leave her wanting.

Colin pulled back, keeping his arm around her to make certain she didn't stumble. She tried to pull him back, to kiss him again, but he edged away. "Do you know what emotion I am feeling now?" he asked, echoing her earlier question.

She nodded.

"I'm pleased we sorted that out." He stepped away from her and straightened the sleeves of his coat. "And since I am a gentleman, I will honor your request and leave the musicale. I'll take Mr. Murray with me, but I may have to promise him you'll introduce him to a chit at some other point." He raised a brow in question.

She nodded again, still staring at him.

"Good night, my lady." He walked out, closing the door behind him. Several of the footmen were still standing on the other side of the door, and they turned to go back inside. Colin shook his head slightly. "Give my wife just a moment. She's a bit out of breath."

And then he walked away. Truth be told, he was out of breath himself. He'd always known he would have to deal with his wife again one day, but he never thought he would find any pleasure in it.

Perhaps he had been wrong.

***

"Daphne," her father said, awakening her from her thoughts as she sat in the morning room embroidering. Well, she was holding her embroidery. She hadn't actually embroidered anything. Her mother and aunt were chatting away, quite ignoring Daphne, but at the duke's entrance, all conversation ceased.

Daphne looked at her father and frowned. She couldn't imagine why he was waving the paper at her.

"Is this true?" he demanded. He was a short man, just a little over five and a half feet, but he had a commanding presence. His hair was white and curled about his face, until it merged into side whiskers that extended to the base of his jaw. She had his eyes, and right now his were a too-bright blue.

She glanced at the paper he held, not able to see anything but the title. "I didn't know you read the *Morning Chronicle*," she said.

He crossed the room and slammed the paper on the couch beside her. Her embroidery bounced off her lap, but she ignored it and lifted the paper.

"What is it, Your Grace?" the duchess asked. The duke ignored her and pointed to the paper.

"Page three," he told Daphne.

Daphne lifted the paper and turned the pages until she reached the third page. Nothing jumped out at her, but by habit she glanced at Mrs. Tattle's Tidbits and Titterings column. She did like to keep up on all the titterings as the Ladies Isabella and Pavenley were sure to mention them.

With a shock, she saw her own name there—not a mention of the Three Suns. She was often mentioned in that way, but she'd been singled out this morning.

Lady D— and her estranged husband shared a breathless tete-a-tete at Lady R—'s musicale last night. One person who was nearby said the gentleman emerged from the servant's chambers tousled and counseled that the lady needed a moment to catch her breath. Is it a bit warm in here, dear reader?

Daphne felt her cheeks flush hot, and to avoid having to look at her father, who had surely read the same column, she read it again. Lord, but she hated Mrs. Tattle.

"Care to comment?" her father drawled.

Daphne shook her head.

"What does it say?" her mother asked.

The duke glanced at his wife. "Only that your daughter was having a liaison with Mr. FitzRoy in the servant's chambers at Rosemont's musicale last night."

Her aunt covered her mouth to stifle a gasp, but her mother did not hold back. "Daphne, really! Have we not raised you better than that?"

She wished the couch would open up and allow her to slide underneath. "Mr. FitzRoy and I were having a private word. That is all." Mostly. "And I should think the real scandal is that Mama sent FitzRoy to follow me like a puppy, not that I was in a room alone with my own husband."

Now her mother's cheeks blushed pink. Daphne was quite satisfied to see it.

"I was only trying to do what was best for you," the duchess replied stiffy.

Daphne rose. "I do not need you to interfere in my marriage."

"What marriage?" her mother asked. "You and FitzRoy never even speak."

This was true, but Daphne did not wish her mother to point it out. "You might have spoken to me about it instead of seeing him without my knowledge."

The duchess rose now too. "I would not have had to resort to such measures if you would do as I suggested and go to see him when he first returned from the war."

"I will *not* chase after him. And you, Mama, had no right to tell him I was in trouble."

"Trouble?" the duke's brow furrowed. "What kind of trouble and why was I not informed?"

Now her mother gave the duke a look full of exasperation. "Warcliffe, the trouble is if Daphne and Mr. FitzRoy do not mend fences soon, the entire *ton* will be talking about it. There is only so much even I can do to keep the gossips at bay."

The duke pointed to the paper. "Articles like *that* will only flame the gossip. But that is not the only gossip. Last night, I heard your name mentioned in the same sentence as Lord Battersea's," her father said, his blue eyes narrowing. "Daphne, I have told you to stay clear of Lord Battersea. He's a bad sort."

Oh, she knew that well enough. "I do stay clear of Lord Battersea."

"But I have seen you in conversation with him," the duchess objected. "And then you still gave me no account for the times you have gone out and no one knew where you were and you came home at all hours."

"I am sure those are simply misunderstandings," Daphne said. She hadn't realized her mother paid that much attention. "That is no reason to go to FitzRoy and tell him to follow me to see what sort of trouble I am in. I am in no trouble."

Her mother crossed her arms over her chest. "What about your dress allowance?"

"What of it? It's the Season. I must have new dresses."

"I agree," her mother said. Then she pointed to Daphne's rose-pink dress with its dozen bows at the hem. "Then why are you wearing dresses from two Seasons ago?"

Daphne looked down at the dress. "I like this dress."

"That may be but where has your dress allowance gone if not to buy new gowns?"

The duke raised a hand and Daphne's retort died on her lips.

"I can tolerate no more talk of gowns or silks or lace. Daphne, answer me this, are you in some sort of trouble?"

"No." It was nothing she could not handle herself.

"Good." He looked at his wife. "You may cease worrying about the matter."

"Warcliffe—"

He held up a hand again. "However, you are right to show concern for her marriage. When FitzRoy was away on the Continent, his absence was unavoidable. And then when he joined that troop, we all thought he would be killed, and Daphne would marry again. I suppose we began to think of you as a widow."

Her aunt nodded her head, obviously agreeing.

"But you are not a widow, and your husband has been home almost two years. I myself have heard the talk about you and FitzRoy, but I chose to ignore it and give you time to remedy the situation on your own."

This Daphne knew was not true. Her father hated FitzRoy and his entire family, and he was happy to pretend her husband didn't exist as long as possible.

"But as you have not remedied the situation, we will take matters into our own hands."

Daphne absolutely hated when her father began speaking in the royal "we." He might be a duke, but he was not the king.

"We will invite Mr. FitzRoy to dinner and discuss the matter. Mary"—he looked at his wife—"I leave the arrangements to you. Daphne…" He sighed. "I expect your full cooperation."

And with that pronouncement, he strode out of the room. Daphne watched him go and then when her mother and aunt tried to speak to her, walked out as well. Back in her room, she sat at her dressing table and stared in the mirror. She supposed she had always known that things could not go on as they were forever. She was a married woman, and while she enjoyed the freedom and privileges that gave her—no chaperones, no marriage proposals—some of that freedom would inevitably end now that her husband was back from the war.

They had said their vows before God, and they were stuck together forever. At one time that idea would have thrilled her. She'd thought Colin FitzRoy the most handsome, most mysterious man she had ever met. He was taciturn and silent, and when she'd been eighteen, she'd thought that romantic.

She'd also thought his personality would change once they were married. She planned to tell him everything, and he would tell her everything. They would share secrets and confidences, not to mention do the things ladies were not supposed to know about.

But her wedding night had quickly disabused her of that ideal of marriage. Not only had Colin shown no interest in talking to her or getting to know her, he'd shown no interest in bedding her. He'd done the act, almost as though it were a chore, and then he'd left her.

She'd lain in bed, alone, wondering what she had done wrong. She'd wondered too why the poets and playwrights wrote about bedsport in such lofty terms. It had hurt, and she had felt no pleasure in it. She could not even be certain FitzRoy had felt pleasure. She certainly didn't care if she ever did it again.

And FitzRoy had not come to her again.

The day after their wedding night, he'd left her father's house on business. He said he had much to do to prepare to go to war. She saw him a few more times after that, and she tried to speak to him, to find out more about him, to try and forge some relationship with him. Before he left to join his regimen, she'd planned to tell him that she loved him. She'd never had the chance.

He'd been cold and remote and uninterested in speaking about anything beyond the prescribed topics of conversation. He'd left without a good-bye, and she hadn't seen him again until the ball the other night.

Now, she was glad she had not told him she loved him. She'd been such a child then. She hadn't even known what she was feeling. It hadn't been love. It was merely infatuation. But she could well imagine what his response would have been if she had said she loved him. He would have said *thank you* or *that's nice*. He hadn't loved her back—not then and not now. He had made it quite clear he did not want her, and that had hurt most of all.

But after last night, she was no longer certain he didn't want her. She'd known nothing of men when she'd been a debutante. She knew a bit more after seven years in the company of the debauched wives of the *ton.* Colin might not love her, but he did desire her. That was clear enough from his behavior at the musicale. Why? Why now?

She looked at herself in the mirror, trying to see herself as he might. She was no longer eighteen, but five and twenty was not so old. She bared her teeth, which were good, and moved her nose this way and that to ensure it was straight.

Daphne's hands then trailed down to her lips. She had thought of the kiss they'd shared almost without respite since arriving home last night. She wished she could give him a taste of his own medicine and reject him as he'd rejected her all those years. But to her annoyance, she had enjoyed the kiss. She'd melted inside and kissed him back. She'd even wanted him to kiss her again. She might even want him to do more than kiss her, except she knew the end result was nothing to shout about. And even if she were to tolerate his bedding her, that alone would not give them any sort of marriage. Marriage to him would be like marrying a rock. Except the rock had more feelings.

It wasn't a life Daphne wanted for herself…even if it was an option. But she couldn't keep pretending everything was fine—in her marriage or in her life. She was in trouble, a lot of trouble, and she could only blame herself for that.

Four

"There she is," Duncan said, pointing across Bond Street to a figure in pink exiting a modiste's shop. "Does the lass always wear pink?"

Colin nodded. "Always. Pink and bows."

Duncan tilted his head. "I doona see the bows."

"Look by her feet. There must be a dozen on the material there."

"Aye. You're right." The two men moved away from the wall and began to follow her on the opposite side of the street. "Why does she dress like she's six?"

It had seemed natural enough when they'd been younger, but Colin wondered why her style had not changed at all. "I think it's because it makes her look sweet and harmless. She lulls her prey into submission then strikes when one isn't expecting it."

Duncan gave him a sidelong look. "Are we still speaking of the lass?"

"You'll see," Colin said.

Duncan shrugged. "I only hope there are other ladies as fearless as you make her oot to be. The lass I was introduced to last night began to cry when I offered to fetch her lemonade."

"I hope you're not taking it personally."

"It isnae easy."

Across the street, Lady Daphne walked on, her footman following close behind. She peered into shop windows and nodded at acquaintances and then all of a sudden she stopped, turned, and looked straight at him. Colin felt the force of her scowl all the way across the street. She lifted her bow-laden skirts, and without even looking to make certain it was safe to cross, she stepped out.

"She's off her head," Duncan said, watching her. Colin didn't agree. She knew what she was about. As she crossed, carts and hackneys slowed and stopped to make way for her. She sauntered across the street and stopped before him without so much as a faltering step.

"Yer a wee bit mad, so you are."

Her eyes narrowed. "A pleasure to see you again as well, Mr. Murray. I cannot imagine why you are not yet wed."

Duncan put his hand over his heart. "Ouch. I'm hit."

Colin saw Daphne's lips twitch slightly and knew she was struggling not to smile. Duncan's charm inevitably won people over. Then she turned her gaze to him, and Colin had the urge to straighten his shoulders. "Good morning, husband."

He inclined his head.

"I was surprised not to see you at Mrs. Fox's dinner party last night. Lately, you turn up everywhere."

He'd dined at the Draven Club the night before, but she did not need to know that. "I don't care for dinner parties," he said.

"Too intimate?"

Like Duncan, he felt the jab. "Too ostentatious. The last one I attended featured thirteen dishes. Not only did the dinner drag on for five hours, it was a complete waste of food as none of us could eat another bite after the eighth course."

Her eyes flicked away, perhaps thinking of the number of courses at Mrs. Fox's dinner party. She opened her parasol, angled it to shield her face from the sun, and held out her hand to the footman. He seemed to know what she wanted because he pulled a sheet of vellum from his coat pocket and placed it in her palm.

"It's too bad you don't care for dinner parties." She offered the paper to him. "My father has invited you to one."

Colin looked at the paper lying on her pink glove like it was a spider. "Why?" he asked, eyeing her suspiciously.

She shrugged. "I suppose he couldn't allow my mother to have all the fun."

"More likely he wants to beat ye senseless," Duncan muttered.

"Will you take this or must I send Daniel to deliver it to your residence? He had instructions to do so later today, but I thought we should take this opportunity to hand deliver it."

"Thoughtful." Colin took the paper, brushing her glove as he did so. He much preferred meeting with her in private. Their encounter at Lady Rosemont's musicale had shown him her haughty exterior could be melted away. Of course, meeting her in private had its drawbacks as well. She made him want, made him *feel*, and both states were to be avoided.

"Do ye have any sisters?" Duncan asked. "I wouldna mind an introduction."

"My sisters are married, Mr. Murray."

"Are any of their husbands elderly?"

Daphne's eyes widened. "No. Why would you—no." She shook her head. "I do not want to know why you might ask that. Mr. Murray, I'm afraid I simply do not know any ladies who would suit you. Perhaps you should see a matchmaker."

"I did. She terminated our business arrangement."

Daphne's parasol slid sideways. "*She* terminated *you*? Shouldn't that be the other way round?"

"I have faith in ye, my lady. Ye'll find me a lass."

With a sigh and a slight shake of the head, she righted her parasol again, almost swiping Colin's face as she did so. He didn't think it was an accident.

"Gentleman, if you will excuse me. I have more shopping."

Duncan said his good-byes, but Colin took her arm and walked with her. She shook him off. "I already have an escort."

"But I want to speak with you for a moment."

"We'll speak at the dinner party. I have no doubt."

He leaned close, inhaling the scent of her perfume as he did so. It was that same heady mixture of tart and sweet. He knew the scent but couldn't quite place it. "You don't want this dinner party any more than I do. Why not just tell me what sort of trouble you are in, let me help you, and we can go back to the way things were?"

She shook her head, angling her parasol so her face was hidden from the gaze of anyone passing. Colin didn't know if she did not want to be seen with him or she simply did not want anyone to observe their conversation. He liked to think the latter, but he could not rule out the former.

"It's too late for that," she said.

Colin paused, catching her arm so she had to stop as well. They stood before a shop with a sign in the window that read *Bond Street Coffee & Tobacco Coming Soon! Proprietor T. Gaines*. As it was not yet open, no one went in or out, and it was the best chance for a private conversation on Bond Street they could hope for. "What do you mean it's too late? For the dinner party or the trouble?"

She looked away, giving her footman a signal to stand out of hearing range. "Both."

Colin closed his eyes in relief. She had finally admitted she was in trouble. At least they were making progress. All he had to do was fix the trouble, and they could go back to leading separate lives.

"You don't really believe that, do you? That we can go back?"

He hadn't wanted to think about it. "You don't?"

"My parents say it's time we behaved like a real married couple. You are back from the war now, and our behavior is causing people to talk."

"God, no. Tell me people aren't talking," he drawled.

She gave him a scathing look. "You may not care, but my father is a duke. He won't have it."

"I don't answer to your father."

"Then perhaps you might answer to me. Why have you avoided me until now? What did I ever do to make you hate me so much?"

His collar felt too tight and he ran a finger beneath it. "I don't hate you."

"Then what *do* you feel for me?"

Bloody hell but his cravat was choking him. Why hadn't he realized Jacobs had tied it too tightly this morning?

"Do you feel anything for me?" she asked.

"I like you well enough," he said, managing to take in some air despite his closing throat.

"Oh, how romantic."

"I am not romantic."

"You don't say."

"Were you always this sarcastic?" he asked. Spots had begun to dance in front of his eyes. He couldn't breathe. He'd probably fall over dead in a few minutes. His one consolation was that he would have an excuse not to attend the dinner party if he was dead.

"It's an acquired skill quite necessary to survive the *ton*."

He nodded, his lungs opening up again now that she had stopped asking him what he felt for her.

She cocked her head. "Are you well? You look a bit flushed."

"I'm fine. You are the one in trouble. I fought Napoleon in the war. I can fix your problem. What is it? Did you spend too much at the modiste?" No doubt her trouble was something minor he could easily settle.

She swung her parasol, and Colin ducked so the edge of it caught the back of his head. Only his swift reaction had saved him a stinging blow. "What the devil is wrong with you?" He wrested the parasol away from her.

"What is wrong with me?" she hissed, keeping her voice low. "How dare you? You think I'm some foolish girl who needs you to sweep in and rescue her? I don't need your help or you!"

"I'll make that decision."

"Go jump in the Thames, you overbearing cretin." She held out her hand. "Parasol."

Still in shock from being called a *cretin*, and an overbearing one at that, he handed her the parasol. She took it and walked away without a backward glance. Her footman scurried after her.

Colin frowned as he watched her go. A moment later, Duncan put his hand on Colin's shoulder. "I may no be the smartest man alive, but even I ken not to tell a woman I'll decide something for her."

"You heard that." Colin scowled as he watched her pink skirts disappear into the packs of other shoppers on Bond Street.

"I'd say a quarter of the street heard it."

Colin lifted his shoulder, dislodging Duncan's hand. "She's impossible."

"She's a woman, so aye. That's a given."

Colin blew out a breath. "And she says *I'm* a cretin."

"If you doona mind me asking, Pretender, why doona you use your skills to find out what her trouble might be?"

Colin cut Duncan a glance. The Scot had a point. Why hadn't Colin thought of it himself? In France, he hadn't walked up to men and tried to find out where Napoleon was moving troops or ammunition. He'd disguised himself and infiltrated their ranks or hid in plain sight among them to overhear their conversations. So why not employ the same tactics with his wife? He could follow her and find out what trouble she was in. She'd never see him, never even know he was there.

"That's not a bad idea," Colin said.

Duncan puffed out his chest. "I have my moments."

Colin considered his next steps. Daphne wanted him to go away, and that's what he'd wanted too. He first wanted to be certain she didn't need help. Once he was sure of that, he would leave her alone again. The duke wouldn't be happy, so perhaps some sort of arrangement might be agreed upon. He would live his life in one part of the country and she in another. They would appear together when necessary. It was not uncommon for husbands and wives to make such arrangements when formal separation was not an option.

And that was what he wanted—to separate from her again. Wasn't it? Being near her weakened his resolve and made him forget that she was to be avoided. The past few days, he'd found himself thinking about her and anticipating when they'd next meet.

But, of course, when they did meet she always asked what he felt for her. Spending time with her was never as simple as a kiss. She wanted more of him. And that was exactly why he had to get away.

"This lass of yours has me wishing for a wee dram of whisky," Duncan said. "Let's go to the Draven Club."

"You go. I will see you there."

"Oh, where are you off to then?"

"I have to go home."

***

Colin took a hackney to the FitzRoy town house on the outskirts of Mayfair. His father, the viscount, swore that in the time of his father or grandfather or great-great grandfather—it depended on the day the story was being told—the house had been in the very heart of London's most desirable area. Now Berkeley and Grosvernor Squares had replaced Clarenton Hill, but the FitzRoys were still there.

Colin did not bother to knock on the door. He could have afforded a bachelor residence, but he usually stayed here when in Town. Of course, lately his three sisters had been in Town as well, and he'd been happy to retreat to Mayne House.

As soon as he entered, Pugsly, the elderly pug who had lived with the family since Colin had been a boy, scampered into the foyer, his nails clicking on the wooden floors. He snorted his happiness at seeing Colin and danced over to him. Colin bent and rubbed his head then the dog's belly when Pugsly immediately flipped over and shamelessly tossed his legs in the air.

"Pugsly, you mustn't be so friendly with strangers."

Colin glanced up to see his sister Louisa standing at the top of the stairs with her arms crossed. She was the oldest of his sisters and the prettiest with her dark curly hair and hazel eyes.

"I'm not a stranger," Colin said.

"You might as well be. You are never here."

Colin knew the admonishment was said out of love. "I am here now."

"Good. Then come up and visit with us."

Colin glanced at the door of his father's library, cracked open so Pugsly could go in and out. "I'd actually wanted to speak with father."

"He has his head together with James. Come up and when they are done, I am sure they will join us."

Colin couldn't see a way to escape. James was the eldest brother and the heir to the title. It was probably best to wait until they had finished their business. Colin started for the stairs and Pugsly tried to follow, hefting his round body onto the first stair then giving Colin a baleful look. Colin reached down and lifted the pudgy little dog and carried him up, scratching behind his ears as he did so. Pugsly's little body twisted with pleasure.

He set the dog down at Louisa's feet and kissed both her cheeks then followed her into the drawing room where his sisters Mary and Anne sat sewing. Colin had noticed his sisters were always sewing something or another. He couldn't imagine what. Since Mary was in Town, and she was the only one of the three to have young children, he looked about for his niece and nephew. "You have come at nap time," she told him, rising to kiss his cheek. She was the shortest of the three sisters with straight brown hair and light brown eyes. "They will be up soon and then all our peace will vanish." Mary was only two years older than he, and growing up, they had always played together as his brothers were twelve and ten years older and already away at school by the time Colin was of any interest.

"Where have you been?" Anne, the middle sister, asked as she too rose to embrace him. She was the tallest of the three and had eyes almost the same green as his and cropped dark hair she wore with a turban.

"Here and there," Colin said, taking a seat on the couch across from Anne and Mary. He would not mention Mayne House or else they would surely come to call on him, out of interest in seeing a ducal house, if nothing else. Pugsly put his paws up on the cushion and snorted loudly, and Colin lifted him to the cushion beside him.

"Would here and there include the Rosemont musicale?" Louisa asked, sitting in her chair and lifting the book she had obviously been reading.

Colin was adept at schooling his features, but he had to choose his words carefully. "Why do you ask?"

"Because we read about you in the *Morning Chronicle*," Anne said. "You behaved quite scandalously."

"And had the bad taste to do so with your own wife," Mary added. "You know the fashion is for scandalous liaisons with women *not* your wife."

"Although I suppose the *ton* will make an exception if the husband and wife in question have not spoken for years," Louisa added.

Colin stroked Pugsly's soft ears. "How do you know we haven't spoken for years?" he asked, tone even and slightly disinterested.

Louisa raised a brow. "Well, have you?"

Colin shrugged. "I spoke to her just this morning."

"Really?" Mary set down her sewing. "Tell us all about it."

That reminded Colin of the invitation to the dinner party she'd given him, and he extricated it from his coat and broke the seal.

"A love letter?" Mary asked.

Colin looked it over and shook his head. "An invitation to a dinner party. You are included as well." He handed the invitation to Anne, who had stuck out her hand in her usual imperious manner. The women passed it around and commented on the paper and the printing.

"Are you shaking in your boots?" Louisa asked.

"Should I be?"

"I imagine the Duke and Duchess of Warcliffe intend to take you to task. It's not as though you and Lady Daphne have a typical marriage. You'll have to acquiesce to the duke's demands. That is, unless you plan to tell him why you detest his daughter."

Colin frowned. "I don't detest her."

"Clearly not, if what the *Morning Chronicle* reports is true." Anne waved the invitation before handing it back.

"You like her then?" Mary asked.

"No one would blame you if you don't," Louisa said. "She's not exactly all sweetness and generosity. Even I fear the censure of the Three Suns when I attend a ball."

"Daphne would never censure you," Colin said. But he didn't know if that was true. He really didn't know her very well at all.

"She has always been very polite," Anne said, clearly being generous.

Pugsly nudged Colin's hand, and Colin stroked him again.

"So you like her then?" Mary asked again. Colin didn't answer, he didn't know what he felt for Lady Daphne, and even if he had, he didn't feel the need to share his feelings with his sisters.

"How are your children, Louisa?" he asked. The three sisters had been sitting forward, waiting for his answer, but now they slumped back.

"We should have known Colin would never talk about his feelings," Anne said. "But you cannot avoid this marriage forever, Colin."

"You are correct, as usual, Anne," said a deep voice, and Colin turned to see his father had entered the drawing room. Pugsly jumped to his feet and then to the floor and ran to the viscount, immediately offering his belly for scratches. The viscount obliged as Colin stood. His father looked older than he had in recent months. His hair, which had once been as dark as Colin's, was now almost completely white, and the viscount moved more slowly these days. He seemed to strain to bend down to rub Pugsly's belly.

"My lord," Colin said. "I hope you are well."

His father straightened. "I'm tired. James asks a thousand questions. They are all good questions, but the answers tire me. I have left him with the accounts."

Louisa rose. "Shall I help you to your chamber, father?"

The viscount smiled. "A nap is in order, but Colin will help me, won't you, son?"

"Of course." Colin offered his arm and the two strode out of the drawing room with Pugsly following. His father's chamber was on the same floor at the far side of the house. As soon as they entered, Colin had to brace himself for the memories of his mother. He could still smell her rose perfume in this chamber, still see her lying in the bed, pale as a ghost.

Now a small set of steps had been placed on her side and Colin watched as Pugsly trotted up them, turned three times, and settled into what was clearly his spot on the bed. The viscount gestured to a grouping of chairs to the side and Colin joined him there.

"Brandy?" he asked.

"No, thank you."

"Will you pour me one?"

"Of course." Colin served his father then sat in the chair across from him as his father sipped the golden-brown liquid and stared into the low flames of the nearby hearth.

"I miss her too," he said after a long silence.

"Miss who?" Colin asked, though he knew very well.

"Your mother."

Colin shifted in his seat, uncomfortable with the conversation. He knew his father missed the viscountess. They all did, but it was not something he wanted to discuss. Silence descended again as, clearly, his father was not comfortable with the topic either.

The viscount sipped his drink again. "I know you only married Warcliffe's daughter because your mother asked you to."

Colin stared at the flames, neither confirming nor denying.

"I didn't like that she asked that of you. I didn't think it was fair for her to ask you when she was ill, but then she was never a woman to play fair. She was an earl's daughter, and she was used to having her way. She wanted Lady Daphne for you, and between your mother and the Duchess of Warcliffe, I fear neither you nor that girl had much say in the matter."

"I didn't mind."

His father winced. "So stoic. Even as a child you were never one to throw a tantrum or cry when you fell down."

Colin didn't think that was quite true, but he'd learned young to hide his hurts. He'd been barely five when his grandfather had smacked him for some transgression. Colin had burst into tears and the man had snapped, "Stop sniveling and act like a man!" Colin had been swatted on the backside again for good measure.

"We'd wanted the clergy for you," his father was saying, drawing him back to the present. "But by the time you were seven, we knew that was out of the question. You have the perfect constitution for the army. Level-headed, unemotional, rational."

Colin nodded. There was no place for sniveling in the army and he'd done well there. He'd even liked it. He hadn't liked the death and destruction, but he'd liked how everything was run. It was efficient, and for the most part, his commanders had been reasonable men. He had seen friends killed, of course. Eighteen of the men he'd served with in Draven's troop had not come back with him. But they had known what they signed up for. They had been prepared to die. Colin tried not to think of them.

"But while those qualities may serve you well in a war, they are the qualities a soldier needs, not a husband."

Colin shifted his gaze back to his father. "I don't wish to speak of this."

"Of course, you don't. But I'm your father, and you must honor me."

"I do."

"Good. Then listen." The viscount sipped his brandy. Colin gripped the arms of the chair and braced himself.

"I do not know Lady Daphne well, but I have observed that she is rather passionate. She cries at the end of a tragedy at the theater. She laughs loud and long at a comedy. She enjoys dancing and conversing. I do believe Lady Daphne is the sort of person who craves an emotional connection. As her husband, she will look to you for that connection."

Her words from long ago flitted through Colin's mind.

Tell me your deepest, darkest secret…

"You are a man who is uncomfortable with emotion. You have shied away from it your whole life."

Stop sniveling and act like a man.

"When your mother died, I saw an even more profound change in you. You built a wall between the rest of the world and yourself, and now none of us can breach it."

Colin practically squirmed in his seat. He might have done if he hadn't been so well trained by the army. "Is this conversation because I have been spending more time away from the town house?" If that was the cause, he would come home more often. Anything to end this torture.

The viscount shook his head. "Colin, my boy, it is not a physical wall. It does not matter where you are. You shut all of us out. You always have to some extent, but the last few years it has been complete."

"I don't know what you mean. I'm not hiding anything."

Silly, little boy.

"Neither do you reveal anything." The viscount set his glass on a table and studied his son. "I knew Lieutenant Draven before you. Did you know that?"

Colin shook his head.

"I see him sometimes and we speak."

Colin wished he had opted to drink that brandy now.

"He told me about your actions during the war. How you were an invaluable member of the team. Your fellow soldiers called you the Pretender because you could disguise yourself as anyone or anything." He paused and seemed to expect some response from Colin. Colin nodded to confirm it.

"You never told us any of that, and yet, none of it surprises me. Of course, you could become someone else. You were always good at blending into a crowd, making yourself invisible. But beyond that, you quite easily divorce yourself from yourself."

Colin frowned. "That makes no sense."

"But it does. You keep all your feelings and thoughts and emotions hidden, even from yourself, and so it makes it easy to become someone else."

"If you think what I did was easy—"

His father waved a hand. "That's not what I meant. I should say, it makes that sort of task possible for you. Other men would fail, or at the very least, be only half as successful because they cannot put who they are and what they feel aside. You can."

"And?" Colin asked.

"And that was an admirable quality during the war, but it's not needed any longer. In fact, it will not serve you in marriage. Your wife wants to know her husband—his feelings, his moods, his emotions. You won't keep her if you cannot give her some of that."

"And who says I want to keep her?"

His father snorted. "I may be old, but I'm not blind. The chit is beautiful. Any man would want to keep her."

"I hope you don't think I'm so shallow."

"You are the last person I would call shallow. No, but I don't think you're blind either. Nor are you stupid. A divorce will ruin us all, if it were even granted, which I doubt. The duke has been more than lenient in allowing the two of you to behave unconventionally. But he will tire of the gossip and whispering and put his foot down. He will expect you to be a model husband to his daughter."

Colin could feel his collar closing in on his throat already. "And if I don't meet his expectations?"

"Then I imagine he will make your life miserable. He has the money and the power to do it."

Colin shrugged, but his father held up a hand. "Before you say *let him do his worst* or some such thing, think about your sisters and your nephews and nieces. Do you want all of Society looking down their noses at them? Do you want to ruin your nieces' chances of making good matches and of coming out? Louisa's eldest will be out in three years. Warcliffe can make sure Eliza is not received anywhere."

Colin blew out a breath and sat back. He detested this sort of thing—men throwing around their power, making others bow to their whims. But if the truth be told, he'd known this day was coming. He'd been waiting for it. "I will meet the duke's expectations," he said, jaw tight.

"And what about your wife's?" his father asked.

Colin couldn't meet his father's eyes. He did not want to admit he would never be able to meet Daphne's expectations.

Five

He had sent his acceptance for the dinner party. Daphne still could not believe it.

Her mother had told her just before they'd entered the carriage on the way to the opera. Her father had a box—he would be coming directly from his club with two of her brothers, and perhaps one of her sisters would be in attendance as well. The box was always full of her siblings and their spouses.

Only Daphne ever had to sit unaccompanied.

But perhaps that would change. Colin had accepted the invitation to the dinner party. She'd expected him to decline. She'd expected her father to have to harangue him, but after one invitation he'd acquiesced.

It was too easy...

"I don't know why I tell you anything," her mother said sharply enough that Daphne turned from the window to look at her. "You don't listen to me."

"I'm sorry, Mama. I was looking out the window."

Her mother frowned. "If you are to use that excuse, you might at least make certain the curtains are open first." She brushed the closed curtains with her hand. "As I was saying, Lord Stockford has lost his entire fortune in some scheme or other. It's quite the scandal."

"I know already."

Lady Isabella had told her all about it, breathless with excitement. There was nothing Lady Isabella and Lady Pavenley liked more than a scandal. Daphne was a little ashamed to realize she had once been the same, eager for any juicy morsel she could spread about. Now she felt sorry for Lord Stockford and his wife and children. "What will happen to them?"

Her mother all but reared back. "I should think they will decamp to the Continent, but I do not know. In any case, that is not the point I wanted to make. You are not to speak to Lady Stockford. Give her the cut direct, Daphne."

Daphne imagined Lady Stockford, who was a pretty woman just two or three years younger than she. She could imagine her face when Daphne turned her back on her.

"You are thinking," her mother observed. "Stop."

"I can't stop thinking, Mama. It's something one does instinctually."

"Yes, well you are thinking hard. I can see the way your forehead wrinkles. Those wrinkles will not smooth out so easily in a few years. Best not to create them."

"I will try, Mama. In the meantime, I cannot help but wonder—"

"Wondering is too close to thinking, Daphne," the duchess said tartly.

"—and yet I wonder if we should really be so quick to cut someone like Lady Stockford. After all, what if Mr. FitzRoy asks for an annulment—"

"An annulment? On what grounds?"

"Very well, a divorce."

The duchess inhaled sharply. "He will *not*! Your father will run him out of Parliament if he dares step foot in chambers with that request."

"Mother, *my* point is that we are none of us without some flaw, some secret, something worthy of gossip."

"And that is precisely why your father has called for the dinner party with Mr. FitzRoy. We will settle this once and for all. Now, about Lord Cheeveton—"

She went on, relating information Daphne already knew. There was little about the goings on in the *ton* Daphne did not know. And it was only because she managed the two biggest gossips in Society—Lady Isabella and Lady

Pavenley—that she was not more of a source of gossip than she was. A little talk was not a bad thing. It made one interesting and mysterious. But she feared the talk about her was growing, even more now that FitzRoy had so publicly sought her out.

She exited the carriage at Covent Garden and went through the motions of greeting people she knew, ignoring those trying to elevate themselves, and ingratiating herself to those above her. How she did grow tired of Prinny staring at her breasts. She shouldn't have worn such a low-cut gown, but she hadn't been thinking when she'd told her maid which dress to press. She'd forgotten Prinny would be here tonight. She'd just wanted something that would look good in the theater's light, and the silver thread worked through the bodice, sleeves, and hem of the bright pink dress always looked very good in dim light. But the dress also had a large pink bow right between her breasts, and it drew the eye—especially the prince's eye.

Using her fan to cover her décolletage, Daphne curtsied and took the first opportunity to go to the Warcliffe box. There she fanned herself and pretended to look out over the mostly still empty seats. Lady Pavenley and her husband had a box to her right, and Lady Isabella had a box almost directly across from them. Her brothers enjoyed that as Lady Isabella had a tendency to lean over to watch the performance and her dress often looked as though it might fail to contain her bosom at any moment. There were usually wagers as to whether a nipple would be visible or an entire breast would pop out.

Daphne's own dress was low enough that she might have the same problem if she had been fond of sitting near the banister and looking over. She almost always sat in the second or third row of seats, though. And her posture was impeccable.

She heard the curtain swish as someone else entered, and she looked behind her, a smile ready. But it wasn't one of her siblings or her parents.

"Lady Daphne, I was hoping you would attend tonight."

Daphne took a deep breath and tried not to panic. "My lord." She gave only a slight curtsey to show the Earl of Battersea she did not hold him in high regard. "You know I never miss the opening of an opera."

He gave her a thin smile, his gaze sharp. "Everyone knows that, but I did think you might not attend tonight. You have been trying so hard to avoid me."

"I don't know what you are talking about."

He moved closer, and she thought, not for the first time, that he moved like a snake. He was tall and sinewy, with copper hair that seemed to signal he was poisonous. "I think you do. You and I both know you are running out of time to pay your debt to me."

She gave him a look of disgust. "How can you be so vulgar as to mention such a thing to a lady?"

He smiled, and his thin lips stretched taut over his teeth. "You have no idea how vulgar I can be, Lady Daphne. But I do hope you will find out." He hissed the last bit, moving closer to her, his eyes alight with what she could only assume was lust.

"I did pay my debt to you." They'd had this conversation before, and she knew what he would reply.

"Not promptly, and you have yet to pay the interest, which grows day by day." He licked his thin lips, and she shuddered. She'd heard rumors he'd played a part in the untimely death—some said murder—of a baroness years ago. The way he looked at her now, she could believe it was true. She looked down at his gloved hands and could imagine them wrapped around her own neck.

"A gentleman does not charge interest," she said faintly, still looking at his hands.

"A lady does not gamble. But you made the wager, and I will be sure you pay." He was close enough to kiss her now. "If not with blunt then with your person." His hand snaked up her arm and caught her painfully where her long gloves ended. She tried to move away, but he was deceptively strong and pulled her closer. "I am done waiting. You have two days. If you do not pay me in full, you are mine." He moved to kiss her, but thankfully, her father parted the curtain in the next moment and the earl was forced to release her.

"Battersea," the duke said, and it was almost a bark. He looked at Daphne then back at the earl. "Good to see you, my lord."

Battersea bowed. "Your Grace. Your daughter and I were just discussing our mutual love of the opera."

The duke looked unconvinced. "You should go back to your seat, Battersea. The opera is about to begin."

"Of course. We will speak more later, Lady Daphne." He took her gloved hand and kissed it, his tongue sneaking out to lick the pink leather. Daphne swallowed her revulsion as the curtains swayed behind him.

"Why was he here?" the duke asked.

"I have no idea. He came in without an invitation and began to talk of the opera."

"He's a bad sort. I've told you to stay clear of him."

"He had only been here a moment before you came in, Papa. I would have dismissed him."

Her father nodded, and she knew he was thinking that she was quite capable of doing just as she'd said. But he also didn't know her secret or that she owed Battersea money. She had wished on so many occasions she could go back in time and refuse his invitation to play a hand of cards. She wished she'd refused to go to the private room with him, refused the high stakes, and walked away from the group of men she hadn't known well. She hadn't wanted to seem afraid. She had wanted to look brave and smart and rebellious.

Now she knew she'd been played for a fool. The earl had made certain she would never be able to repay her debt. She'd planned to ask him for more time, but she could see that would be pointless. He wanted her to default on her debt. He'd never give her more time.

"Good," her father said, apparently mollified. "I am sure you have heard rumors about him, and I will not expound on those, but suffice it to say, he is not the sort of man you should involve yourself with."

"Of course not, Papa. I am married."

He blew out his breath, clearly not pleased by that response.

She didn't blame him, but she'd rather speak of FitzRoy than Battersea. She could never tell her father what she had heard of Battersea. Ladies weren't supposed to discuss what was rumored to happen at his country house parties—drinking, opium, prostitutes, and orgies. The rumors had made him seem dangerous, and it had been amusing to flirt with that danger. Until it had gone too far.

Now she would have to take drastic measures. The problem was that she would have to take them soon. Very soon. And that dratted dinner party with her husband was tomorrow night.

Her second to oldest brother and his wife entered, and she was happy to abandon the topic and speak of the business of a charitable organization with Lady William. Then two of her sisters and their husbands arrived with her mother and soon everyone was talking over everyone and no one quieted until halfway through the first act when the soprano sang so loudly they could not help but pay attention.

Daphne sat in the second row of seats, her mother, father, brother William and his wife in the first row. Her sisters and their husbands shared her row, and she was on the end closest to the stage and feeling a bit crowded. One row of chairs had been placed behind her in case her other sister or one of her other brothers made an appearance. She might have sat there except she would have had to sit alone. Daphne had quite forgotten it until she sensed someone sitting in the seat directly behind her.

At first she caught her breath, fearful it was Battersea. But no, she knew where his box was, and he was in it, leering at the courtesan seated beside him. She glanced at her siblings and their husbands, but they were all either watching the stage or the others in the audience. She saw her two brothers-in-law exchange coins and glanced at Lady Isabella, who was indeed tucking her bosom back into its meager confines.

Slowly, she turned her head and looked into the gaze of Colin FitzRoy. He was watching her, not the stage, not Lady Isabella's chest. *Her*.

Her first impulse was to ask what he was doing there, to stand up and demand how long he had been sitting there, but she was aware that she, like every other person in a box, was on full display. People were watching her and hoping for the scandal broth her mother so wanted to avoid.

"What are you doing here?" she whispered.

"Watching the opera, what else?" he replied, his voice low but not quite low enough. One of her sisters turned and looked at her. Her eyes widened as she noticed Colin. Daphne gritted her teeth.

"You know want I am asking. What are you doing in my box?"

"Would you like to come to mine? The view is not quite as good, and my sisters will assuredly shush you."

As if to underscore the differences between their families, Lady Cora, one of Daphne's sisters leaned over. "Do speak up so we can hear, dear. It strains my ears, all this whispering."

"That's it." Daphne rose and exited the box, the red velvet curtains swishing in her wake. For a moment she stood in the deserted corridor behind the box, wondering if Colin would follow her, then the curtains parted and he emerged, looking amused. He propped one shoulder against the wall separating the Warcliffe box from the one adjacent and looked down at her.

"Now," she said quietly, "why are you here? You are never at the opera."

He shrugged. "You are here, wife."

It seemed as though he mocked her with the words. "Don't call me that. I'm no more your wife than…" She looked about and watched a woman re-enter a box far down the corridor. "Than she is."

"Not true. You and I exchanged vows."

"As though that means anything."

"Your father thinks it means something, else he wouldn't have summoned me to a dinner where, no doubt, he intends to take me to task for neglecting my husbandly duties." He looked at her, his green eyes on her face. "Does he know about the trouble you are in?"

"No. I mean, I am not in any sort of trouble." Dratted man! When he looked at her with those eyes, she practically forgot how to speak.

Colin smiled. "Right."

"Go away." She started back through the curtain, but Colin caught her by the waist and pulled her gently back. She tensed until his lips brushed her ear.

"I'm not going away."

She shivered at the way his warm breath caressed her ear. But she was all too familiar with this unfulfilled promise. "We'll see," she said, loosing his fingers and stepping out of his hold. She pushed aside the curtain and re-entered the box. But Colin was right behind her, and he cut off her path to the chair she'd occupied. Instead, he directed her to a seat in the third row of chairs, pulling it out for her then taking the one beside it.

She sat, back stiff and straight, and concentrated on ignoring him. She'd almost succeeded too when he took her hand. She jumped at the warm contact as his gloved hand covered hers. She tried to pull hers away, but he held on. She glanced across the theater and saw Lady Isabella watching her, brows raised. Daphne pretended to watch the opera again. She would have had to make a large gesture to free herself, and that would have only set tongues wagging.

She could allow him to hold her hand. It wasn't as though they were actually touching. She kept her attention on the opera, not able to fully enjoy it with him so close. Finally, after a few moments of the soprano's aria, he leaned over. "My Italian is a bit out of use. What is she singing about?"

Daphne didn't believe him for a moment. She'd heard he was able to speak several languages. She couldn't imagine Italian wasn't one of them. But if he wanted to play this game, she would show him who was the master. "She is singing about the night she spent with her lover," she murmured, turning her head slightly in his direction. "His kisses set her heart on fire. She longs for his touch. She is lost without him."

"Bereft," he said, leaning close. "That's stronger than *lost*."

She cut a look at him. "I thought you didn't understand Italian."

His eyes, dark in the dimly lit rear of the box, looked into her own. She felt her heart speed up.

"I understand a little." He looked back at the stage, and she was thankful for the break in eye contact. But just as she was able to breathe again, he tilted his head until his lips were close to her ear. "I don't suppose you understand what she is singing about."

Daphne stiffened. "What sort of question is that?"

He shrugged. "The sort a husband might ask. After all, I didn't make you feel any of that fire on our wedding night. I have wondered if some other man has managed to enlighten you."

Daphne's jaw dropped, and she turned her head to stare at him outright. Colin looked at her, his gaze unwavering. "What shocked you more? That I admit I was a poor lover or that I ask if you have a paramour?"

She opened her mouth then closed it again. "You weren't—"

He smiled and shook his head. "Don't. I had no idea what I was doing." The hand holding hers dropped to her knee, resting there lightly. "But if we tried again, I'd make sure you enjoyed it."

Her chest felt tight and when she tried to breathe, her hardened nipples were so sensitive that they chafed when they brushed against the soft fabric of her chemise. Her body betrayed her, but her mind cleared. "Because now you have had so much practice," she said stiffly. "All of those French girls, I imagine."

"You imagine wrong." His gaze shifted back to the stage, and he seemed utterly transfixed by the singer. Daphne watched her too, but she couldn't stop wondering what he meant.

You imagine wrong.

I'd make sure you enjoyed it.

Finally, she could not take it anymore. She turned her head to look at him. "What do you mean, I imagine wrong?"

She saw the ghost of a smile play on his lips. "Watch the opera or people will talk."

"People will talk anyway," she said, but she turned her head to the stage again. After a moment, he leaned toward her. To anyone who watched them, it would appear as though he was enraptured by the singers.

"We spoke before of our mutual friend."

She closed her eyes briefly, attempting to ignore the warmth of his body beside hers and the low timbre of his voice resonating through her, and to focus on his words. "Mr. Beaumont?" she asked, finally.

"Rafe, yes. Do you know what he was called during the war?" Colin asked.

She shook her head.

Colin leaned closer, so close she felt his lips on her jaw, just below her ear. "The Seducer," he murmured.

She exhaled a slow, shaky breath. The way Colin's voice sounded on that word, *seducer,* made her belly tighten.

"We often worked together. I would be in disguise, and he as well. But I would stand in the corner, unobtrusive, observing and gathering intelligence by seeming to become one with the men of the town or the French officers, depending on where we were. But Rafe would sit down at a table and within minutes, he'd have three or four women at his side. He'd charm them until they told him practically everything he wanted to know.

"If he needed more information, he'd take them to bed. Sometimes even when he didn't need more information. It was my task to gather the information the women didn't know. We worked in tandem for month after month. I couldn't help but learn a few things about what pleases a woman. What gives her pleasure." The hand on her knee moved slightly, one of his fingers tracing a slow circle on her gown.

That circle seemed to be made of fire. Her skin, under her brightly-colored gown, felt itchy and uncomfortable. She wanted him to stop. And yet, she wanted him to move his hand higher.

And then, as though she'd spoken her wish aloud, his hand did move slightly higher, the heat of his touch radiating through her body like a newly lit fire on a cold winter evening. She should tell him to stop. She should put her hand over his and force him to stop, but her hand stayed on the arm of the chair, and her eyes were on the stage, though her entire being was compressed into that one location on her body.

"These are just observations," he said, tearing her mind away from the mesmerizing feel of his hand on her thigh. "Perhaps you could confirm." His hand slid higher. "Being that you are"—and higher—"most definitely"—and higher—"a woman."

His hand slid over the V between her thighs and she all but jumped out of her seat. One of her sisters turned to peer at her curiously, and Daphne kept her eyes on the stage while surreptitiously sliding Colin's hand back down her leg.

She held his gloved hand tightly in hers for several minutes then leaned over and whispered, "Don't toy with me."

"And here I thought I was seducing you."

"Why? What do you hope to gain?"

He was silent for a long time, and she finally turned to look at him. His expression was, as ever, unreadable, but she thought she saw sadness. "You've been in London too long," he answered. "You think everything is about winning or losing. I am on your side, Daphne. You don't lose if you admit you need help."

It was on the tip of her tongue to claim she didn't need help, but she feared that would amount to protesting too much. And as she considered other retorts, her gaze drifted to Battersea. His courtesan was whispering in his ear, but his gaze was on her, hungry and knowing. He knew he had her right where he wanted her, and nothing except acquiescing to his whims would save her from ruin.

Except giving in was its own sort of ruin.

"Fine," she said quietly, her gaze still on Battersea. "I'll tell you everything at the dinner party."

"We aren't likely to have a moment alone."

"I can arrange it."

"No doubt you can. And you will tell me everything?"

"Yes." Her gaze went back to the stage again. She couldn't tell him everything. She couldn't tell him even half of it, but if pressed, she would tell him something. It would buy her some time, time she needed to work out the details of her plan.

"Then I will speak to you more tomorrow." He moved his hand out of hers, and she'd almost forgotten she was still holding it. The sudden loss made her feel very alone.

He rose then, quietly and without seeming to draw the attention of the others in the box. But before he departed, he leaned over her chair and whispered into her hair. "I have ways of finding out the truth. I want to give you the courtesy of confiding in me first. If you haven't after tomorrow, I will use my skills."

She turned to glare at him, to offer a rejoinder. But he was already gone. Daphne turned back to the stage, but the soprano sounded too high and shrill, and though she was surrounded by people and the air in the box a bit stale and warm, she shivered with a sudden chill.

Six

Colin adjusted his neckcloth once last time, ignoring the noise of the household around him. His sisters were arguing over lace or gloves, Pugsly was barking, and one of his nieces or nephews was crying.

It was a contrast to the usual quiet calm of the FitzRoy town house, but it presaged what was to come. The Duke of Warcliffe's dinner party would be anything but calm and quiet. Colin found that he was ready for the dressing down Warcliffe was likely to give him for his inattention to Lady Daphne. Colin realized he deserved it. He supposed he'd been waiting for someone to say something to him for a long time and was only surprised that it had taken this long.

He'd been given his share of reprimands in the army. He'd neither been the perfect husband or the perfect soldier. He'd disobeyed commands, he'd countermanded orders, he'd failed at times in his missions. But when he'd gone against authority, he always had a good reason.

And he had reasons for keeping his distance from his wife. They were not reasons he wanted to look at too closely, but he'd been forced to do so the past few days, and the undeniable truth was that Lady Daphne was a threat. It wasn't her beauty or her cleverness or even her strength that kept Colin at arm's length. There were other women who possessed those same qualities, though not in the same measures, of course. Colin didn't find those women threatening. He didn't want to slide his hand up their skirts at operas or whisper seductive promises in their ears or find every opportunity to spend more time with them.

But Lady Daphne made him do things he wouldn't otherwise do. She made him feel things he wouldn't otherwise feel. Things he did not want to feel. Things he did not want to do—oh, very well, he did want to do them. He just didn't want to face the consequences of what came after.

Because he wasn't like Rafe Beaumont. He couldn't take a woman to bed and then forget her the next day. A night with Lady Daphne would change everything. Though for Rafe as well there had finally been a woman he couldn't easily forget. And look what had happened to him—depending on the story one believed, Rafe was either dead, turned traitor, or languishing in America.

Colin didn't know what was worse.

He wanted to tell himself that if he solved Lady Daphne's problem, all would go back to the way it had been. But he'd been a fool to tell himself that lie. He'd been telling himself another lie as well. He'd let himself believe he was devoid of emotions, of *feelings*, but the few interactions he'd had with Daphne had shown him that was a falsehood. He had plenty of feelings, and the truth was, the depth of those he felt for her frightened him. It wasn't something he wanted to admit, not even to himself. And the problem was that he couldn't escape dealing with his fears. It was time for his life—for their lives—to change. He had to begin to behave as a husband when they were together. Perhaps if he could limit his interactions with her to a few days out of every year, he could keep his feelings from rising to the surface.

"You look like you've just seen a ghost."

Colin turned to see James, his eldest brother, standing in the doorway that connected their rooms.

"I don't believe in spirits."

"Of course not," James said with a smile. "You've never been fanciful. I have the feeling you are not eager to attend this dinner."

"An evening with the Duke of Warcliffe is hardly my idea of entertainment."

James shrugged. "I rather like the man, though he is loud and a bit pompous, but what do you expect from a duke?"

Colin made a sound of agreement and gave his neckcloth one last tug.

"You could have avoided this, you know."

"Tell me this isn't the part where you give me brotherly advice on how to be a perfect husband."

"Hardly. Let George do that. He is the perfect husband. I'm no example. Why do you think my wife prefers to stay in the country while I spend so much time here? We can barely speak two civil words to each other."

Colin lifted the glass of brandy he'd poured earlier and then forgotten. "I feel so much better now."

"I'm not trying to make you feel better. I'm saying marriage isn't the end of the world. But you have to stop running and do your duty."

Stop sniveling and act like a man.

Colin sipped his brandy, aware his facial expression was calm while inwardly he fumed. His brother was forever telling him truths he had already deduced himself.

"But at least you've finally secured us an invitation to the duke's house. Anne, Louisa, and Mary can't praise you enough."

"We'll see if they're still enthusiastic after they spend the evening with the Warcliffes."

"Truer words, Colin." He took Colin's unfinished brandy and drank the rest of it. As the eldest, he was used to taking what he wanted. Colin had never before minded very much. But he found at this moment he would have liked to hit his brother hard in the jaw.

He refrained and instead followed him out of the room and into the drawing room where his father and sisters had assembled. A nanny was reading quietly to the children, and his sisters seemed to have solved their disagreements. They all wore gowns in shades of blue or green. Mary held a Catarina lace handkerchief in one hand, and Colin realized that must have been the item the ladies fought over. He had surmised from all the discussions he had been subjected to that Catarina lace was the latest fashion.

"There you are," the viscount said. "The carriages should arrive in just a moment. I thought we should take two. No point in trying to fit seven in one."

"Seven?" James looked about the room. "Is one of the children coming?"

Colin closed his eyes, already knowing what his father had in mind. "He means the dog," Colin said quietly.

"Oh, no, my lord." Louisa shook her head. "You can't take Pugsly."

"Of course, I shall take Pugsly. He is well-behaved. Why should I leave him behind?"

"What if the duke does not like dogs?" Mary asked.

"Not like dogs?" The viscount sounded appalled. "What sort of man does not like dogs?"

"Not the sort I wish to know," Anne said. She wore a turban wrapped about her cropped hair. The shade of green matched her gown.

The viscount pointed at her. "Precisely." He bent and scooped up Pugsly. "Let us go down."

At the bottom of the stairs, the servants helped the ladies into wraps and the gentlemen into greatcoats. Then everyone stood shuffling about, waiting for the carriages. His father moved close to Colin and murmured, "You would do well to not make a muddle of this."

"Thank you for the encouragement," Colin said drily.

Louisa linked her arm with Colin. "Father means that it wouldn't hurt for you to try and be charming and romantic. Sweep Lady Daphne off her feet. Tell her how you adore her, how lovely her brown eyes are, how supple her lips."

"How supple her lips?" James looked slightly ill.

Louisa huffed. "It doesn't hurt to be romantic."

"It would probably do me no good to compliment her brown eyes as her eyes are blue," Colin pointed out.

Mary cooed. "You know the color of her eyes! That's a good start."

"Forgive me." Colin untangled himself from Louisa's grip. "I don't recall asking for advice."

"Another mistake," Louisa observed.

The carriages finally clattered to a stop at the door and the ladies took one while Colin, James, Pugsly, and the viscount climbed into the other. Fortunately, James and his father were more interested in talking politics than women, and Colin didn't have to speak or think about much more than what shade of pink Daphne would wear and how many bows would adorn the dress.

Although it was only a short distance to Mayfair, the streets were clogged with carriages bearing others to the numerous events of the Season, and it took a half hour to arrive in front of the duke's town house. It was large and white and practically an entire army of footmen awaited their arrival on the front drive. Colin passed through that army unscathed and soon enough he was blinking in the bright light of the chandelier, divested of his greatcoat and hat, and set like a sacrifice in the center of the drawing room.

He accepted a glass of claret from the servant beside the duke, who slapped him a bit too hard on the back and called him *son*. "So pleased to have you back from the Continent," the duke said when Colin had made the appropriate greetings. "We heard you made quite the name for yourself."

"I did my duty," Colin said. Daphne had not come down yet and neither had the duchess. One of her sisters, Clara or Cora—he could never remember their names—had taken his sisters aside while the Marquess of Shorstow, the heir to the dukedom, was speaking with James and the viscount who still held a softly snoring Pugsly.

"No need to be modest, my boy," Warcliffe said. "You can tell me how many Frenchies you killed. I'm not in the least squeamish."

Colin drank more claret. "I'm afraid I didn't count, Your Grace."

"That many, eh?"

Colin was searching for some other topic of conversation when the drawing room doors opened, and the duchess, followed by her youngest daughter, entered. Colin had a moment to note the duchess looked quite regal and sparkling in jewels before his breath caught as Daphne came into view.

Pugsly woke then and barked, causing everyone to look in his direction. Everyone except Colin. He couldn't look away from Daphne.

There was no question as to why she always wore pink. It was her color. She was naturally pale, and her silvery blond hair did not add any color to her features, making her vivid blue eyes stand out in stark contrast. But the pink of her clothing always seemed to make her look healthy and warm her complexion. Her dress tonight was composed of a rose overdress with a paler pink dress underneath. The sleeves were long and tight, small bows at the cuffs. The overdress closed around the underdress just below her breasts with a satin sash that was also tied into a bow. Colin did not know if the bow was decorative or not, but he ached to rip it off.

Instead, he bowed. "Lady Daphne." He caught Louisa glaring at him and added, "You look very healthy."

Louisa rolled her eyes.

Daphne curtsied. "Thank you, Mr. FitzRoy. As do you." She addressed the room then, turning away from him, and he noted the pink rose caught up in the twist of her hair. "I do hope you stayed warm on your journey here. The weather has certainly grown unseasonably cool."

Pugsly struggled free of the viscount and ran about, sniffing the duchess's feet. She ignored him, but Lady

Daphne bent and scratched him behind the ear. "I haven't seen you in so long, dear Puglsy."

Pugsly snorted happily. Daphne looked up and caught Colin staring at her. Her cheeks seemed to turn a deeper shade of pink before she looked away. He wondered if she thought he disliked her display of affection. On the contrary, he was surprised she not only remembered the dog but took time to give him affection.

After a few minutes, Pugsly sniffed about and the butler offered to take him to the kitchens for a bit of dinner. Pugsly happily complied when he heard one of his favorite words. With no further distractions, Colin was subjected to a quarter hour of discussion on the weather, and while he might have marveled at his wife's ability to speak at length on every topic of polite conversation, his mind was occupied with how he might speak with her alone so she could make good on her promise to tell him everything.

"My lady," he said, when she had paused to take a breath. "I wonder if you and I might speak privately for a few minutes." He thought he saw fear flash in her eyes before she was saved by the gong. The butler announced that dinner was served.

They took their place in the procession down the dining room, Daphne forced to link her arm with him. Colin didn't wait for another opportunity to speak with her. "You promised to tell me everything tonight," he said quietly.

"And I will," she murmured back. "Later."

"Tell me now."

She shook her head. "Then you'll have nothing to look forward to."

As it was considered vulgar for husbands and wives to sit beside each other, he was seated by Cora or Clara while Daphne was beside James. Considering the whole idea of the dinner party was to mend Daphne and Colin's marriage, it seemed rather absurd to follow the protocols, but he dutifully listened to Lady Clara/Cora expound on the virtues of lace. He'd been distracted by the sound of Lady Daphne's laugh and had accidentally responded to one of Lady Cora/Clara's remarks with the observation that he had met Catarina Draven, the Catarina of Catarina lace, and Daphne's sister had not ceased going on about it.

Finally, about the time the roast was served, the duke turned to the topic they had all been anticipating. "Mr. FitzRoy," he said, causing both James and Colin to turn his way. Colin envied James then as he could go back to eating while the duke bored holes into Colin with his eyes the same color as his daughter's. "Now that you are back in England again," the duke went on, as though Colin hadn't been in

England for many months now, "where do you plan to live? We like to have our daughter close, of course, but this time of year one has to take what one can get."

Colin did not miss the directive implied in the question—*it's time you and my daughter lived under the same roof.*

Colin cleared his throat. He was tempted to glance at Daphne but resisted. Another look at the bow straining beneath her breasts wouldn't help him any. And he supposed it *was* time he lived with her. There was no acceptable reason not to—other than the fact that once she lived with him a few weeks, she'd want to move out again as soon as possible. He was not the sort of husband she wanted.

Tell me your deepest, darkest secret...

"I hadn't really thought about it, Your Grace."

"Do you know," the duchess began obviously trying to sound nonchalant, "this reminds me of a house I saw for let just the other day. It was small but quite charming. I think it would be perfect for you."

Daphne raised her brows at her mother, obviously no more fooled than Colin or anyone else. "Imagine that," Daphne said. "This late in the Season."

"I know. It's quite providential. Why don't we three"— she looked at Daphne and Colin—"go take a look at it in a day or so? If you like it, we'll lease it. It will be our wedding gift to you."

Colin recalled the duke and duchess had leased them a house seven years ago, when they'd first married, as a wedding gift. He'd never even stepped foot into it. He wondered if Daphne had.

Colin looked about the table and noted everyone was waiting for him to respond. He took a breath. "Thank you, Your Grace. I'd like that." It would be as pleasant as swallowing glass.

The dinner dragged on. Colin tried not to stare at his wife, but every time he looked up from his plate, there she was. It would have been easier to ignore her if she'd been beside him. Instead, he had to watch James converse with her. From what he could tell, they didn't speak of anything particularly interesting, but Daphne always looked interested. She smiled and laughed and at one point, put her hand on James's arm. Colin began to rise from his seat when he saw that, but Lady Cora/Clara spoke and he remembered himself and sat back down.

"Are you quite well, Mr. FitzRoy?" the lady asked.

"Yes." Why had he never thought about Daphne touching other men before? Why had he never imagined her dancing with other men, flirting with them? Why had he not cared?

No, he amended, nodding politely as Lady Clara/Cora discussed a recent outing to Vauxhall Gardens and bemoaned its shabby state. It wasn't that Colin didn't care what Daphne did. It was that he could not allow himself to care. He could not become attached to her, could not begin to care for her. That path would only end badly. Not only would she never return his affection. She would never trust him after the way he'd treated her, and who could blame her?

The viscount had read her well when he'd said she needed an emotional connection. That was why she enjoyed the theater so much and the opera. That was why she discussed novels with James, tears in her eyes, across the table.

That was why Colin would never make her happy. He was uncomfortable just thinking about those displays of emotion.

And yet, he had little choice but to do his duty. He must at least appear to act the role of the husband. He'd done it before. He could do it again—hopefully, a bit more skillfully this time around.

Finally, the last course was eaten, and the dishes were cleared. The ladies adjourned to the drawing room and the men were left with cigars and port. As the ladies rose to exit, Daphne glanced at Colin. The look on her face was a mixture of guilt and regret. He would have liked to follow her, except the door closed, blocking his view of her. Colin tried to think of an excuse to go after her, but the duke was already passing out glasses of port.

"If you'll excuse me," Colin said, rising. "I'll find the retiring room."

"No need," the duke said, pulling a chamber pot from beneath the sideboard. "Here you are."

Colin took the thankfully unused chamber pot and set it back down. "I'll wait."

"Pass it here then," James said. Colin did so, trying not to cough when the cigar smoke wafted his way. He'd been in many places over the years—battlefields, taverns, ships, sewers—but he had never felt so out of place as he did in his father-in-law's town house.

"So," the duke said, sitting back with his cigar in one hand and his port in the other, "I expect you will want to relocate to your new house by the end of the week."

Colin didn't see as he had any choice but to agree. "Yes, the end of the week."

"Good. By this time next year, I expect I will be a grandfather again." He gave Colin a long look. Colin gave it back to him. "You are capable of giving me grandchildren, are you not, Mr. FitzRoy?"

Colin had the urge to hit him at that moment. His father, sensing trouble, broke in. "Of course, he is. Colin loves children. You should see him with my grandchildren."

"Good, good. Daphne needs children to keep her busy. That girl too easily falls into trouble." The duke sipped his port and exchanged a look with his son, whose lips thinned.

"What sort of trouble?" Colin asked. "The duchess mentioned some trouble to me before, but Lady Daphne has not been forthcoming."

The duke nodded. "It's good to see you take an interest. I think we both know that the duchess's mention of trouble was a ruse, but I have noticed that Daphne hasn't been herself lately. I thought it might be because you had returned, but it seems there is more to it. I have no proof, but…"

He trailed off. If Colin knew anything, it was how to listen, how to ferret out information. If he kept silent, the duke would say more. He would probably say more than he wanted. Unfortunately, Colin could not count on his father or brother to know the rules, and he dared not leave it to chance. "Go on," he said. "What do you suspect?"

"Something with Battersea," the duke said, surprising Colin. He'd thought the duke would wave a hand and dismiss the matter.

"Who is Battersea?" he asked.

"He's an earl," James said. "Something of a reprobate from what I've heard."

Colin nodded. "I'll look into him." Rather, he would ask Jasper Grantham to find out what he could. One of his fellow soldiers, Jasper practically lived in the rookeries as he often worked as a bounty hunter for hire. He knew every sort of vice in the city and who perpetrated it.

Colin stood.

"It can wait until tomorrow," Daphne's brother, the Marquess of Shorstow, said.

Colin didn't think so. "If you'll excuse me." Colin bowed and left the dining room. He stopped in the drawing room, intending to take his leave of the ladies and perhaps have that private conversation with Daphne. Now if she hesitated, he would ask her about Battersea.

"Ah, Mr. FitzRoy." The duchess nodded at him then looked behind him expectantly. She was seated on a couch, listening as her older daughter played at the pianoforte. Mary, Anne, and Louisa were listening politely. "Are the other gentlemen not coming?"

"Not yet." Colin scanned the room and frowned when he didn't find a splash of pink amongst the other ladies' gowns.

"She has a megrim," the duchess said. "Cora, do stop playing for a moment.

Ah, so it was Cora.

Lady Cora played a wrong note and huffed.

"As I was saying," the duchess continued, "Lady Daphne has a megrim and went up to her room."

"It was only a few minutes ago," Louisa added.

"We do hope you will call on her tomorrow," the duchess said, eyes wide with expectation.

Colin almost nodded and agreed. Then he remembered he was married to Lady Daphne. She didn't have the luxury of avoiding him any more than he did her.

"I'll just go up and check on her," he said.

The duchess's eyes widened with shock and also pleasure. "Oh!"

All three of his sisters sat up and looked interested now. Even Lady Cora looked away from her music to stare at him.

"Her chamber is still the same?" He ignored the many pairs of eyes fixed on him.

"Yes." The duchess's cheeks had turned pink, and Colin wanted to roll his eyes. As though he would run upstairs to ravish his wife when her head was pounding—though, as to that, he didn't believe her excuse for an instant.

He bowed and started for the stairs, taking them two at a time so that he was practically breathless by the time he reached the floor where the family had rooms. He went straight for Daphne's chamber, rapped on the door three times, then waited.

No answer.

He knocked again. "Daphne, may I come in? It's FitzRoy."

Still no answer. Was she asleep? Was she ignoring him?

He clenched his hands. Or was she not in her room at all?

He tried the handle. It was unlocked, and he swung the door wide. Her room was just as he remembered it—pink, with a white coverlet on the bed. Daphne was not in the bed. Her robe and nightrail had been laid out by her ladies' maid and a fire burned in the hearth, but Colin didn't need to step inside to know the room was empty. He did anyway, just to be doubly certain.

A few moments later, he was back in the drawing room. The duchess and Lady Cora had been whispering together and they broke apart almost guiltily when he entered.

"You're back," Anne said, as though warning the others he was now present.

"That was certainly quick," the duchess said, disapproval in her tone.

"She's not there."

"Not there?" the duchess looked confused. "Yes, she is. I saw her go up myself. She was going straight to bed." The other ladies nodded in agreement.

"Is there anywhere else in the house she might be? Perhaps she went to the kitchen for a tonic."

The duchess rang a bell and a moment later the butler entered. "Yes, Your Grace?"

"Dowling, have you seen Lady Daphne? Is she in the kitchen, perchance?"

"No, Your Grace. The last I saw her, she was slipping out the back door."

"What?" The duchess practically screeched. "But she's supposed to be in her room!"

Colin didn't wait for the duchess's shrill cries to bring the duke and the rest of his family running. He walked out, down the stairs, and through the front door.

If he hurried, he could catch her.

Seven

Daphne adjusted her sister's navy cloak and pulled it closer
about her face. She'd pilfered it from the room where the
footman had stored it, and she didn't feel guilty because
she'd return it tomorrow. The cloak's dark color hid her hair
and dress. She didn't want to be seen by the carriages passing
the duke's residence, and the best way to avoid notice was to
travel along the lane in the back where the mews were
located. She moved toward the back of the house and was in
the midst of the servants' yard, where laundry was hung to
dry and rugs were beaten, when a loud *yip* rent the air.
Daphne turned to find Pugsly hunched low and with his fur
bristling.

"Pugsly," she hissed. "It's me. Daphne."

Pugsly's head cocked to the side, but when she moved
closer to him, he backed away and yipped in warning.

"Pugsly! Shh!" Daphne lowered the hood of the cloak,
and seeing her face, Pugsly straightened and trotted to her.

Daphne petted him, obliging him when he rolled over to have his tummy scratched. Then she rose. "Quiet, boy. Sit."

Pugsly sat, blinking at her with those big, dark eyes. Daphne pulled the cloak back over her hair and started again toward the mews. She'd lost precious time, but if she hurried, she would still be able to escape before anyone realized she was gone. The men would spend at least another quarter hour with their port and then they would join the ladies. Even then, they would have no reason to question that Daphne was ill. No one would come and check on her for at least another hour.

She had plenty of time to make it to St. James and the gambling hells. There she would find a game of vingt-et-un or piquet, both card games she knew well and almost always won, and would win enough money to hold Battersea off for another week or so. She didn't know what she would do after that. She'd given him her pin money and pawned all her jewelry worth anything. But she'd paid the last of debt late, and he'd charged her interest—an exorbitant amount of interest she could never hope to pay, even if she won heaps in St. James's hells. And every day she was late on the interest, he added more.

She'd think of something. She had to because the alternative…

She opened the back gate, slipped through it, and shut it behind her, leaning against it with relief. She reached into a pocket of the cloak and withdrew the silver filigreed half mask. She'd intended to wear it to hide her identity. She wished she had a dress to wear that was not pink or a wig to hide her hair, but there was nothing for it. Anyone who knew her would still recognize her. At least the mask would allow her to pretend she was not Lady Daphne, even if the ruse fooled no one.

Lowering her hood, she placed the mask over her face and caught hold of the black silk ribbons on the side, pulling them behind her head to secure the mask. But it slipped and she had to position it again then fumble with the ribbons.

"Allow me to assist you," came a masculine voice from behind her.

"Thank y—" Daphne whirled around, praying she would see one of the grooms there. But she knew even before she saw him who it would be.

Colin FitzRoy.

She stared at him then looked back toward the house, whose windows were still lit up. She could even see shadows moving about behind the lighted windows of the drawing room.

"Surprised to see me?" he asked, stepping out of the shadows.

"How long have you been there?"

"Not long." His gaze traveled down her body, taking in the cloak. "You were almost safely away." His eyes lingered on the mask she still held. "Going to a ball?"

"Yes," she said, grasping onto the idea as though she were drowning and the suggestion was a rope. "I must have forgotten to mention the invitation I received to the masked ball."

"Did you forget to mention it to your mother as well?" He took the mask from her hand and studied it. "She seems to think you are in bed with a headache." He made a circling motion with his finger, and since she couldn't immediately think of a reply to his last statement, she gave him her back. He moved closer, the heat of him warming her through the thick woolen cloak. His arms came over her head, and he secured the mask over her eyes and the upper part of her face. Trailing his fingers along her temples, he tied the ribbons behind her head and knotted them tightly. He took her by the shoulders and moved her to face him. His gaze bore into her for so long that she finally looked away.

"Will I do?" she asked.

"I don't know. Where are we really going?"

"*I* am going to a ball."

"If we were really attending a ball, you would do nicely. But if you actually need to hide your identity, you're wasting your time."

She was caught as surely as a fish who had eaten the worm. She could feel herself dangling above safety, gasping for her last breaths.

"Are you ready to tell me the truth yet?"

"Why? So you can lecture and berate me?"

His green eyes narrowed, the only indication he was concerned. "Will lecturing and berating help the matter?"

"No."

"Then I'll save that for another time."

Daphne touched the mask, the delicate pattern pressing into the flesh of her face. She would have to tell him something. She couldn't avoid it now.

"Go on," he said, his tone that of a parent scolding a child. "It's easier if you say it quickly."

"Odious man." Why were men always shouldering their way in where they were not wanted? At least this particular man was not telling her to go inside and finish her embroidery. She might as well tell him. She could always try for St. James's again later tonight.

"I need money," she said.

His expression didn't change. "Why?"

"Does it matter?"

"Probably."

"I just need it. I was planning to go to one of the gaming hells on St. James's Street and win at cards."

Colin stared at her for a long moment as though waiting for her to say more. "You're actually serious," he finally said. "This was your plan." He indicated the mask and the cloak with a wave of his hand. "You thought to waltz into a gaming hell, play a few hands of Loo—"

"Piquet."

"Even worse—and walk out with a fortune?"

Annoyed now, she stuck her hands on her hips. "And what's wrong with that? I'm a good card player. I could beat you."

"Do you know anything about these gaming hells you think to fleece? They would not stay in business if the players won."

Daphne shook her head in disbelief. "You mean they cheat?"

"Not the more reputable ones, but you wouldn't gain entrance to any of those. You have to pay for a membership, and ladies are not admitted. You'd only be allowed in the worst sort of places, and you'd be cheated blind. After that, you'd probably be accosted."

"I'm prepared for that."

His brow rose, and to prove her point, she reached into an inner pocket of her dress and pulled out a gold bouquet holder encrusted with jewels.

Colin looked at the small ornament. "You'll present your attacker with flowers?"

"No." She pulled off the end of the handle to reveal a dagger. "This was my grandmother's, passed down to me."

"Why the hell did your grandmother have a knife hidden in a bouquet holder?"

"She was in France during their revolution. She needed a way to defend herself when she fled the guillotine."

"And you intend to do what with that?" He gestured toward the sharp point. "Stab a man?"

"I could."

His mouth thinned.

"I could!" she insisted. "If my life depended on it."

"Stab me then." He stepped closer to her.

"What? No." She stepped back.

"I'm an attacker. Stab me." He said opening his arms wide.

"Stop it."

He lunged toward her. Startled, she brought the bouquet holder up sharply.

"Good. Now do it."

"I can't!"

"Do it!"

"Fine." She sliced at him, intending to make a shallow cut, but he moved more quickly than she'd anticipated, feinted to the left, reached out, and snatched the bouquet holder from her hand. He tossed it aside then pushed her up against the gate, his arm across her chest.

She gasped in outrage. "Those are real rubies you just tossed to the ground!"

"You should be worried about more than rubies. It took me all of ten seconds to relieve you of your weapon. What will you do now?"

"Release me," she said in her most authoritative voice.

"I'm an attacker, Daphne, not a gentleman."

"Then I'd fight you." Her gaze met his, and she felt a little shiver of pleasure at his closeness.

"You'd lose. I'm stronger than you."

She nodded. She could feel his power in the press of his leg against hers and the firmness of his arm across her upper chest. "You've made your point."

"I hardly believe that. As soon as I let you go, you'll wait until you think I'm gone and try again."

He knew her better than she thought. They stood there for a long moment, breathing heavily, his body pressed against hers. She wasn't thinking about gambling any longer. Her body was tingling, and her throat had gone dry. "Colin?"

He made a sound like a grunt.

"What will you do now?"

"I don't know. I'm considering my options." His voice was low and ragged.

"So am I."

"I don't suppose one of them is to go inside and go straight to bed."

"No." She shook her head slightly.

"Is one to tell me more about this money you owe?"

"No." She wet her lips. His gaze lowered to her mouth, and a stab of hot desire speared through her belly.

"I'm out of ideas," he murmured.

"I'm not." She leaned forward and brushed her lips over his. His arm was still pinning her shoulders to the wall, and she couldn't raise her hands to touch him, but he didn't move away. He held perfectly still while her lips caressed his with feather-light touches. "Lower your arm," she said, her own voice low and breathy. She couldn't seem to take in enough oxygen.

His arm dropped, and she was suddenly free. She had not thought he would actually do as she asked. She moved closer to him. He didn't move, not even when she ran her hands up his chest and then high enough to knock off his hat. She could see his face more clearly now. See that dark hair she always wanted to touch. She curled her fingers in the hair at the base of his neck and tugged his head down. He could have easily resisted, but he went willingly. They both hesitated for a moment, and then she couldn't hold back. Her lips collided with his. As soon as their mouths touched, heat rushed through her. The cloak was too warm, her clothing too tight, the distance between them too great. She moved closer, flicking his lips with her tongue until he opened for her. She kissed him deeper, wondering if he would stop her. He hadn't kissed her back.

But then her tongue slid against his, and he made a sound like a low growl. She was suddenly thrust against the gate again. His hands were on either side of her head, and his lips were doing things to her that she had never imagined. She was dizzy with pleasure and only vaguely aware that she was making small mewling noises.

"You like that." His mouth trailed to her neck, and he bestowed kisses there then bit her earlobe gently.

Daphne felt her legs go weak as heat surged straight into her lower belly. Who was this man? She'd never seen him show even an ounce of emotion and now here was passion so hot she could hardly remain upright.

His lips moved down to her shoulder, where the cloak covered her skin. She wished she could throw it off. She wanted his lips on more of her skin. His hands moved under the cloak as he kissed her neck. She felt them on her waist as they moved slowly higher.

"Yes," she murmured. Her breasts ached to be touched. All of her ached at that moment.

But instead of easing that need, he stepped back.

She opened her eyes. "What?" She could barely speak; she was panting so hard. He was out of breath too. His chest rose and fell as though he'd been running. He jerked his head to the left, and she saw two footmen walking toward the mews. They were having a discussion and hadn't spotted her and Colin yet, but they would in another moment.

And they were her father's men. She knew the livery.

Colin seemed to know exactly what to do. He reached down for his hat, took her hand, then pulled her along the garden wall until they were standing in deep shadow. "We'll wait until they're gone," he whispered.

Daphne nodded, but she couldn't help but wonder what would happen when the footmen had gone back inside. What were they waiting to do? Would he kiss her again? Ravish her? Make her go back inside? Take her to St. James's Street?

She wanted to ask but didn't dare make any noise. The footmen were too close now, and they'd reached the mews. One went inside, and she heard him speaking to the groom. The FitzRoys wanted their carriage.

She glanced at Colin, but he was already looking at her. Heat boiled up in her again, the desire that came with it was so strong she had to bite her lips to stop herself from making a sound. His eyes, though too dark to see well, seemed to glitter. She moved then, careful to stay in the shadows as she pushed him against the garden wall.

He gave her a warning look, but she wasn't deterred. She leaned forward, cupped the back of his neck, and kissed him hard. He responded immediately, kissing her back and pulling her roughly against him. She'd never felt anything like this before. Sparks seemed to ignite each time their lips touched, and she was almost surprised not to see them flare in the darkness.

Finally, when her breathing had grown so ragged that she feared she was too loud, he pulled her against his chest and held her there. She could hear his heart hammering as fast as her own. So the man was not completely without emotions. How she longed to incite them again. She liked this side of him.

"I have to get you out of here," he said, low enough so only she could hear.

She nodded, eager to go with him. She'd been afraid he would tell her to go back inside. She was prepared to tell him she'd only go to her chamber if he came too.

He pulled her hood up then tugged her along the narrow alley, making her walk so quickly she almost had to run. Stones in the street jabbed into her feet and she hissed with pain. She tugged on his arm to dislodge a stone, and he looked back at her. "What's wrong?"

"My shoes." She lifted the hem of her skirts to show the thin slippers she wore.

Colin stared at her as though she were a complete imbecile. "I'll hail a hackney," he said.

"Where are we going?" she asked as they stepped out onto the street just a little way down from her father's town house. She looked in that direction, watching as the FitzRoys' grooms calmed the horses standing on the street outside. Any minute the FitzRoys themselves would come out.

"Somewhere we can talk," he said, raising a hand to a hackney whose driver immediately turned his horse toward them.

"I told you I want to go to St. James's Street," she protested.

He cut her a glance. "I'll take you later. If you still want to go."

The hackney stopped, and he opened the door for her. As she climbed in, she heard him give the driver the Duke of Mayne's address.

***

Mayne's town house was only a short distance, but Colin didn't trust himself. He sat opposite Daphne and made a point not to look at her. What the devil was she about, kissing him like that on a public street? What was he about, kissing her back? Given about three more minutes, he would have had her half-undressed. Every time he saw her, his appetite was whetted. Now he was practically ravenous for her.

The difficult thing was that even though she was his wife, taking her to bed wasn't that simple. It would be the start of something—and he was none too certain what exactly that something might be. What were the rules? What would she want from him?

He knew what he wanted. He knew *exactly* what he wanted, but somehow he doubted that orgasm after orgasm after orgasm was all she was after.

But perhaps he could make her forget that if he got her into bed.

And wasn't that exactly why he was taking her to Mayne's house? Because he wanted her alone?

He shook his head.

"What's wrong?" she asked.

Obviously, she was watching him.

"Nothing."

"Why are you taking me to the duke's house?"

"Because we can talk privately there," he said. That was what he had to remember. That he needed to talk to her. Needed to find out what had made her desperate enough that she was willing to put on a disguise and risk the gaming hells on St. James's Street.

"And what if I have nothing more to say?" She rose, and he realized she intended to move to sit beside him. He pointed at her.

"Stay where you are."

She cocked her head. "Why? Afraid you'll kiss me again?"

He didn't answer. That was it exactly, but he didn't have to admit it.

"All these years I thought you didn't want me. That's not really true, is it?"

Colin gave her a sharp look. "Why would you think that?" But as soon as the words were out, he realized it was a stupid question. And he was a stupid man. How had he never considered what his avoidance of their marriage might mean to her? Of course, she would think he didn't want her.

"I suppose because on our wedding night you were so…perfunctory."

"I didn't want to hurt you, and I didn't know what I was doing." The words came out somewhat choked. It was not as easy an admission as he made it sound.

She crossed her arms over her chest. "Then why not just say that? I was nervous as well."

"I was not nervous." He'd been terrified.

She gave him a long look, but he wasn't backing down.

Finally, she sighed. Heavily. "No. You aren't ever nervous. I'm sure you never feel any of the normal human emotions."

"Forgive me if I don't want to spend hours talking about my *feelings*."

"Then you admit you have them?"

"I'm feeling one right now." The annoyance in his tone should have quieted her, but the woman was relentless.

"And I daresay you were feeling something when we were near the mews. Is that the extent of your repertoire then? Impatience and lust?"

"You've forgotten frustration."

"Ooh, I rather like that one." She pushed her hood off her hair and undid the fastening at her neck. Sliding the cloak off, she revealed the dress she'd been wearing at the dinner party. His gaze went immediately to the bow under her breasts. "Is it hot in here?" she asked, watching him.

"No."

"Are you sure?" She tugged at the fingers of her gloves.

"We will be there in a moment. Don't take anything else off." His mouth spoke the words, but his body was not in agreement. His cock was hard and stiff, and his mouth was practically dry at the thought of seeing her bare arms. Which was ridiculous. He had seen much more than a woman's bare arms before. He might have honored his wedding vows and resisted temptation all these years. But even if he didn't touch, that didn't mean he didn't sometimes look. And there were usually plenty of women who were eager to lure him to their beds.

Daphne tugged at another finger of her glove then another until the top slid down, revealing the pale skin just above her elbow. She pulled gently on the white silk until a fraction more of her soft flesh was revealed. He meant to look away, but he couldn't seem to stop watching as inch after inch of her arm was revealed to him.

Colin shifted in his seat, trying to find a comfortable way to sit. He felt like a boy again. He was hot and flushed from the mere glimpse of cleavage. Daphne pulled the rest of the glove off, revealing long, thin fingers. "That's better," she said. She looked at him, her blue eyes glowing with mischief behind the mask she still wore. Oh, she knew exactly what she was about. "Will you hold this for me?" She tossed it to him, and he caught the glove mid-air.

"No more," he said, his voice hoarse.

"Why not?" She tugged at the other glove, and it slid down quite easily. He watched its progress over the inner skin of her elbow, and he wondered how she tasted there, if she was sensitive in that spot, what she would do if he teased her with his tongue right where the glove had been.

The glove lowered further, dragging his gaze down with it.

"Feeling anything new?" she asked, her voice low and seductive.

He didn't answer.

"Are you sure you don't want me to come sit beside you? You look a little frustrated."

That was an understatement, but thankfully the hackney slowed and the jarvey called out their destination. Colin jumped to his feet, opened the door, and gulped in the night air. The hackney hadn't felt warm when he'd first climbed inside.

He held out his hand to assist the now cloakless and gloveless Lady Daphne. Colin tried not to notice her bare shoulders and arms, encased only in a thin, gauzy material that was certainly more for show than function. He tossed the jarvey a handful of coins and started up the walkway just as Mayne's butler opened the door.

"Good evening, Mr. FitzRoy. Lady Daphne." Banks greeted them as though he had been expecting them. "Would you like to join the others in the drawing room?"

Colin halted. "Others? Is Mayne back?"

"No, sir. But Mr. Fortescue and Mr. Murray have stopped in."

"Not the Scot," Daphne murmured, but it was too late. Duncan was already on the stairs.

"Just the lass I wanted to see," he said, coming down a few steps. He took in her mask and paused. "I dinnae ken there was a masque tonight. Let me find something to wear, and I'll join you."

"We didn't come looking for you," Colin said.

Duncan folded his arms over his chest. "I must say, yer lass is doing a puir job of finding me a bride."

"Is this your wife, FitzRoy?"

Colin blew out a breath. Now they had Stratford *and* Duncan to contend with. "Lady Daphne, may I present—"

"Mr Fortescue," she said. "We know each other, of course. How is your cousin?"

"Unfortunately, she has a sniffle tonight," he said, not looking the least bit troubled by that fact. "Else I would be squiring her about."

Daphne gestured to Duncan. "Why not introduce her to Mr. Murray? He is looking for a bride."

Duncan held up a hand. "I'm beginning to think matchmaking is nae your forte, lass. My mother won't have a woman like Fortescue's cousin." He lowered his voice. "She's far too mannish."

"I say, Murray." Stratford turned on him. "She's as much a lady as any other. She just has ideas."

"Why would I want a bride with ideas?"

"Yes, by all means, marry a witless girl," Daphne said, her voice full of exasperation. "I do not know why I am even here. I have somewhere more important to be."

"Oh no, you don't." Colin grasped her arm. Her bare arm. God, had he ever felt skin so soft? "Lady Daphne and I have a matter to discuss," he told his friends.

"What aboot the masque?" Duncan asked.

Stratford put his arm about Duncan's shoulders. "Not tonight, friend." He called down to Colin. "We'll be in the drawing room for at least another hour or so." He winked.

Daphne blew out a breath. "Really. Don't you men have a club or something?"

"We do, actually. Banks, I believe we will use the parlor again."

"Yes, sir. Would you like wine?"

"No." Colin ushered Daphne into the parlor, closing the door behind him. The fire had already been lit, as though he had been anticipated. Daphne went immediately to one of the green chairs and sat.

"Will this take long?" she asked. "I have a gaming hell to visit."

Colin went to the hearth and leaned against the mantel. "I told you I'd take you."

Her eyes narrowed. "Surely there is some condition."

"Take off your mask," he said.

She frowned, clearly surprised at his words. But he couldn't see her face as well with it in place, and he wanted to be able to read her expression.

"Why?"

"Nevermind. I will do it for you." He moved behind her low-backed chair and loosed the silk ribbons. She caught the mask and set it on the table beside her.

"That actually feels much better," she said. "I hadn't realized it was sticking to my skin. And my head really is beginning to ache." She reached up and pressed a hand into her tight coiffure.

"Take it down then," he said, his voice far lower than he would have liked. Her hand stilled, and he saw her slight shiver. "Allow me." He took hold of a pin that was already out of place and plucked it out. One lone curl descended, and he moved closer, bending to kiss the spot it grazed. Daphne inhaled sharply as his lips brushed against the back of her neck.

Slowly, he rose and studied her silvery hair again. He plucked out another pin and then another and more hair tumbled down to the middle of her back. He unwrapped a coil of it and she let out a soft moan and rolled her neck. Seeing no more pins, Colin brushed her hair back off her face and threaded his hands through the thick mass. He found her scalp and gently massaged.

Daphne made a sound of unmistakable pleasure. She let her neck fall back, and he pressed against her temples. Her eyes closed, and he tried very hard not to look down the front of her gown. He moved his hands, massaging the base of her neck, and her head fell forward.

"Where did you learn to do this?" she asked, her voice thick with pleasure.

He didn't think mentioning a brothel in Spain was wise. "Here and there," he said, then moved her hair to the side and stared at the delicate flesh of the back of her neck. He bent and placed a kiss there, and her hand came up cupping him around the base of his neck. She turned her face and kissed him full on the lips. Colin's hands landed on her shoulders as her mouth moved against his. He slid his palms down to the silk of her gown, feeling the ridges of the fabric-covered buttons securing the gown. His fingers felt big and clumsy on the small round buttons, but he managed to loosen one and then another.

Daphne stopped kissing him and pulled back, her vivid blue eyes meeting his. He didn't mistake the desire in her eyes. He knew she saw it in his own, and he knew that this was a sure way to entangle himself further with him.

But there was no altering course now. It would happen tonight or another night, and he would have to find a way to deal with the emotions that came with their lovemaking. They were married, and he couldn't escape her forever.

Nor did he want to.

He undid another button and the fabric of her bodice slid down, revealing the pale pink of her stays. His gaze slid there and to the flesh that had been lifted by the undergarment. The bow beneath her breasts was still in place, which meant he had only a glimpse of the top of her breasts. But it was enough. He moved around the chair and knelt before her. She stared at him, watching to see what he would do next, her breath coming quickly. He reached out, fingered the bow, ran the soft material through his hands, then yanked. It came loose, and the bodice dipped lower, revealing the lacy stays with a pink bow right between her breasts. He couldn't remove the stays. Not without taking the rest of the garment off and then unhooking the undergarment. It was all a froth of silks and muslin to him, and he'd probably never get her back into it if he managed to get her out. But he told himself this was enough. He only wanted to look at her, and perhaps taste.

He put his hands on her knees and opened her legs. She resisted for just a moment then allowed it. Her skirts gave way as he slid between her legs and took her face in his hands.

Her breath was audible now, hitching in her throat. "Kiss me," she ordered him.

He did. He kissed her long and hard and until she was whimpering for more. When he drew back so they could both catch their breath, she closed her legs about his waist, keeping him in place. He gave her a long look then drew a line from her swollen lips to her chin, down over her throat. She shivered and arched back, and he couldn't resist. He pressed his mouth to the half-moons of her breasts, inhaling her sweet, tart scent and feeling the silky skin against his lips.

Her hands threaded through his hair as he kissed her warm flesh. He tugged at her stays, managing to free first one rosy nipple then another. Colin drew in a breath, certain he would never be able to look at her dresses in the same way. Her aureoles were pale pink while her nipples were a dusty rose. He ran his tongue over one and watched as her skin pebbled. Her hands in his hair tightened and he took the hard bud in his mouth, sucking lightly.

Daphne moaned and arched, giving him more access. He teased and licked before moving to the other nipple. While his mouth worked, his hands dove between them, inching up her skirts. When he reached the tie of her garters, above her knee, she jerked at the feel of his bare hands on her leg. She pushed back, giving him a lovely view of her upthrust breasts. Her gaze drifted down to where his hand made a small hill under the fabric of her gown.

"Unlock your knees," he murmured, stroking the knee she had clamped at his waist. "I promise I'm not going anywhere."

He thought she might argue or protest, but she released him, her eyes glittering with interest. His hand slid higher, over skin so soft and smooth he would have sworn it was the most expensive silk. Her eyes fluttered closed, and he watched her face, enjoying the way her lips parted when his fingers brushed over the damp curls at the juncture of her thighs.

"I've never done this before," he said, leaning forward and kissing one breast. His heart pounded with desire and alarm at what he'd just admitted. If he opened himself a little, would she wedge her fingers in and pry him open all the way? He wanted her enough to risk it. "I've been told there's a small nub that will bring you pleasure. But I'm not certain I can find it." His tongue slaked over the hard point of her nipple. "Will you help me?" Those last words were the hardest. His throat had closed, and he'd had to force them out.

"Yes," she breathed on a moan, not seeming to notice the difficulty he had even with this small admission.

His hand slid higher, cupping her. She was hot and pushed against his hand, her slick flesh sliding easily against his fingers. "Is this it?" he asked, parting her outer folds.

"No," she whispered.

He stroked her, finding her opening and pausing. "Here?"

"Colin," she breathed, her sex tensing against his hand. He slid higher, and he didn't need to ask if he'd found the spot. She jumped, and her eyes flew open to meet his.

"Here?" he asked, sliding one wet finger over the small bud.

"Please," she moaned, moving against his hand. Her cheeks were flushed, her eyes bright, and her chest heaving. He had never seen a more perfect image in his life, and he would never forget how ravishing she looked in that moment. He'd taken a risk, and the benefit had been priceless. His thumb circled her, and she threw her head back. "Yes. Oh, don't stop."

He should tell her to lower her voice, but truthfully, he wanted more. She sounded so husky and raw. He watched her reaction, learning what she liked and responded to. When she cried out and grasped the arms of the chair, he knew he'd brought her pleasure.

The only question was what would happen when it faded.

Eight

Daphne felt too good to be embarrassed. She knew she'd behaved in an unladylike fashion, but she really didn't care. She opened her eyes to find Colin's beautiful green ones watching her. He had a smug smile on his lips, and for once she didn't feel like wiping it away. She'd give him that smile. He'd earned it.

She leaned forward, watched as his gaze dipped to her bared breasts, then up to her lips. She kissed him, pulling him close. She couldn't seem to get enough of his hands and his mouth. She wanted more.

And then something else occurred to her. She pushed him back and quickly yanked up her stays. His brows rose, but he didn't look surprised. He looked as though he expected this. "I see what you're doing now," she said. She pushed him back, closed her legs, then rose. The back of her gown was still unfastened and her bodice gaped, but she pushed down her skirts and held her bodice up with one hand.

"What am I doing?" he asked, resting one arm on his bent knee. He hadn't even bothered to rise from the floor.

"You're trying to distract me. You don't want me to go to St. James's Street."

His face darkened. "Of course I don't want you to go to St. James's, but if you think this"—he gestured to the chair—"was about me trying to trick you, you are wrong."

"What else could it be?" she demanded. "Don't tell me you couldn't resist me. You've resisted me for seven years." She had thought he'd been swept away by passion, as she had been, but she was a fool. He didn't suddenly care for her. He'd more than proven he cared nothing at all for her.

Colin rose slowly and deliberately. "I told you I would take you to St. James's if you wanted to go."

"Fine." She gave him her back. "Do me up. I want to go."

For a long moment she thought he would argue or walk away, but then she felt the heat of him behind her. His hands ran down her back, and he closed the first button. "If we're to go to a gaming hell, we need a plan. Fortunately, we have one of the best strategists in the country upstairs."

She whipped her head around to look at Colin. "Murray?"

"No. Mr. Fortescue."

Daphne shook her head and faced away again. "No. I don't want him to know. I don't need his help."

He sighed quietly then said in a resolute tone, "What is your plan?"

"I'll wear the mask and find a game I like. If possible, I'll find a game where the other players are deep in their cups. I can smile and flirt and leave before I win too much. Then I'll move to the next club."

His hands paused at her buttons. "That's not half bad."

"Thank you." She straightened her shoulders.

"But it won't work."

She swung around to face him. "Why not?"

"Because this isn't a card party or a ball. The games are run by the management. You go to a table with a dealer. He won't be drunk, and if you start to win, the management will replace him with someone who will make sure you start to lose. I told you. These places wouldn't stay open if they lost money."

"I have brothers, Colin FitzRoy, and I hear them talking about winning fifty or seventy pounds all the time."

"And how much do you need?" he asked.

She opened her mouth to tell him then closed it again.

He let out a breath and closed his eyes. "That much?"

"I don't know why I told you anything." She pushed past him. "I knew you wouldn't help."

"I can't help if you won't tell me anything. How much do you owe? It has to be an exorbitant amount or you would have asked me for the money."

She couldn't argue. He was no duke, but he was far from poor. He was the son of a viscount, one of the older titles in the realm. By all accounts, he had a sizeable yearly income.

"It's more than I have," she admitted grudgingly.

"Why not tell the lady who holds your vowels you'll pay in installments? Surely your father gives you generous pin money."

"It's no lady, and if I don't pay soon, he'll—" She broke off. She didn't want to admit what a fool she'd been. She'd been playing so well. She had not believed she could lose, but she'd been an idiot. She was the one being played all along.

Colin grabbed her arm before she could escape. "He'll what?"

"Nothing."

"Who is it?"

"No one you know. Now, will you take me to St. James's Street or not?"

"No."

"Then I'll go by myself." She pulled loose, gathered her cloak, and started for the door. But when she opened it, she found Stratford Fortescue and Duncan Murray blocking her path.

Mr. Fortescue's eyes widened slightly, and she realized her hair was still loose and her bodice not quite repaired. Murray seemed not to notice. "I told you the lass would change her mind," he said. "Tell us where the masque is and we'll escort you."

Colin stepped out from behind her. "We're not attending a masque," he said to his friends. To her he said, "And we're not visiting St. James's Street. You don't need to win at the tables to fix this. I have another plan"

She stared at him, waiting for him to go on.

But he glanced at his friends. "I'll explain more later. Right now, I'm taking you home. We have a busy day tomorrow. Your mother is taking us to see our new home."

"You have a town house?" Fortescue asked. "Where?"

"I have no idea."

"My mother won't be up before noon," Daphne said. "It's not even two in the morning. Tell me your plan now."

He shook his head. "It needs a bit of polishing. I promise to tell you tomorrow."

She didn't believe him. How could he possibly make a plan when he didn't even know how much she owed or to whom? On the other hand, he'd made her reconsider traipsing down to St. James's Street and gambling the night away. What if winning was not as easy as she thought? What if she only found herself in more debt and with a ruined reputation besides?

"Fine. Take me home," she said, fumbling with her cloak. Mr. Fortescue helped her with it, but when she had it fastened at her throat, she noticed Colin was speaking quietly with Murray.

"Don't tell me *he's* part of your plan."

Colin smiled. "Fine. I won't."

"I'll hail the hackney," Fortescue said.

"You?" Daphne looked at the three men. "You're all coming?"

"No sense wasting a perfectly good hackney," Murray said with a wink. Daphne wanted to hit him. The last thing she wanted was to be trapped in a hackney with these three men. Fortunately, Murray and Fortescue went on their way when she and Colin departed the hackney at the corner near her father's house.

"I'll just make sure you get inside," Colin said, leading her around the back, past the now quiet mews. She couldn't help but dart a glance at the place he'd kissed her before. She had the urge to kiss him again. But she had to remember that it was all calculation with him. He didn't really feel anything when he was with her. It was a means to an end, and she would not allow him to break her heart again.

And so she left him at the gate and went inside, straight to her chamber, without being seen. She could not stop thinking that she was out of time with Battersea. He would come for her soon.

But when she reached her bedside, she had the sense Colin was still near, and she went to the window and parted the curtains. She didn't see him, but she knew he would stay close. The thought of him nearby eased her mind enough that she could sleep.

***

The duchess had arranged for Colin and Daphne to visit their new house at half past three in the afternoon. This was undoubtedly so the couple could be seen riding together after the visit at the fashionable hour. Colin could appreciate the Duchess of Warcliffe's strategic mind. She could have challenged Stratford Fortescue for his role in Draven's troop.

Her daughter was equally cunning, so Colin had watched the town house for another half hour the night before until the servant he'd paid had come out to tell him Lady Daphne had gone to sleep. The maid swore she'd seen the lady in bed and asleep.

He'd gone home and prepared for the morning. It was not hard to discover Lady Daphne's daily routine. She was at home to callers Tuesdays and Thursdays. She made calls Mondays and Wednesdays. Fridays she visited her modiste, a dark-skinned Frenchwoman who had a shop near Bond Street. Colin took up residence across from Madame Renauld's shop, dressed as one of the lower classes, the sort of man a shop owner might employ as a bully to keep the rabble and thieves away. He doubted Daphne would recognize him but was sure of it when the Earl of Shrewsbury leapt out of his curricle and threw Colin his reigns before escorting his wife into a hat shop. Shrewsbury was the brother of his friend Jasper, and the earl and Colin had met on several occasions.

Colin didn't mind being given the task. It made his disguise more authentic when the Duke of Warcliffe's carriage turned into the small square and a footman helped Daphne out. She told the coachman to return in an hour and went into Madame Renauld's. The footman waited outside.

Daphne came out twenty minutes later, followed by a seamstress who handed the footman a package. The servant followed Daphne to the café next door where she usually took tea until the carriage returned. If Colin knew her routine this well, it wouldn't be difficult for someone else to learn it. He'd been there long enough to see all the people who went in and out of the modiste's shop and the café, and now he moved so he could see into the café a bit better. No one had entered who he thought might have anything to do with Daphne and the money she owed. There were a few debutantes with their mothers and an older couple. Daphne seemed to take no notice of them.

But she owed someone money and the debt was due, else she wouldn't have been so desperate to visit the gaming tables on St. James's Street last night. And whoever was in her debt would want to speak to her sooner rather than later.

Just then a man in an expensive greatcoat and carrying an ebony walking stick rounded the corner on the other side, entering the square. Colin went on alert, but his attention was diverted when Shrewsbury returned and threw him a few coins before taking his reins. Colin moved along the street, finally spotting the man again in front of the modiste's shop. He went in, which Colin found curious as he had no lady with him.

"Can you spare a ha'pence, sir?"

Colin glanced down at the urchin looking up at him, hand outstretched. Of course, he didn't fool the street urchins.

They knew who belonged and who didn't. Colin dug out a penny Shrewsbury had tossed him and gave it to the lad. "You can have another if you tell me the name of the man that just went into that dressmaker's shop."

The boy's eyes lit up. "The nob?"

"Yes."

The boy's eyes narrowed. "She'll throw me out. Don't like anyone not a customer to come inside, and she already has a boy who fetches and carries."

"Then you'll have a penny for your trouble. Hurry up and decide."

The boy looked at the penny in his hand, then the shop, then darted across the street and slipped into the shop. Colin melted back into the scenery, his gaze alternating between the modiste's and the café.

A moment later the modiste's door opened and a seamstress bodily threw the urchin out. He made a rude hand gesture then crossed the street, rubbing his ear. He looked up and down for a moment until he spotted Colin.

"I think I deserve two pence for what she did to my ear. It 'urts like the dickens."

"Who is he?" Colin asked, without preamble.

The urchin held out his hand. "I like to be paid up front."

Colin tossed him the penny. The boy examined it then said, "The man's name is Battersea. 'E's a lord, but I don't know what kind."

Colin doubted the presence of the Earl of Battersea was a coincidence. "What else?"

"Says 'e's shopping for ladies' gloves, but 'e wasn't looking at them."

"What was he looking at?"

"More like looking around, if you know what I mean."

"I do." Colin gave him another penny. "Now take that money to your mother so she can buy something for your family to eat."

The boy made a face. "She'll just spend it all on gin."

"Then you buy food and share it. Off with you before one of the bigger boys decides to shake it out of you."

The boy tapped his cap and started away. "Will you come back?" he asked.

"I don't know."

"If you do, I'll go in the shop for you again."

"Good to know." But Colin's eyes were on the modiste's shop. Battersea had emerged, and, presumably not having found Daphne in the dressmaker's, was now heading toward the café.

He went in the café, and Colin crossed the street. Colin couldn't go in the café, not dressed as he was, but he stood to one side of the window and watched.

As soon as Battersea entered, Daphne stiffened and rose to leave. Battersea, the picture of politeness, seemed to accidentally step in her path and apologize. Daphne barely looked at him as he spoke, keeping her head high. Her cheeks turned pink, and she nodded slightly before moving past him toward the door. Colin checked the street. Her carriage had not returned yet and would not for another quarter hour or so. That would give Battersea plenty of time to threaten and cajole.

She stepped outside, her gaze sliding over Colin as she looked around the square. "William, go fetch the coachman, will you?" she asked.

"Yes, my lady." The footman rushed away.

A moment later Battersea stepped out of the café and stood behind her. Daphne's eyes closed, and Colin imagined she realized her mistake then. She was alone on the street with nowhere to escape.

Colin intended to stand by and leave her to her fate. After all, it was full daylight in a well-trafficked square and her footman would return with the carriage shortly. But Battersea made his own error. He came up behind Daphne and took her arm.

She wore a pink cloak, and the man probably couldn't feel much more than the material of the garment, but Colin did not like seeing the other man's hand on her. "My lady," Colin said in his best lower-class accent. She glanced at him in surprise but still without recognition. "I'll escort you if you're ready to go."

"Go away," Battersea told him. "She's already sent the footman to fetch the carriage."

Colin could see the man clearly now. He had red hair and dark eyes. He was tall and wiry under his clothing and his lips were thin, his cheeks elegant slashes. Colin knew without a doubt this was the man she owed money to, and he was not a man to be trifled with.

Not that Colin cared one way or the other. If he didn't take his hand off Colin's wife, the man would find his nose on the wrong side of his face. Colin kept his head bowed and his expression placid, mirroring none of the anger building inside him.

"Then my lady has time to stop in and look at the hat shop."

"My lady is speaking with me. Go find your coin elsewhere." He tossed a coin to the ground, but Colin ignored it. It was then that Daphne really looked at him. No man truly in his position would ignore the coin. "As I was saying," Battersea began.

Daphne pulled her gaze from Colin to frown at Battersea. "My lord, I believe I said we would have to speak of it later."

"We'll speak of it now."

Colin couldn't seem to stop looking at Battersea's gloved hand on Daphne's cloak. His grip had tightened and looked far too possessive. Colin grabbed the hand and shoved the man back. They were of a similar height and Battersea stumbled.

"What is the meaning of this?" Battersea righted himself and came for Colin, who stood his ground.

"She said she'll speak later."

"I will have you locked away for this, you filthy piece of offal. How dare you put hands on me?" He raised his walking stick and swung it at Colin's head. Colin caught it and shoved Battersea back again.

"My lady, we had better walk away now," he said quickly.

She nodded, staring at him as though she'd seen a ghost. Colin took her wrist and pulled her toward Bond Street, where presumably the carriage had been driven to wait. They walked quickly as Battersea sputtered behind them.

"That was foolish," she said. "He'll kill you."

"He was hurting you," Colin answered.

"Yes, but…" She stared at him. "Do I know you?"

Colin lifted his chin and looked her directly in the face. She stumbled and went pale. "Oh, my God."

"Now just you wait!" Battersea yelled. "I said halt!"

Colin could hear his footsteps pounding behind them, and at the last minute he pushed Daphne aside. "Stay there." He swung around in time to duck Battersea's fist. Battersea had swung hard and expected to make impact, so he was not ready for Colin's counterattack. Colin brought his right fist up for a swift upper cut to Battersea's jaw. Battersea grunted and landed a punch in Colin's ribs. He huffed out air but ignored the pain and swept Battersea's leg. When he was down, he kicked him in the belly.

Breathing heavily, Colin held out his arm to Daphne. "Shall we?"

"You're mad," she breathed, but she was smart enough not to hesitate. Daphne jumped away from the wall and took his arm. As they walked, she looked over her shoulder.

"Eyes forward," he said, gritting his teeth against the burn in his ribs.

"He's standing up. He looks angry enough to kill both of us." She trembled, and Colin realized she truly was afraid.

"Son of a bastard." His rib must be bruised. It felt like a knife in his flesh.

"This way," she said, arrowing for the modiste's shop.

"He'll just follow us inside." Colin could picture it now. They'd exchange punches, turning over tables of muslin and causing bows to flutter all over the floor.

"Have some faith in me," she said.

Since he didn't relish the idea of continuing the fight with an injury, he followed her through the door. As soon as they entered the cool, dim interior, the clerk was beside them. "My lady, did you forget something?"

"No, but I need your help, Miss Phaedra."

"Of course."

"Tell the man who comes in next we went out the back," Daphne said.

"I will, but—"

"Is anyone in the private parlor?" She was tugging Colin toward the back staircase.

"No, but we have a customer in"—she checked her pocket watch—"three quarters of an hour who will need it."

"We'll be gone by then. Hurry."

Colin followed her, wincing at the effort it took to climb the stairs. At the top, he heard the bell jingle and the clerk ask if she could be of assistance. Battersea yelled for her to move out of the way and fired off a litany of questions.

Finger on her lips, Daphne silently opened the door at the top of the stairs and slipped inside. The parlor was cool and dark, and she led him to a couch that was so soft he practically sank into it. She went to the window and glanced out the heavy drapes. "My carriage hasn't returned yet."

"It will take a little time at this hour," he answered, gingerly probing his ribs.

She closed the heavy drapes and moved back toward him. Colin couldn't help but look about the room with interest. When he'd been younger, he'd always hoped to get a peek at the secret places ladies retreated. He'd been sorely disappointed the first time he'd stepped into a dressmaker's shop. It was just fabrics and trims, nothing scandalous at all. This room held a grouping of chairs, a raised platform where a lady might stand to be measured, and a sewing table with patterns and scraps of paper laid out. No lacy underthings to be found.

Except under his wife's dress.

He knew he'd given her pleasure the night before. What he hadn't expected was for her to think his actions were some sort of ploy to distract her from traveling to St. James's Street. The truth was he'd just wanted to touch her, watch her face as she climaxed. But he'd ended up making her question his intentions. Colin supposed his presence here this morning wouldn't change any of that. Now that he knew who he was dealing with, however, he could put his plan into action.

She stood before him, her eyes sweeping over his attire. "You really are good with disguises. I didn't recognize you."

"I've had a lot of practice."

"And today you thought to practice on me? How many times have you followed me around, spying on me?"

Colin felt the couch cushion sink lower. "I needed to know who you owed money to in order to finalize my plan."

"Your plan? It's too late for that now. My time is up, and he'll come for me." She clasped her hands, looking young and frightened.

"I won't allow that." His confident tone was belied by the sound of Battersea's angry outbursts drifting up from below. "What is he threatening? To make it public you, a lady, owe him a significant amount of money?"

She looked away. "Yes. But it's worse than that. He is the Earl of Battersea."

"So I'm given to understand." He rose with some effort, feeling uncomfortable sitting while she stood. "But I've heard very little of him."

"I forget that you've been away, and since you've been back haven't taken much interest the *ton*."

"I take an interest in you." He rather wished she would remove the pink cloak so he could see what her dress looked like today.

"Battersea is not the sort of man any lady wants to be associated with. I shouldn't have been playing cards with him, and I was a fool to allow myself to be drawn in to losing so much money to him."

Colin refrained from agreeing with her. "We can discuss the specifics later, but the question I want answered is what happens if you don't pay your debt? It must be something unpleasant if it would drive you to the more unsavory parts of St. James's Street."

She took a deep breath. "I lost a thousand pounds to the earl. I paid it, but it took me time to gather the blunt, and the interest is four thousand pounds."

"Interest?" No gentleman would ask a lady to pay interest.

"I told you I made a mistake. I was playing so well, and I didn't think it would matter."

"So he tricked you."

"Yes, and either I pay the earl the four thousand pounds interest or he makes it known that I am in his debt. That will be scandal enough, considering he is extremely disreputable, but it's my understanding that the last person who didn't pay him was found dead."

Colin crossed his arms. "Are you saying he killed someone? A peer?"

"Either that or he had her killed. She was the wife of a baron."

"A baroness murdered? Why isn't it all over the papers?

"Because it was made to look like an accident, and her family took great pains to have the story suppressed. That is the rumor, at any rate. Of course, you know how the *ton* behaves. Now that he's been labeled *dangerous*, Battersea is even more popular than before. It's so amusing to invite a man of mystery to a ball, but I've been afraid for several weeks now that the rumors about the baroness are true."

Colin touched his ribs again, which were beginning to ache.

"Battersea has threatened me to either pay or end up like the baroness. Except…" She shook her head.

Colin raised a brow. "Except?"

"The baroness was older. I don't think he would kill me. I think I would just"—she shrugged her shoulders— "disappear."

"Explain."

Her cheeks turned pink. "I don't have to pay my debt in pounds," she said.

Colin went very still. "What are you saying?"

"I'm saying, he's willing to take other forms of payment. That he added the interest in the hopes I would not be able to pay."

Colin did not move for three fast heartbeats, then he turned and started for the door. Daphne went after him, grabbing his arm. "What are you doing?" she hissed.

"I'll kill him."

"You can't kill him. You'll be hung."

"I don't care."

She managed to dart in front of him. "I do. I have enough problems without being married to a murderer." She held out her hands to stop him. One hand glanced off his injured ribs and he hissed in pain.

"You're injured!"

"Not enough that I can't kill him."

Daphne pressed herself against the door, and Colin frowned at her. "Move out of the way."

She shook her head. "And to think, all of this time I thought you were a gentleman."

"I *am* a gentleman."

"No gentleman dresses like you are or fights the way you fought. Gentlemen don't kick."

He placed on hand on the door frame beside her head and leaned close. "I learned a few things from the war, sweetheart, and one of those is that the enemy doesn't care who your father is. They'll kill you just the same."

She reached out and touched the rough material of his coat. "I rather like this look on you. It's…dangerous."

"And you have a taste for danger? Isn't that what landed you in this trouble in the first place?"

"Probably. But one does tire of shopping and gossiping all the time." Her hand trailed over to his ragged waistcoat and thin linen shirt. He knew what she was doing. She was trying to distract him from going after Battersea this moment, which would undoubtedly be a mistake. So perhaps he could allow himself to be distracted.

"And now you wonder what it would be like to kiss a common man or perhaps even a ruffian?" he asked.

"It has recently crossed my mind." She looked up at him, and he didn't mistake the look in her eyes. It was pure arousal.

He moved his free hand to her cloak and freed the fastening. It slid from her shoulders, revealing a dark pink gown with huge bows on the shoulders. No bow beneath her breasts, unfortunately. She moved forward, pressing her breasts against his chest. "Colin?"

"Hmm?"

"Kiss me."

He obliged, but he wasn't gentle. She wanted a taste of danger? He would give her that. He claimed her mouth hard, and she gasped in what sounded like a mixture of shock and pleasure. He needed to claim her at the moment. Needed to know she was safe and his. Since he was not playing the gentleman, he cupped one of her breasts, fondling it until she was wriggling against him and breathing hard.

"Is this what you want?" he asked, voice rough.

"Yes, more."

Ignoring the sharp pain in his rib, he swept her up into his arms and carried her to the couch. But he didn't lie down beside her. Instead, he took the hem of her skirts and began to raise it.

Nine

She'd never done something like this before. Yes, she liked to play at breaking the rules, but Madame Renauld or one of her seamstresses could walk in at any moment. And what would they see? Daphne sprawled on the couch with her skirts at her knees and what looked like a common street bully between them.

Of course, the bully was her husband, but he didn't look like it at the moment. He hadn't shaved this morning so a rough layer of shadow darkened his jaw. His light green eyes seemed darker under the cap he hadn't even taken off to kiss her. His clothing felt rough on her skin, and his touch, while not rough, was none too gentle. His hands slid up her calves and paused at the pink bows of her garters. He looked at them for a long time then bent and kissed them.

"What are you doing?" she asked, both scandalized and aroused.

"Something I've wanted to do for a long time," he murmured, his stubble rasping across the bare skin just above her garters. She squirmed as heat began to throb between her legs.

Her heart thudded faster as his hands slid higher. Her first thought upon waking this morning had been the feel of his fingers on her sex. Just the thought was enough to make her nipples hard. They were tight points right now, chafing against her chemise. "Touch me again," she said, knowing she would be horrified by her behavior later but wanting it too much in the moment to care.

"Not this time," he said, and his tone held a threat. Her gaze flew to his face and the slight smile on his lips. She watched as he slid her dress higher, uncovering her thighs. He parted her legs, holding them open with his broad shoulders.

"Then what?" she asked. He hadn't loosed the fall of his trousers. Not yet, at any rate.

His gaze lowered. She knew she was exposed to him. Knew he was looking his fill at that most secret place. He moved one hand from her knee and slid it down the inside of her thigh. She groaned softly and arched her hips. He made a sound like a growl as he slid his fingers over her exposed flesh.

"You're wet," he murmured.

"I take it that's a good thing."

"A very good thing as I want to taste you."

She frowned. "What do you—" But she broke off when his mouth began to follow the same path his hand had a moment before. His stubble tickled her, but as he neared her sex, she began to tremble. His lips were so warm, his tongue so wet when it darted out to lick the skin of her thigh. She looked down at his head between her legs, his cap still on. She knocked it off, and he glanced up with amusement in his eyes.

"Is my hat not to your liking?"

"I want to see you."

The amusement fled his face, and his eyes darkened. "Then watch."

He lowered his head again, and she felt his tongue probe her sex. She gasped and took hold of his shoulders as he licked at her, exploring. Daphne tried to speak and found she couldn't. This was the most wicked thing she had ever done. And even worse, she was doing it on Madame Renauld's couch above the shop where her staff was working.

And then Colin found the spot he'd teased last night, and she didn't care where she was. She spread her legs wider to give him access.

"So you like this?" he murmured, his breath making her quiver.

"Don't stop," she begged, half ashamed of herself, half afraid he might break off. She needed him to continue. His tongue touched her again, and she bit her lip to keep from crying out. Her entire body was shaking, every single sense centered on the way he licked and laved and flicked at her.

And then the world seemed to go dark before exploding into a thousand tiny pinpricks of light. She couldn't stop a cry of *Yes* before biting her lip hard to contain any other outbursts. Her hips bucked, and he slid one finger inside her, bringing his palm up to press hard against where he'd licked a moment before. To her great horror, she ground against his hand and her body seemed to want more of him.

"Colin, more," she all but sobbed.

"Not here," he said, but he pressed his hand harder against her and slowly, very slowly, she began to descend.

She lay very still then, feeling completely drained, far too warm, and sated. This was what it must feel like to be debauched. Her hair was probably a wreck, her skirts up to her waist, her legs spread, and Colin's hand was still stroking her sex lightly.

"That was better than I imagined it might be," he said.

"I'd say you are a quick study," she murmured.

"And you are beautiful," he said, his hand coming up to cup her cheek. He'd never called her beautiful before. Many men had given her compliments, but never him. And while she'd always enjoyed the compliments of other men, none made her heart swell painfully in her chest as it did now.

But she didn't want to feel this way about him. He'd hurt her before, and she was afraid if she allowed him into her heart, he would do it again. There was obviously physical attraction between them. He lusted after her. She couldn't think of any other reason he would put his mouth…where he had put it. Or perhaps he felt the need to prove himself after her less than glowing critique of their wedding night. But lust was not all she wanted from him, and she knew better than to hope for anything more.

She turned her head, and his hand fell away. He moved back and she closed her legs and tossed her skirts down over her legs. "We had better go down," she said. "Madame Renauld will need this room soon, and surely Battersea has given up on us."

"Not to mention we have an appointment with your mother later." He pushed off the couch and hissed in a breath.

Daphne was beside him in an instant. "I forgot you are hurt!"

"I'm fine."

"You're not fine. You just winced. Where are you injured?"

He pushed her hands away and straightened. "A bruised rib. I've had far worse."

"Let me see."

He gave her a look. "You just said we should be on our way. This isn't the time for me to undress."

"This will just be a moment. And if it's serious, we can send for a physician."

A quiet tap sounded on the door. "My lady, have you finished your, er—shopping?"

Colin smiled. "Shopping. I like that."

"Yes, and we were just leaving," Daphne answered, going to the door and opening it. "Is the man who came in after us gone?"

Phaedra nodded. "Yes, my lady. He stormed out in a fit of pique." Her dark eyes darted past Daphne to Colin. They were both completely dressed, but Daphne doubted the dressmaker missed how rumpled her skirts were or how tousled her hair.

"Your coach is waiting outside," Phaedra said.

"Thank you." Daphne looked at Colin. "We shouldn't be seen leaving together. You go out the back, and I'll go out the front."

"Is that really necessary? What if Battersea is out there?"

That was a concern, but all her father's servants were well-trained. "My coachman will protect me. Besides I don't wish to anger Madame Renauld. She will not be happy with me if a man who looks like a ruffian is seen leaving her shop by the front door."

Obviously, he could see the logic in that statement because he agreed. But he watched and waited until she was in the carriage and safely away. She found that gesture oddly charming. She'd always had a footman or maid or her mother watching over her. After she'd been married for a few years, her mother gave her a bit more freedom. Daphne had thought it was high time.

But it turned out all she had done was embroil herself in a situation that could not help but end in scandal—or worse. She didn't think Battersea would kill her, but she knew he would not have the slightest qualm about having one of his men snatch her off the street and carry her to the country for one of his infamous house parties. If she wasn't a willing participant in the debauchery, she'd be locked in a room and plied with opium or drink until she was more malleable.

It would be rape all the same.

She covered her eyes with her hand, wishing for the thousandth time she could go back and do it all differently.

***

Colin went home, shushed Pugsly before the dog could alert Louisa, Mary, and Anne of his presence, went straight to his room, and ordered a bath. A cold bath. He needed something to cool his ire and his desire. He wasn't certain which was stronger at the moment, but they were definitely in a brawl for first place.

His valet, Jacobs, returned with the water quickly—probably because he did not have to heat it—just in time to assist Colin with his shirt. Jacobs was used to seeing Colin in a variety of clothing and disguises. Jacobs had been in the theater when he'd been younger and knew as much, if not more, than Colin about the art of creating a character. But Jacobs raised his brows when he saw Colin's chest.

"Find yourself in a bit of a scrape, sir?"

"A bit." Colin walked to the mirror to peer at the area where he'd been hurt. The skin was already turning slightly yellow.

"Shall I ask Cook for her salve?"

"No. It smells like piss, and I have an appointment later today." Colin shed the rest of his clothing and stepped into the tub, sitting with his knees up to his chest.

"A brandy then, sir?"

"I wouldn't say no." Colin soaped his arms then sat for a long moment, shivering. "Jacobs, what do you know about the Earl of Battersea?"

Jacobs paused in the act of pouring the brandy and cast a look at Colin over his shoulder. "I know his servants don't stay in his service long. He takes liberties with the female servants and bullies the males if they speak out."

"If I gave you the afternoon off, do you think you could find time to loiter about his town house and learn more?"

"I can try, sir."

"Then try."

"Shall I shave you before I go, sir?"

"I suppose you'd better. And get out my good coat. I am going house shopping."

The term *shopping* made him warm all over again. He could easily picture Daphne's face after he'd pleasured her. Her cheeks were pink, her lips parted, her blue eyes even brighter than usual but with a sated, heavy-lidded look. He wanted to do it all over again, just to see that look on her face.

He wanted to do much more than that.

But he was playing with fire. They couldn't keep having these intimate rendezvous. When he kissed her and touched her, emotions swelled in him that he didn't understand. He did not know what to do with them, how to store them. He wasn't a man easily frightened, but some of what he felt made his lungs tight and his heart hammer. It wasn't lust; it was fear. The more he was with her, the more he wondered about that fear, and the more it tried to escape. Colin had decided years ago it was not a box he would open.

Besides, she would never be content with a purely physical relationship. She would want to know what he was thinking and feeling and then be disappointed when he wasn't thinking about anything other than seeing her naked.

Jacobs had finished shaving him by then and as soon as the valet had assisted with the most difficult aspects of dressing with bruised ribs, Colin sent him on his errand. He slipped out of the house again, after deciding that mentioning Battersea to his sisters was a bad idea. They probably knew something about him. They were much more inclined to read the scandal sheets, but they'd ask too many questions.

He'd have to go somewhere people didn't ask unwanted questions. Or if they asked and he didn't answer, they wouldn't peck him to death.

The Draven Club was situated on King Street in St. James's Street. Lieutenant Draven had opened it as a place for his men to congregate after the war. There were thirteen members, including Draven himself. They were the thirteen who had come back from the Continent alive.

As usual the Master of the House seemed to know he'd arrived even before Colin did. Porter opened the door just as Colin was about to knock. "Mr. FitzRoy, come in," Porter said. Colin entered the wood-paneled vestibule. It was just after one and the chandelier had not yet been lit. Even without its light he could make out the shape of the enormous shield mounted on the wall opposite the door. An equally impressive sword bisected the shield. It was too shadowy to see the pommel molded into the shape of a fleur-de-lis or the skull on the cross guard. He didn't need to see the smaller fleur-de-lis around the shield, symbols that honored the eighteen Survivors who hadn't returned from the war.

"Is the Duke of Mayne here?" Colin asked. Phineas was the most social of the group and, as a duke, the most likely to have been to the same functions as an earl.

"No, sir."

Colin hadn't really expected him to be back in Town yet. He was probably happily ensconced in some little cottage in Berkshire with his new wife. He'd wanted to talk all about his *feelings* the last time Colin had seen him, and Colin had been forced to grit his teeth for almost three minutes and listen. No doubt the duke had no interest in reviving all the stories in the papers about him and his bride by making an appearance in London just as the scandal had died down. The scandal being that his new wife was quite a bit older than he and past childbearing years. This was a problem for a duke without offspring. But Phineas hadn't seemed to care that some distant cousin or other would inherit.

Still, he'd have to come to Town periodically to sit in the Lords. As much as Colin had been at Mayne House lately, he'd thought he might see his friend more.

"Mr. Murray and Mr. Fortescue are in the dining room, sir," Porter told him. Colin shook his head. He did not want to listen to them bemoan all the balls and fetes they'd been forced to attend nor did he want Duncan badgering him as to when Daphne would find him a wife.

"Then I'll go anywhere but the dining room." And too bad as Colin had not eaten since the night before.

"Lord Grantham is in the card room."

Jasper. His presence here was perfect as it fit right into his plan. "Thank you, Porter."

Colin ascended the blue carpeted staircase. The dining room was at the top, so he slipped by the open door as sleekly as possible so Duncan and Stratford wouldn't see him and call him in. Colin stopped outside the card room. The green baize tables were empty at this time of day. Jasper stood at one staring intently at a deck of cards. He wasn't wearing his mask. He hadn't worn it as much since his marriage, though he'd almost never worn it at the Draven Club anyway. They'd all been there when Jasper, Ewan, and Peter had been ambushed by the French. Jasper and Ewan had managed to fight back the French soldiers, but Peter had been trapped inside a burning building. Jasper had gone in to save him and had been felled by a burning piece of debris that left a scar on the upper part of his face.

Jasper had survived thanks to Ewan. Peter was now represented by one of the fleur-de-lis on the shield in the vestibule.

Jasper looked up, even though Colin hadn't moved or made a sound.

"Good. I need a mark," Jasper said.

Colin shrugged. He liked Jasper. The man didn't bother with all the social niceties unless he had to. Colin supposed that was because his work as a bounty hunter often took him to the less savory areas of the city.

Colin entered, eyeing the cards Jasper was shuffling so quickly they looked like a blur. "Putting on a magic show to amuse your son?"

Jasper almost smiled at the mention of the boy. "Learning a few card tricks so I'll fit in with a group of swindlers. They have information I want. Now, you stand there and pick a card." He fanned out the cards in front of Colin with an admirable flourish.

"Any card?"

Jasper shook the cards at him impatiently. Colin selected one and looked at it. "Ten of hearts."

Jasper tossed the cards on the table in exasperation. "You're not supposed to tell me what card you took."

"Then you should say that at the start."

Jasper snatched the ten of hearts out of Colin's hand and shuffled again.

"Speaking of wanting information," Colin said.

"No. I have to concentrate. Now, pick a card." He held out the fanned deck again. "Any card and don't tell me the card you pick."

Colin picked one and looked at it. This time he'd chosen the seven of diamonds.

"Remember your card," Jasper said smoothly. Colin nodded. "Then slide it back into the deck. Anywhere you like," Jasper instructed.

Colin slid the card back into the deck, and Jasper shuffled again, the cards flying by in a whirl. He set the cards on the table. "Cut the deck."

Colin did. Jasper lifted half the deck, pushed the other half away, and said, "Cut again."

Colin obeyed. Jasper lifted one side of the deck and showed the bottom card. It was the seven of diamonds. "Is this your card?"

"Yes."

"Bloody Christ, I did it." He frowned at Colin. "You're not at all impressed?"

"I saw you slide the card out of your sleeve the second time I cut the deck."

"How the hell did you see that? You're supposed to be cutting the cards and watching them."

"You need to establish your character so when your hand moves to your sleeve, it doesn't draw my attention."

Jasper sank into a chair at the table and slid the cards across it then flipped them over. "I need to what?"

"Establish your character. You're playing a role. Who are you?"

"A card swindler."

"Then everyone will be looking for you to trick them. Better if you were new to doing these tricks and a little nervous and unskilled. You could have a tic."

"A tick? Is that like a flea circus?"

Colin refrained from rolling his eyes only because Jasper would probably hit him if he did. "I'll show you." Colin held out his hand and Jasper slapped the cards into it. Colin cleared his throat and spoke in an uncertain voice. "Would you like to see a trick?" He pulled nervously at the cuff of his coat and shuffled the cards every bit as skillfully as Jasper had done.

"It took me two days to learn to do that," Jasper muttered.

"Want to see a trick?" Colin asked again in his performer voice.

"Sure," Jasper answered.

"I'll just shuffle once more." He did then held the deck out. "Pick a card, any card, and—er, don't tell me your card. Don't let me see it either."

Jasper yanked a card out.

"Now look at your card." Colin slid the deck closed and tugged at his coat cuff again as though uncomfortable or too warm. "Do you have it?"

Jasper glared at him. Colin fanned out the deck again. "Slide it back in wherever you like." Jasper did and Colin shuffled the deck, sliding Jasper's card to the top. "Now, cut the deck." Colin set the cards down and tugged at his coat, sliding the chosen card in his sleeve.

Jasper cut the deck, and Colin set half to the side. "Did you shuffle again here?" he asked in his normal voice.

"No," Jasper said.

"You might consider it. It would add a bit of flourish."

"Shut up and tell me to cut the deck again."

"Cut the deck again." Jasper did and Colin tugged at his sleeve, sliding the card out and to the bottom of the cut deck when he lifted it. "Is this your card?" He showed the three of spades.

"Yes."

Colin spread his arms. "There you go. By the time you cut the deck, you were used to my habit of pulling on my cuffs and didn't note it when I did it."

Jasper gathered his cards. "I'm going home."

"Fine. I'll walk with you."

"Why?" Jasper asked, sliding his half mask on and tying it.

"Because I need information on the Earl of Battersea."

Jasper's hand dropped. "Why?"

Colin considered. He trusted Jasper, but the fewer people who knew about Daphne's debt, the better. "Just tell me what you know."

"Let me just say that among people who have a bad reputation, he has a bad reputation."

"His purported vices?"

"He doesn't drink to excess, but he likes to gamble. He always wins, so I assume he cheats. Though I take it he loses often enough in the drawing rooms of Mayfair so as not to raise suspicion. But when he's slumming it's a different story. He likes women and men too. He'll often round up a group of whores and molly boys and bring them out to a house party for a few days to entertain the guests." Jasper put his hands on the table. "Not all of them always come back, and those who do, don't go again."

"What happens at these house parties?"

"No one is much inclined to say, and I've never pressed. The earl generally keeps away from the debutantes and Society virgins, so I've not had any irate fathers knocking on my door."

"What do you know of his finances?"

Jasper rubbed a thumb along his chin. "Not much. Something to do with shipping possibly? He doesn't have much family money. His father was a profligate." Jasper finished with his mask. "Do you want me to look into him further?"

"Not if it takes you away from your card swindlers."

Jasper stuck the deck in his pocket. "I'm interested now. You've been staying at Mayne's?"

Colin shifted. "I may be moving soon. I'm looking at a town house today." He paused and decided he might as well say it. "With my wife."

Colin couldn't see Jasper's brows under the mask, but he imagined they rose.

"Leave the address with Porter. I'll come see you and Lady Daphne if I find out anything."

"Good. You should, er, bring your wife. We'll have dinner."

Jasper's mouth quirked up. "And here I thought we would all die in the mud in France."

"We've come a long way from scavenging for food and sleeping propped against a tree."

"Somehow I never thought you would be the one planning dinner parties." Jasper started for the door. "I'll tell Neil and Ewan to bring their wives."

"Wait. What?"

Jasper continued walking. "You should probably ask Draven to bring his bride. And we don't want to leave out Mayne, even if he is the biggest scandal of the moment."

"I never said—"

"Thanks for the help with the card trick."

And he was gone. Colin could hear him chuckling as he walked away. He was annoyed Colin could do the trick as well, if not better, than he. That was why he'd threatened to invite half the Survivors to a dinner party.

It had been an empty threat. Colin hadn't even seen the town house yet.

It had to be an empty threat, didn't it?

The clock chimed, and Colin realized he'd be late if he didn't hurry. He forgot to slip unnoticed past the dining room, and Duncan called out to him. Pretending he hadn't heard, Colin continued walking. That didn't deter Duncan, who caught up to him in the vestibule.

"Why the hurry?" Duncan asked, hands on his hips.

"I have an appointment. Thank you." He accepted his hat from Porter.

"With yer wife?"

"As it happens, but why should that matter?"

"As you ken, I need to have a few words with the lass. I'll come with ye."

Colin took the hat Porter held out to Duncan and handed it back to the Master of the House.

"No, you won't. Her mother will be there as well."

"I will. If the lass willnae introduce me to any ladies, then I'll ask her for a list." Duncan grabbed the hat and shoved it on his head. "Where are we headed?"

Colin shook his head and started for the door. Outside, he gave Duncan a sideways look. "This is harassment, you know."

"You say harassment. I say persistence. Besides, I'll entertain the duchess while you slip away with yer lady." Duncan waggled his brows. "That's the best way to ken if the bed chamber suits."

And this, Colin thought, is why Duncan was called the Lunatic. The problem was that the plan wasn't half bad. Colin did need to speak to Daphne in private. He supposed Duncan had his uses and would appeal to a lady looking to rebel. But it would take more than a little rebellion to convince any well-bred lady of the *ton* to consent to live in the wilds of Scotland with the Lunatic and his dragon of a mother.

Ten

"Who is that with him?" the duchess asked as she and Daphne stood in front of the town house in Oxford Square on the outskirts of Mayfair, the leasing agent checking his watch nervously beside them.

Daphne closed her eyes. Colin wouldn't. But, of course, he had. "It's no one, Mama. I'll send him away."

"See that you do."

Even though the skies threatened no rain, Daphne opened her parasol and spread it out behind her then moved forward to intercept her husband and Mr. Murray. She gave them a tight smile, keeping her gaze mainly on Mr. Murray as looking at Colin would remind her too much of what had happened this morning at Madame Renauld's.

"The lass has fire in her eyes," Mr. Murray said to Colin, probably thinking she couldn't hear.

"Mr. Murray, how kind of you to escort Mr. FitzRoy to see us." It was a clear dismissal. The men paused before her and gave polite bows. Colin's was graceful as usual while

Murray's was more gallant than she might have expected from such a large, seemingly uncouth man. She moved to take Colin's arm, but Murray surprised her again by intercepting her and wrapping her arm around his. Then holding it in place.

"Actually, I came to see you, Lady Daphne." He began to walk with her, very slowly, toward her mother, whose gaze had narrowed. "You see, I havenae met any suitable lasses yet."

She tried to tug her arm away, but he just patted it. Colin covered his smile with one hand.

"The Season is young, Mr. Murray. I don't even believe all the families are yet in Town."

He gave her a wide smile. "Och, I didnae ken. I was wondering if you would do me one more kindness, lass. Perhaps make me a list of the lasses you recommend."

She gave him a sharp look. "Women are not like tailors or bootmakers, Mr. Murray."

"Aye. I didnae intend to pay the lasses. Just woo and wed one then take her back to Scotland with me."

It seemed a fate she would not wish on her worst enemy. "I beg your pardon, Mr. Murray, but as I have said before, I do not think I can be of assistance." She finally freed her arm.

Her mother gave her an impatient look as the men were now standing before the duchess.

"Your Grace," Colin said, "may I present Mr. Duncan Murray. He fought with me on the Continent."

The duchess held out a stiff hand and Murray bent over it. "A pleasure, Your Grace. I believe you ken my mother."

The duchess started. "I think that unlikely, Mr. Murray."

"My mother was English, the daughter of the Earl of Montleroy."

The duchess's blue eyes widened. "Lady Charlotte? But she ran off with…" She trailed off as she assessed Murray.

"A Scotsman? James Murray, me father and the brother of the laird of Clan Murray." Murray spread his arms. "And now Lady Charlotte has sent me to find a bride."

"Charlotte. I haven't thought of her in years." The duchess appeared to be staring across the street, but Daphne thought she looked as though she'd gone decades into the past, perhaps reliving her own Season as a young debutante.

"Your Grace," the leasing agent said timidly. "Might I show you the house now?"

"Of course."

The leasing agent ascended the steps and led them inside, Murray escorting the duchess. Daphne wondered if what he had told her mother was true. If it was, Duncan Murray's uncle was the Duke of Atholl. It was very difficult to picture the Scotsman as part of such a noble family. Colin offered his arm to Daphne. She closed her parasol and took it.

"Why is he here?"

"You try putting him off," Colin answered.

She had and thus far her efforts had been futile. Her mother was still chatting with Murray about his mother, who had apparently been a good friend of the duchess's, and waved Colin and Daphne ahead. "I have seen the house," she declared. "You two look around. I will wait in the parlor."

Compared to the Warcliffe town house, this building was small. But Daphne supposed they did not need much room as it was only the two of them. The first floor held what she immediately thought of as the pink parlor. The walls were a pale rose and the furnishings in shades of cream or blush. She knew she would love spending mornings in that room. It opened into a library, which was quite bright and airy as libraries went. Books lined the shelves and a writing desk faced the window. It was a large window that opened to the garden, and Daphne could see rose bushes already had been planted and tended. They would bloom soon. She'd have to see what color the roses were. If not pink, she'd have some planted.

"I can tell you like it," Colin said.

She glanced at him. "You don't?"

He shrugged. "One house is much like another." He spoke to the agent. "Might we see the dining room?"

The agent led them across the foyer and opened the doors to the dining room. It was a good size, not so large that she would feel as though the two of them were separated by miles if at opposite ends of the table, but not so small that her parents or siblings could not dine with them.

"It's a bit small," Colin commented.

She chuckled. "It's not as though we plan to have grand dinner parties." She might enjoy Society, but he had made clear he did not. And she did not mind. She was tiring of the endless rounds of social engagements.

"I don't know about *grand,* but it will be difficult to fit six couples."

"Six couples?"

"My friends and their wives."

She gaped at him. He had friends? But then she knew that. There was Murray and Fortescue and the Duke of Mayne, she supposed. But of those, only Mayne was married, and she certainly did not intend to invite a woman known as the Wanton Widow to her home. Although now that the widow had married the duke, perhaps people would give her another moniker.

"The garden is large enough," she heard herself saying. "We could dine al fresco."

"Even better, I can tell Mayne he has to host. Phin is much better at that sort of thing than I am." He seemed relieved, but as they followed the agent up the stairs, it occurred to her, for the first time, that Colin actually intended to live here.

She intended to live here.

They would live here together.

Yes, she'd always thought she wanted a real marriage, but now that she was faced with the prospect, it was a bit daunting. She'd never spent above a few hours with Colin. She barely knew him. What would they talk about at breakfast? What would they do in the evenings? Where would he sleep when he went to bed?

She got a glimpse of the drawing room, her mind too occupied with thoughts of Colin in bed with her to notice much of it. Then they were shown to the bed chambers. The agent informed them there was one large one with a sitting room attached on the first floor and two others above. Those above were smaller—perfect for servants or children.

Daphne felt the blood rush out of her head at the mention of children. There was only one way to beget children, and she hadn't particularly enjoyed that act the last time.

I'd make sure you enjoyed it.

She was beginning to believe he would too.

But this was all so very much to take in. Years ago, she'd fancied herself in love with him and had been thrilled to marry him. But that was before he'd abandoned her, making her feel a fool for ever having cared for him.

And she didn't have the luxury of playing at being a new bride. She had Battersea demanding payment, and he would not wait any longer. He would come for her. After this morning, she couldn't seem to stop looking over her shoulder. Once or twice, she imagined she spotted him following her, but it must have been her imagination. One of these times, she'd be right and he'd snatch her away and force her to pay her debts on her back.

Colin's voice startled her out of her worrying. "Give us a moment to speak in private," he said, ushering the agent out. Daphne watched, feeling a bit dazed. He closed the door of the bed chamber, leaving them alone.

"There's only one bed chamber," she said. Her parents had adjoining chambers and their own beds.

"And you don't want that?"

She sank into a wide chair upholstered in velvet. "I don't know what I want. How can I even think of this with

Battersea demanding his payment? What am I supposed to do? Pick out china?"

"I'm sure the house comes with china."

She rolled her eyes. "You know what I mean."

"I do, and I have already begun investigations into Battersea." He crouched before her, his arms resting on his knees.

"How will that help? Everyone knows his reputation. Even I knew. I was such a fool."

"You made a mistake. You're trying to fix it."

"How? I didn't even make it to the gaming hell to win the money I need."

"By trusting me to help you."

"You can't don disguises and run away from him forever." It all seemed so hopeless.

"But I can see if he has any vulnerabilities. Perhaps he has secrets he doesn't want made known. He might be willing to forgive your debt in exchange for your silence."

She blinked at him. She'd never thought of that. It hadn't even occurred to her, and it rather surprised her that it occurred to Colin. She hadn't known he was so devious.

"Do you really think he has any secrets we could use against him? Something provable, not just rumors about his part in the baroness's death."

"I intend to find out." He looked about the bed chamber. "Do you like the house?"

She shrugged. "Does it matter? My parents have already leased it for us. Don't you like it?"

He shrugged. "Like you, I'm not sure what I want." His gaze moved to the bed. "With a few exceptions."

She was careful not to look at the bed. "Do you actually intend to live here then? I thought perhaps you went along with the idea so my mother would leave you alone."

"I'll admit that was a factor I considered, but right now you need to be kept safe."

Her shoulders slumped. "Oh, good. So you will live with me not only out of obligation but duty as well."

He looked a little surprised by her outburst. "That's not all."

Daphne told herself not to hope. She told herself not to wish. He'd never cared for her. He probably didn't have the capability to care for anyone. She'd never seen him express any strong emotion other than the rare flash of anger here and there. "It's not?" she asked, cursing her heart, which sped up even as she told it not to.

"I'd been thinking I needed a place of my own for some time. And this location is more convenient to my club."

Daphne stiffened. She would not say a word. She would not react.

"Not to mention, it gets a bit crowded at my father's house when my sisters and all their offspring are in Town from the country."

Daphne sprang to her feet. She couldn't keep quiet. The humiliation of it all was too much. "So you want to live with me out of convenience? Duty, obligation, and convenience!"

His eyes narrowed as he rose slowly to his feet, wincing slightly. Obviously, his ribs still pained him. "It might be less convenient than I supposed."

"I daresay it will." She faced him, hands on hips. "I am not a convenience! Do you know how many men asked me to marry them?"

His brow clouded.

"I'll tell you. Dozens!"

"Well, you did have a formidable dowry," he said. Obviously, he did not realize how close she was to clobbering him over the head. Would he never see her as desirable, someone of worth?

"Fine. Then do you know how many men asked me to run away with them after you and I married? How many men propositioned me, wrote me love poems, begged me to return their affections?"

"I don't think I want the answer to that."

"But maybe you need it because it will show you that not everyone sees me as just a *convenience*!" She was shouting now, but she didn't care. For his part, Colin looked unperturbed.

"I said the house was convenient. Not you." He ran a hand through his hair. "I'd never call you that."

"Oh, so now you insult me."

He blew out a breath, his only sign of frustration. "So I'm not to think of you as convenient or inconvenient. What is it you want from me?"

"I want you to feel something for me! Something other than lust. Something more than indifference."

He took a step toward her, his green eyes fixed on hers. "I'm not in the least bit indifferent to you," he said. He took another step and she moved back slightly. "I'll admit to the lust, but that's not all there is."

"Then what else is there?" she asked, her voice little more than a whisper.

He stared at her for what seemed a very long time.

"Hate?" she prompted. "Love? Some other feeling?"

He swallowed. "I don't know."

Daphne closed her eyes. He did not know what he felt for her. He couldn't even say whether it was closer to love or hate. This man, who was so much a part of her life and yet who had never been *part* of her life, couldn't even answer a basic question as to how he felt about her.

She could not do this anymore. She could not keep hoping he might someday feel something for her, might someday want her, want to build a life with her. "I am done here," she said. She pushed him away and walked toward the door, the tears she held back stinging her eyes. She would make some excuse when she was downstairs. She would tell her mother she was not feeling well and needed to go home. But she didn't even reach the door.

Colin's hand closed on her arm, his grip gentle but firm. She looked back at him, prepared to shake him off and tell him where he could go. Something in his eyes stopped her. Was it fear?

"I like your bows," he said.

Daphne blinked. "Pardon?"

"Your bows. I like them. I like seeing where you will wear them." He gestured to her dress, which had a row of pink bows from her throat to the floor. "I like thinking about untying them when we're alone."

She felt her cheeks heat but ignored the sudden rush of arousal at the image his words created. "That's just lust again."

"Yes, but lust for you. I don't look at other women's clothing and think about undressing them. I don't even notice what they're wearing."

She nodded. "I suppose that might border on affection. What else?"

He gaped at her. "I have to say *more*?"

"Do you want me to talk about how I feel about you?" She wasn't sure what she would say. Not the entire truth, that was certain. He would probably pass out if she told him how she really felt.

He looked as though he were ready to pass out now. "No! You needn't start talking about your *feelings*. I'll think of something else." He put a hand to his forehead, pressing it hard as if thinking very intently. His gaze roamed over her face then down to her bosom.

"No more physical attributes," she qualified.

He gave her a murderous look. "Fine." He looked down, then away, then up at the ceiling.

"If this is too difficult for you—"

"I like that you're brave," he said.

She raised her brows. She didn't think she was particularly brave. She'd never gone off to war and faced the enemy on a battlefield. Apparently, that was a good deal easier for him than this.

"You walk into a ballroom and never seem to worry that everyone looks at you and judges you. And the other night, you were ready to run off to St. James's Street. Although that might have been more foolhardy than brave." He took her other arm, so he held both of them. "Don't give up on me," he said so quietly she almost couldn't make out the words.

She stared at him, and for once his face looked so open and vulnerable. And she realized she had been right earlier when she'd thought she'd seen fear. It *had* been fear, and now he was afraid she would walk away from him.

He felt something for her. She could see it now. He just couldn't say it. Not yet.

Her first impulse was to throw her arms about him and kiss him and tell him she loved him, but that would only terrify him back into silence and stiffness. And she couldn't risk his rejection again. So she notched her chin up. "Fine," she said. "I'll give you another chance."

The fear in his eyes turned to annoyance, and she liked that much better.

"You may kiss me, if you want," she said, her tone regal and long-suffering.

"May I?"

"I suppose." She shrugged. But as soon as his hand came around the back of her neck, she lost all semblance of false apathy. He slid his other arm around her waist and pulled her hard against him.

"May I do this?"

She took a shaky breath. "If you must," she whispered.

"I must." He moved backward, taking her with him until he had her pressed up against the wall. She could feel his hardness pushing against her belly. "How is this?"

"Acceptable."

"Just acceptable?" He slid a hand down her arm until she trembled. "Now, do you *want* me to kiss you?"

"Yes," she murmured.

"You want me to tell you how I feel?"

She nodded.

"Then pay attention." His mouth closed over hers, taking her breath away. She closed her eyes, holding on to him, and allowing the sensation of his lips on hers, his arms around her, to take over. There was more than lust in this kiss. There was passion and reverence and need. And just as she tried to respond to that need, he pulled back. He rested one arm on the wall and looked down at her. "When are we moving in?" he asked.

"Now?" she whispered. She wanted him to lead her to the bed. Better yet, she would lead him. She'd strip off his clothes and kiss him in all the places where she ached right now. She'd like to see his reaction to that.

His mouth quirked. "Too ambitious. The day after tomorrow."

Daphne did not want to wait that long. She wanted him to do what he'd done to her this morning again. Now.

"Daphne!"

Daphne closed her eyes and gritted her teeth. It was her mother.

"Duncan said he would keep her busy, but even he has his limits," Colin said. "Listen to me, stay home tonight and tomorrow night. Say you have an ague or whatever it is ladies say. Just be careful until you're back with me. I can't follow Battersea and keep an eye on you, and I don't want to have to rescue you should he see a chance at abduction."

"As though I would need rescuing."

"Daphne! Where are you?"

"Just do this one favor for me, will you?"

The door pushed open, and the duchess stepped into the bed chamber. Colin looked over his shoulder, and Daphne caught her mother's wide-eyed look. The shock quickly turned to pleasure. "Oh, I didn't mean to interrupt."

Colin stepped away from her. "We were just discussing when we should move in. The house is perfect, Your Grace."

"Oh, good! Well, continue your, er, discussion. I'll wait downstairs." And she was gone, closing the door behind her.

Colin looked back at her. "Well?"

Daphne's own eyes widened. Did he mean to take advantage of this opportunity to—

"Will you stay home, stay safe, for a couple of nights and days?"

"Fine," she said. "But this is my problem, and I want to deal with it. I'll accept help, but I won't sit home forever and embroider while you fix everything. Once we move into this house, my father will release my dowry. We can use that to pay the interest on my debt to Battersea."

"No," Colin said.

Daphne narrowed her eyes.

"We're not paying him a penny. Besides, if you think he'll be satisfied with that, think again. It was you he wanted all along. If you paid the debt and the interest, he would find another way. All the money in the world won't be enough to satisfy him."

"But you think we can blackmail him?"

"I don't know. I hope so. I'll know more when you see me again." He kissed her lips briefly. "In two days."

She wanted to pull him down for another kiss, but he stepped back and released her. She felt chilled without him, and two days of not seeing him seemed a long time. But then there would be the first night in their new home.

I'd make sure you enjoyed it.

Taking a deep breath, she decided she could wait just a little longer.

Eleven

Colin had followed Battersea from the earl's club—where he'd waited outside as he wasn't a member—to a rout—where he'd pretended to be a servant to move about the festivities. He'd seen Daphne's friends, Lady Isabella and Lady Pavenley, but they were without their third tonight.

For once Daphne had done as he'd asked.

Battersea must have also gone in the hopes of seeing Lady Daphne. He made a circuit of the room, stayed as long as etiquette demanded, and then departed.

Colin followed Battersea to a raucous street just outside Mayfair where a bawdy house catering to wealthy men was situated. The bawd seemed to be having her own rout that evening as noise filtered out and culls streamed in. Colin tucked himself just around the corner, keeping out of sight of the bullies at the door but close enough so that the entrance to the house was in view.

"Not going inside?" a voice said from behind him. Colin tensed and put his hand over the dagger he carried hidden under his coat. He turned slowly, then loosed his grip when he saw Jasper behind him. Jasper wore all black and, with his half-mask in place, he blended in with the shadows.

"You're following Battersea too?" Colin asked.

"I heard he frequents this house. Thought I would see for myself. Interesting attire." He glanced down at the livery Colin wore.

"I was at a rout earlier. I'd have to change to go into the bawdy house, and I'm not sure it's worth the trouble. I wouldn't be able to move about freely, not with the ladies doing their best to empty my pockets."

"The whores in the rookeries know about Battersea. He will round up a half dozen when he has a house party in the country. Apparently, they don't always come back."

"I heard something to that effect." Colin studied the door of the bawdy house again, knowing it was too early for Battersea to emerge but diligent in his observation nonetheless.

"We'll have to do more than follow him from whore to whore in order to find out anything compromising."

Colin looked back at Jasper. "What are you suggesting?"

"We worked together a few times on the Continent before…" He trailed off, and Colin knew he was thinking about the fire that had scarred him.

"We did," he agreed. "As I recall, we were generally successful."

"Why don't we visit Battersea's shipping offices? See what we can find," Jasper suggested.

"You confirmed he has investments in shipping."

"I did, but I'm still poking around. I'd know more, but…" He spread his hands and a card seemed to appear from nowhere between two black-gloved fingers.

"Card swindlers," Colin supplied.

"Exactly. It's too late tonight. By the time we reached the docks and started looking, it would be too close to dawn, and we'd risk being seen. I know you blend in, but in the daylight, I'm better off staying out of sight." Jasper gestured to his mask.

"Tomorrow night then?" Colin asked.

"Meet me here at ten."

Colin nodded, looked back at the bawdy house, then back at Jasper. "What about your wife?"

Jasper seemed to start in surprise. "What about her? Planned that dinner party already?"

"I'm told our dining room might not suit for a large dinner party."

"We'll have it at Mayne's house then. He has enough room to feed an army."

"Good luck persuading him to return to London." Colin paused then decided to ask the question in the back of his mind. "About your wife. She doesn't mind you roaming London every night?"

"I don't roam every night, but she understands the nature of my work. And I'm usually home to wake her up." His mouth curved into a smile, indicating he rather enjoyed his method of waking his wife from sleep. "But you're not really interested in my wife. You're thinking about how to manage yours."

Colin raised his brows. "I doubt she'd like having it put that way."

"Then don't put it that way. And you're better off not asking for my advice. I don't know what the devil I'm doing most days, and Olivia is practical and prefers a quiet life. Your wife—" He shook his head.

"What does that mean?"

Jasper laughed. "And here I thought you didn't like her. I only meant that she seems to enjoy balls and the theater." He paused. "And musicales, fetes, routs, dinner parties, tea parties, garden parties—"

"I take your point, Grantham."

"And all the pink and the bows and the frothy lacy stuff she wears. She's not one to stand in a corner and blend in."

Colin understood exactly what Jasper was saying, and he already knew he and Daphne were opposites. But there was more to her than her popularity in social circles. And he was more than a man who pretended to be someone else on demand. He just wasn't certain she would like who he was under the disguise.

"Do you plan to stay here until he emerges?"

"Yes." Colin studied the bullies at the door again. "I want to make sure he stays away from Daphne. She's at home tonight with some illness or other."

"I assume it's fabricated."

"She will be ill again tomorrow evening, so I will see you at ten."

"Dress as a sailor," Jasper said a moment later. Colin had actually thought he'd gone.

"A sailor? What will you dress as?"

"Myself. But if we need a distraction, I'll look to you. You *can* play the role of sailor?"

Colin scowled at him as though the question was an insult. Jasper laughed, probably only asking it to elicit Colin's annoyance. As Colin watched, Jasper melted away into the darkness and was gone.

He went back to watching the whore house and tried not to think about where he would be and with whom a few nights hence.

***

Daphne held a handkerchief to her nose and pretended to sniffle as Lady Isabella and Lady Pavenley delicately sipped their tea in the sitting room of her bed chamber. They'd come to call on her and offer their wishes for a quick recovery. At least, that was what they'd said. Daphne thought it was more likely they hoped to see her red-nosed and feverish and looking her worst.

They seemed disappointed.

She had actually enjoyed staying in last night. She'd felt some guilt at lying to her mother, who had also stayed in to watch over Daphne. But it had been surprisingly pleasant to spend a quiet evening reading and sipping tea with her mother. And when her father had come home from the Lords, they'd all played cards games she remembered from when she'd been a child.

Her mother had worried she would tire herself and sent Daphne to bed early. Daphne didn't mind at all. It had been ages since she had gone to bed before three in the morning, and when she'd woken this morning, she'd felt refreshed and in perfect spirits.

That was until the other Suns called on her. While Daphne could tell other callers she was not at home, she could hardly refuse her best friends. If she had, who knew what rumors they would circulate? The papers would claim she was on her death bed.

"I do wish you could have been there," Lady Pavenley said. She was going on about Lord and Lady Richelieu's rout. Daphne had been looking forward to the event, but she found she hadn't missed it at all. "Everyone asked about you."

"Quite tedious," Lady Isabella said, nibbling on a biscuit. "We told everyone you would be at Lord Forsythe's ball tonight."

Daphne did enjoy dancing, but she had promised to stay home until tomorrow. "I don't think so," Daphne said, dabbing her nose again. "I'm still not feeling well, and I have to supervise the packing."

"Oh, yes!" Lady Pavenley set her teacup down with a clink. "You and Mr. FitzRoy have finally secured your own residence. Where is he, by the way?"

Daphne had no idea, but she was not about to admit that or explain that Colin hadn't been in her father's house above a handful of times. "At his club, I suppose." She waved a hand.

"But you cannot miss the ball," Lady Isabella said, her brown eyes wide. "It's the event of the Season."

"Oh, bosh. It's far too early in the Season for such hyperbole. And anyway, I will only sneeze on all my dance partners. I will simply have to stay home one more evening. Perhaps I will feel up to the theater later this week."

"Lord Battersea was looking for you last night," Lady Pavenley said, lifting her teacup again and peering over the rim at Daphne.

Of course, he was. He was undoubtedly looking for an opportunity to get a taste of what he thought she owed him. Or perhaps he planned to snatch her away from the ball so she was never seen again.

Panic swelled within her, but she couldn't allow her guests to see it. She took a breath.

"Was he?" Daphne made her voice as flat as possible. She did not know how the other Suns knew something had occurred between Daphne and Battersea, but they did. They wouldn't be prodding her so if they did not. They just didn't know what. And they would never know. She had to remember Colin had said he would help her. Once she and Colin put their plan in motion, this ordeal would be at an end. Perhaps her husband already had incriminating evidence against the earl.

"We told him you were home, and he said he would call on you when you were better."

"My father would not admit him. He dislikes Battersea."

"The earl is always so interested in you, Lady Daphne," Lady Pavenley said. Then she lifted her reticule and opened it, removing a small envelope from inside. There was a red seal on it.

Daphne narrowed her eyes. "What is this?"

"Lord Battersea asked me to give it to you." Lady Pavenley held it out to Daphne. Daphne stared at the envelope as though it were a viper. She did not want it and certainly did not want to know what Battersea had written to her. Finally, Lady Pavenley waved the envelope impatiently, and Daphne was forced to take it. She looked at the seal, which appeared unbroken, but that did not mean Lady Pavenley hadn't gone to some trouble to remove it so she could read the contents and then reseal it. Perhaps Battersea had anticipated this since the seal was rather wide and thin. Daphne did not think it had been tampered with.

"Why don't you open it?" Lady Pavenley asked.

Daphne glanced at her. Her violet eyes were fixed on the envelope. She looked like a kitten eyeing a bowl of cream.

"Later," Daphne said, slipping it into her bosom, where it burned like a hot coal.

Lady Isabella and Lady Pavenley exchanged looks. They had obviously discussed what the contents of the note might be and hoped to have their suppositions confirmed or denied this afternoon. But Daphne felt a real headache coming on and pretended to cough into her handkerchief. She coughed for about another ten minutes, each time one of her friends asked a question, and finally the ladies departed. As soon as she was certain they were gone, Daphne jumped up, raced to her bed, closed the curtains about it, and opened the missive.

My Dear Daphne,

Daphne recoiled. She had not given him permission to use her given name.

I was so distraught to hear of your illness. I do hope you will be well enough to attend a small gathering at my country house.

Daphne wondered if this was the sort of note the baroness had received before he'd killed her.

As we have yet to settle our debt, perhaps we can do so at the event. I will collect you very soon.

Daphne read that line again. *Very soon.* What did that mean?

Yours affectionately,

B

Daphne read the letter again then stuffed it under a pillow and leapt out of her bed. "Mama!" she called. "Mama!"

"What is it?" her mother asked, coming up the stairs. "Are you feeling worse?"

"What?" She'd forgotten she was supposed to be ill. "Oh, yes. I feel awful. You will stay home with me again tonight, won't you?"

"Brown!" When the maid didn't appear, the duchess tugged at the bell pull. "I will have Brown put you right to bed. You shouldn't be up. Your color is quite high. Your friends have worn you out."

"I'll go to bed." Daphne pushed back the draperies and climbed in. "But you'll stay home with me again, as you did last night?"

"I can't, darling. You know Lady Forsythe is the Chairwoman of the Hyde Park Annual Flowershow and Botanical Festival. If I don't attend, she'll assign me to the flowering shrubs this year, and you know I want to present the roses."

Daphne stared at her mother. How could she say she feared for her life? If she did, she'd have to reveal the whole affair with Battersea.

"Brown will stay with you, darling. And I won't be long at the ball." She tucked the covers around Daphne, then surprised her daughter by leaning down to kiss her forehead. "After tonight you will have to ask your husband to stay with you." She gave Daphne a fond look. "My last little chick leaving the nest."

Daphne gave her a weak smile then lay still and listened in the enclosed bed as her mother gave Brown instructions. As Daphne saw it, she had two choices. She could stay home and hope Battersea did not come for her. Or she could go after him herself. Her friends' visit had already shown her that Battersea was looking for her. If he followed the same system as he had the night before, then he would stop in at the Forsythe ball. When he saw she was not there but her parents were, he would come looking for her here. Her father had a large, competent staff, but they would not be expected to guard the perimeter of the house in case an earl decided to abduct Daphne. Many would have the evening off, and the others would be belowstairs until the duke and duchess were expected to return. Only Brown would be with Daphne, and she would be little use against Battersea.

Daphne sat and peered through the bed curtains into her bed chamber. It was empty, the window curtains drawn and the lamp turned low. She climbed quietly out of bed, tiptoed to her desk, and eased the drawer open. She withdrew a sheet of vellum and scratched off a note to Colin. He had told her to remain home, but that had been before she'd received the note from Battersea. Besides, she had created this problem. She could very well help solve it.

She added one more line to her note, enclosed Battersea's with it, sealed it, and tugged the bell pull. Brown appeared in less than a minute. "I thought you were sleeping, my lady."

"I'm feeling better."

"But it's only been a few minutes."

"Brown, take this letter and have a footman deliver it to Mr. FitzRoy."

Her maid looked at the letter. "Where shall I say to find him?"

"Have the footman begin at the viscount's residence. If my husband isn't there, they will know where to find him."

"Very good, my lady."

Daphne climbed back into bed, knowing she would have to pretend to rest for a few hours and feeling the task would be impossible.

"My lady, should the servant wait for a reply?"

Daphne considered. If she waited for a reply then it would appear the matter was up for debate. "No reply necessary," she said, lying back and closing her eyes.

She did fall into a light sleep, which she thought might serve her well if she were to be up and out most of the night.

When she woke, she called for Brown who told her the footman had discovered FitzRoy was at his club, the Draven Club, and had left the letter with the Master of the House.

Now Daphne did wish she had asked for a reply as she didn't know if Colin had actually received the letter and she couldn't help but wonder what he thought of her plan. She supposed she would know in a few hours. A little while later her mother came in to check on her. She was dressed in red and smelled of lilacs. She glittered in rubies and diamonds and was warm when she kissed Daphne's cheek. "I'm having dinner with friends before the ball. I will check on you when I return."

Daphne pretended to flutter her eyes sleepily and then closed them and feigned falling back asleep. A quarter hour later the house was quiet and the last echoes of the carriage's wheels clattering on the street had died away. The hay used to muffle the noise of passing carriages needed to be replaced, but for the moment Daphne was glad for the noise.

"Brown," she called as she rose from bed and went to her clothes press. "I need something dark to wear."

Brown came in from the sitting room, her arms full of ribbons. She was obviously packing for the move tomorrow. "Something dark to sleep in, my lady?"

"I'm not sleeping, Brown. You and I are going out."

"But, my lady! You are ill."

"I'm perfectly fine, but I don't want to go alone."

"I wouldn't allow it, my lady."

"Then find me something dark. I don't want to be seen."

Brown set the ribbons on Daphne's dressing table. "There's the cloak you wore the other evening."

Daphne shook her head. "I returned it to my sister. A gown will have to do."

The maid opened the clothes press and stared at the profusion of pink. "I don't think you have anything in dark colors, my lady."

"Nonsense!" Daphne went through her gowns herself. Brown was right. She sighed then whirled on the maid. "I know! What about the gowns I wore when Great-Aunt Clotilda died? I had to wear black for a year, it seemed."

Brown frowned. "It was no more than a month, my lady, and that was several years ago."

"Where are they?"

"Perhaps packed in a trunk in one of the storage rooms."

Daphne shooed at her. "Go find them. I'll put my hair up while you do."

"*You* will put your hair up, my lady?"

Daphne put her hands on her hips. "I can dress my own hair, Brown."

Brown looked dubious as she left to look for the mourning gowns. In the meantime, Daphne managed to fasten her hair in a tail down her back. She intended to stuff it into one of her father's hunting caps at any rate. It didn't have to look fancy.

She paced the room, checking the clock on the mantel impatiently. Parliament would adjourn soon, and then she did not know how much time she had until Battersea came looking for her. She wanted to be well away before then.

Finally, Brown returned, carrying a dove gray cloak and a black silk dress with jet beading on the bodice. Daphne remembered wearing it to the theater and hating it as her mother hadn't allowed her to order Madame Renauld to add any bows to it. Hopefully the beading would not catch too much light. As it had been an evening dress, the bodice was low enough to show off any black enamel jewelry. Daphne didn't bother with adornments. She donned the dress and threw the cloak over the dress and her hair. Then she gave Brown a once-over. The maid was already dressed in dark blue. Daphne told her to leave her apron on the bed and put on a shawl. On the way out the door, Daphne took one of her father's hunting caps.

It was a short walk to Oxford Square, where her new home stood. Brown stayed close to her, and Daphne was glad as any little sound and every man they passed made her heart pound in fear. Finally, they arrived at the town house.

"My lady, it's dark," Brown said.

Daphne had seen that as well. She'd expected Colin to be there already and to have lit at least a candle for her. "Perhaps he hasn't arrived yet. It's not a problem. Mama gave me a key."

She pulled it from her reticule, which she had kept tucked under the cloak as it was pink, and as Brown held the lantern for her, she inserted it into the lock and heard the click as she opened the door.

"I'll go first, my lady," Brown said. Daphne thought she should argue or at least pretend to be brave, but she couldn't seem to make her mouth object when Brown pushed the door open and entered. Daphne followed Brown into the shadowy vestibule. There was no sound other than the swish of the ladies' skirts. Daphne turned in a circle, then screamed as a man stepped out of the shadows.

Brown turned and shrieked as well even as the masked man held up two hands in a universal gesture promising no harm.

"Who are you? What do you want?" Daphne demanded, pushing Brown behind her. "Are you a highwayman? We don't have any valuables."

"I'm not a highwayman," the man said. It almost sounded as though he were laughing. Footsteps sounded on the marble and then Colin ran into the foyer, holding an unlit lamp and a jug.

"What the devil?"

"It's a highwayman, Colin," Daphne explained. "I told him we don't have any blunt. Just give him what you have, and he won't hurt anyone." She looked at the highwayman. "Isn't that right?"

"That is right. Give me your blunt, Colin."

"Stubble it, Jasper."

Daphne looked from one man to the other. "You know the highwayman?"

Colin set the lamp on the entryway table and produced a tinder box. "He's not a highwayman. We're not even on the highway."

"If he's not a highwayman, why does he wear a mask?"

"I was injured in the war, my lady. I wear it so you won't scream, though it didn't seem to help much this evening."

The lamp flared to life, and Colin held it up, illuminating the room. "Lady Daphne, may I present Lord Jasper. Lord Jasper, my wife."

Twelve

Jasper gave an exaggerated bow, and Daphne gave a more perfunctory one, obviously not quite sure she believed the ruffian in her soon-to-be foyer was actually a gentleman. He certainly looked more highwayman than marquess's son, but then Colin was dressed as a sailor, so who was he to judge? For her part, Daphne wore a gray cloak he'd not seen before. He wondered what she wore underneath.

And then he caught a glimpse of her maid, her face pale and her eyes large, and pulled a chair away from the wall and set it behind the woman. "You had better sit down, miss."

The maid sank into the chair without a word.

"Why are you dressed like that?" Daphne asked a moment later, when she'd had time to notice his clothing. "And you might have warned me your friend would be here."

"I'll just take a look in the parlor," Jasper said, sliding through the door and out of sight.

"I went to the butler's pantry to find lamp oil. I didn't know you'd come as I'd just stepped away." He took her arm and shuttled her into the dining room. "And it's not as though you gave me any time to warn you of anything. You informed me you'd come here and demanded I join you."

"I included Battersea's letter. What else was I supposed to do?"

He looked down at her and had to stop himself from throttling her. "I can think of a hundred better options than for you to go out into London alone at night to come to an empty house. What if Battersea had been waiting for you?"

Daphne swallowed, her expression filled with fear. "I knew that was a possibility, but I am supposed to attend the Forsythe ball, and I think he will look for me there. Besides, I am not alone. I have Brown with me."

"The maid who is sitting in that chair looking as though she might faint at any moment?"

"And the house isn't empty. You were here waiting for me."

He gave her a mocking bow. "As you can see, my lady, I am your servant, as always."

She snorted.

"I can see why you would be concerned after that letter from Battersea." It had taken Neil Wraxall, Stratford Fortescue, and Draven himself to persuade Colin not to go and kill the earl on the spot when he'd received her note at the Draven Club. Colin couldn't remember ever reacting the way he had. He'd been so furious that he would have murdered Battersea with his bare hands if he'd had the opportunity. Colin hadn't even realized he had such strong emotions.

He'd managed to contain them again before finding Jasper and changing their plans to first meet Daphne here. Of course, the part he hadn't worked out was what to do with her while he and Jasper searched Battersea's shipping offices.

"My parents had to attend the Forsythe ball tonight. I didn't want to be home when Battersea realizes I'm not at the ball. I'm…" He could see the admission was difficult, but she closed her eyes and said it. "I'm afraid he will come to the town house and try to abduct me. Colin, I'm truly scared now."

Colin took her in his arms and held her for a long moment. She was shaking, and he rubbed her back until she stilled. The truth was, he admired her for taking action rather than being passive and waiting for Battersea to come for her. After he'd seen that note, he didn't like the idea of her alone at home any more than he liked her here. Some of the staff would be home, of course, but no one would be paying attention to Lady Daphne or her maid.

If he were Battersea, he would have taken the opportunity.

Colin opened his mouth to tell her what she should do now, then closed it again and reconsidered. He'd grown up with three sisters. He should apply what he'd learned. He stepped back to look at her face. "What is your plan?" he asked.

"You said you'd know more about Battersea tomorrow. I thought I could help with your research. Or have you finished?"

Colin shook his head. "All I found out last night was which bawdy house he frequents."

Her eyes widened and her lips thinned. "Are you saying while I was home, pretending to be ill, you were enjoying yourself at a bawdy house?" She took a menacing step toward him, and Colin was relieved there were no sharp objects nearby.

"I didn't go in. Lord Jasper and I stood outside. We were following him."

She looked at him for a long moment, assessing his words. "Why is Lord Jasper following him?"

"I asked him to help. He tracks people and stolen items for a living. He was the best tracker we had in the war."

She glanced over her shoulder at where the parlor would be. Colin could see he was winning her over.

"He also knows people you and I don't have access to—people in the underworld."

"Criminals?"

"Men of dubious character, like your Battersea."

"He's not *my* Battersea. Where are we searching tonight? Back to the bawdy house or in a rookery?" Her tone was clearly one of suppressed excitement. Colin would wager all he owned she'd never seen a bawdy house or set foot anywhere near a rookery.

"You aren't—" Colin stopped himself. "Don't you think it's best if you and your maid wait here until we return? Battersea won't know where you're moving or think to search for you here if he does."

Daphne gave him a look she might give a lunatic. "I'm not staying here. I'm coming with you. After all, this is my problem to solve. I cannot leave it all to you. I can stand outside a bawdy house as well as you."

"We're not returning to the bawdy house. Jasper heard Battersea has investments in shipping. We plan to search his shipping offices."

Daphne frowned. "How will you do that?"

The woman did not have a devious bone in her body.

"Break in. That's why I'm dressed as a sailor. We don't want to look suspicious. You will draw attention to us, and I'd rather not have to explain all of this to the magistrate."

"But I won't draw attention to you." She unfastened her cloak and laid it over one of the dining chairs. "I'm wearing all black, and I brought this cap to hide my hair." She pulled an old hunting cap onto her head.

Colin stared at her. She looked…he didn't know how she looked. Adorable? Yes. Kissable? Yes. Inconspicuous? No.

"Daphne, the black was a good choice, but you still look like what you are—a well-bred lady."

"Then Brown and I will switch clothing. I'll look like a servant with the night off or on the way to visit friends."

She would never look like a servant, but it wasn't a wholly ridiculous idea. And he knew he would have to waste half the night arguing with her if he didn't give in.

"Fine. You and Brown change. I'll tell Jasper."

She blinked at him, her blue eyes speculative. "That's it? No more arguing?"

"Would it make any difference if I did? I can see you are determined to go." And truth be told, he understood her reasoning. This was her doing. Why should he step in and fix all the broken pieces as though she were a child? All her life she'd been catered to and told not to do this and not to do that. He knew because he'd lived much the same sort of existence before the war. But she was a woman, not a child, and he didn't intend to treat her as one.

"I am determined, and I can help."

"That remains to be seen. But you'll get your chance." He opened the door. "Brown?" The servant looked up from the floor.

"Yes, sir?"

"I believe Lady Daphne requires your services."

Then he crossed to the parlor and closed the door. Jasper was looking through a crack in the curtains. He didn't bother to glance at Colin. "This is a bad idea."

"You haven't even heard the idea yet."

"She wants to come with us, and you agreed."

Colin scowled. How the devil did he know that?

Jasper looked at him. "It didn't take me but thirty seconds to realize you've been lying to us all these years."

Colin stiffened. "I beg your pardon."

"I should beg yours. You've always made it seem as though you were forced to marry Warcliffe's youngest and that you didn't care a whit for her. That's not true—at least not the part about not caring for her."

"I don't want her raped or abducted by a known abuser. I should think no gentleman would accept that."

Jasper shook his head. "It's more than that." He moved closer to Colin, circled him. Colin watched him warily. "But maybe you're not ready to accept that you care for her." Jasper was behind him and leaned in close, whispering, "Maybe you really think you don't have feelings."

Colin turned to look at him. "Don't tell me you want to talk about *feelings*."

"Not particularly, but I can acknowledge I have them. I love my wife and my son."

Colin felt his collar was too tight, even though he wore a shirt open at the neck. "Moving on."

Jasper strolled around the room, ignoring him. "And I suppose I feel something akin to love for the Survivors. I was close to Rafe, but he's gone now. Neil and Ewan and I had a few close calls. Draven's always been something of a father to me, and you—"

"Stop." Colin's throat was so tight he had to push the word out. "This is unnecessary."

"Is it? What if we die tonight? What if the devil comes looking for us, wearing his dancing shoes?" It was a phrase the men of Draven's troop had used before a mission. "I want you to know how I feel."

Colin might have stared at him in stupefaction if he hadn't seen the ghost of a smile on Jasper's lips.

"You think you're amusing, don't you?"

Jasper doubled over laughing, while Colin crossed his arms in annoyance. "I don't see what's so entertaining."

"You should have seen your face," Jasper said between chortles of laughter. "You looked like you'd just had cold water thrown over your head."

"I'll throw cold water over *your* head," Colin muttered.

Jasper straightened and wiped his eyes. "But in all seriousness, FitzRoy, what are you frightened of? She's your wife. It's perfectly fine to be in love with her."

"I'm not in love with her." He realized he'd said it too quickly because Jasper gave him a look of warning. But then Colin frowned—Jasper wasn't looking at him. Moreover, he would have joked that Colin protested too stridently, not given him an expression designed to shut him up.

Slowly, Colin followed Jasper's gaze. There was Daphne in the parlor doorway, dressed in the maid's uniform, which was too tight over her breasts and too short, showing her ankles. She looked nothing like a servant, especially not with the angry look on her face.

"Daphne, I—"

"Yes, I heard," she said curtly. "You don't love me. Well, that suits as I don't love you either." Her voice was cold, but he thought he saw a flash of hurt in her eyes. "So perhaps we should finish this night's work so we can go back to ignoring each other."

"Lady Daphne," Jasper began. "Colin and I were discussing…when he said…you see I goaded him…"

"Lord Jasper, do you plan to stand here all night tripping over your tongue or shall we go?"

Jasper closed him mouth. "I suppose I prefer to go."

"Then let's be off." And she turned her back and strode toward the door as though she were a queen.

Jasper looked at Colin. "She looked so pretty and sweet."

Colin gave a bark of laughter. "At least you can admit you don't know everything."

***

She knew Colin didn't love her. She didn't need to be told that. She hadn't needed to be told when they were betrothed. She hadn't needed to be told when he did his duty on their wedding night, his attitude perfunctory and resigned. She hadn't needed to be told these last seven years when he all but pretended she didn't exist.

Colin FitzRoy did not love Daphne Caraway.

But she did not need it rubbed in her face, especially when the last few days she had begun to hope that maybe he would love her *some* day. Or maybe he at least liked her. Gone were the dutiful pecks on the hand or cheek. He kissed her as though he liked her. He touched her as though he liked her.

He touched her with an emotion much stronger than mere *like*.

But what if she'd misunderstood all of it? What if she had mistaken lust for something more? Women did it all the time, and men too. She had seen enough scandals in her time in London that she should have been immune to making such amateur mistakes. She wasn't an ingenue who threw herself at the first man who whispered pretty words in her ear.

Or perhaps she was, because she had never been able to resist Colin, and he had done much more than give her pretty words.

But he'd said it loud and clear tonight. *I'm not in love with her.* She could stop hoping and pretending and wishing it were different or might someday be different. Yesterday, in this very house, he had asked her to give him a chance. Not to give up on him. She'd thought he had shown genuine emotion, but what if it was just a way to convince her to move in here or stay out of his way for a few days? What if all he cared about was that the duchess stopped badgering him to act like a husband?

And what if she was poised to act a complete fool all over again and have her heart broken to pieces?

"Daphne," Colin said behind her.

She didn't look around.

"Daphne, allow Lord Jasper to lead."

"I'm perfectly capable." They were out of the house now. She'd sent Brown back to the Warcliffe town house as soon as they had exchanged clothing. She supposed at least she'd been spared the indignity of her maid hearing her husband's declaration. So it was only the three of them now, walking along the dark street.

"I am certain you are capable, my lady," Lord Jasper said from behind her. "But you are walking in the wrong direction."

She turned and followed him, aware this was yet another instance when she looked like a fool. Lord Jasper led and Colin walked behind her as they wound through dark streets and rank alleys. Brown's feet were smaller than hers, so they had not traded footwear, and Daphne was glad she wore her sturdiest half-boots. She'd learned her lesson from the slippers the other night.

But even with the half-boots, her legs were beginning to hurt, and she was slightly out of breath.

"We're almost there," Colin said, coming up behind her and putting a hand on her elbow.

She snatched her elbow away, not wanting him to touch her. "I'm fine. I don't need any help." She increased her pace. "Especially not from you," she muttered.

She knew they were nearing the docks by the smell. There were places on the Thames that were pretty and smelled fresh and lovely. And then there were the docks, which smelled like rotting fruit, dead fish, and fouled water. In the distance, she could see the tall masts of the ships crowding the sky. Lord Jasper led them toward the warehouse and customs buildings, which was away from the taverns and inns the sailors and dock workers frequented.

They seemed to pass building after building after building until Daphne was hopelessly lost and certain she would never find her way home again if separated from her companions. Finally, Lord Jasper stopped before a building and said in a low voice, "This is the one."

"How can you tell?" Daphne asked, looking up at the structure. It looked just like all the other buildings.

"Because I can," he said. She wanted to roll her eyes.

"We should go in the back," Colin said, looking around them. They were actually about to break in. Daphne could not believe she would be a criminal after tonight. What if they ended up finding incriminating papers or documents and taking them? She would be a thief, not merely a...whatever the name was for someone who broke into buildings.

She followed Lord Jasper around the back and stood to the side while he bent to the lock. She saw no lights and heard nothing but the sounds of men's voices, but those were distant and not a worry at the moment. Still, her heart pounded in her chest so loudly she thought Colin could surely hear.

Finally, the door swung open and Jasper stepped out of the way. "Ladies first." But she did not want to go into the dark building first. Colin seemed to sense this and moved past her. Once inside, Jasper closed and locked the door again then lit the lantern he had with him. He pointed to the office on the first floor. "Anything worth anything will be up there. You two start there. I'll search down here."

Colin climbed the steps, but they were stymied at the closed door by yet another lock. "Give me a hairpin," Colin said.

She reached up and took one out then handed it to him. "You know how to pick locks?"

"I know a little." But after a few minutes of fumbling and two more of her hair pins, he called for Lord Jasper. She held the lamp while Lord Jasper used his own tools to pick the lock. He swore several times, but as it was nothing she hadn't heard from her brothers, she ignored it.

Finally, the door clicked open. "You're bound to find something here," Lord Jasper said, indicating the office. "That was a well-made lock and not cheap. He's protecting something."

He stayed until Colin lit the lamp in the office with the lantern Jasper held, then went back to the ground floor to "look around and keep watch."

Daphne entered the office and shivered. She couldn't remember ever having smelled Lord Battersea, but this place carried his scent. It was something dark and heavy. It made her stomach turn.

"Do you want the desk or those file drawers?" Colin asked.

"I'll take the file drawers."

He nodded, lit a lamp for her, then brought his to the desk. He sat behind it and opened the first drawer.

Daphne stared at all of the drawers, finally deciding to begin with the first one. That was the most logical method of proceeding, but it was probably not the quickest. She opened it and lifted out the file on top.

She and Colin worked in silence for some time, he leafing through papers from the drawers and she opening file after file and seeing nothing that looked in the least interesting or suspicious. If only she knew what she were looking for.

"I didn't mean for you to hear that." Colin spoke, breaking the silence. His voice startled her, and she whipped around to look at him. As soon as she realized what he'd said, she wished she had left her back to him.

She turned back to her file. "I don't know why it should matter. It's not as though you said anything I don't already know."

"Daphne, I spoke out of frustration. Jasper can be an arse, and he'd annoyed me."

She set the folder she held on the floor and looked at him. "Then you do love me?"

It would have been comical to watch him squirm and his mouth open and shut like a fish if the question hadn't meant so much to her.

Why had she even asked? Did she want him to hurt her? "Never mind. I think your silence says everything."

"It's not that I don't…" He swallowed. "Care for you."

"Oh, you *care* for me? Like you care for Pugsly?"

"Daphne." He rose and crouched beside her on the floor. "I can honestly say that I would never, ever kiss Pugsly."

She smiled despite herself. "And we are back to lust."

"It's not lust." He ran a hand through his hair and when he looked at her again, she arched a brow. He sighed. "There's some lust. I'm a man and you're...well, look at you."

She looked down at her drab, ill-fitting livery. Her hair had come loose from its pins—the ones still in place—and she was seated on the floor.

"I look a mess."

He shook his head slowly, and the look he gave her sent heat straight to her lower belly. Why was it so hard to resist him?

"You have no idea what I'd like to do to you right now."

She looked about. "Here?" The idea sent a little thrill through her.

"I didn't say it was logical. I've been wondering for the past hour if the stitches in that bodice will hold."

She looked down at the taut fabric straining to contain her breasts.

"I've been hoping it wouldn't."

He lifted a hand and traced one finger over the exposed tops of her breasts. She inhaled sharply and their eyes met. She couldn't seem to stop herself. Just as she couldn't seem to stop acting like a ninny. And here she went again. Daphne grasped his coat and kissed him hard. He fell against her, toppling them both to the floor. She didn't care. She needed his mouth on her. She needed the feel of his body against hers.

He kissed her with all the passion she felt, leaving her breathless and wanting more. And when he pulled back and traced a line of kisses down her throat and to her collarbone, she arched her head back. After tonight they could do this every night, in a bed. She would undress him, touch him everywhere, wake up beside him…

Or would she? Maybe he would just take his pleasure and leave as he had on their wedding night. Because maybe all there was for him was lust. But couldn't lust turn into more? Perhaps it already had, and he just didn't know how to admit it. She hadn't asked him to apologize—not that he had apologized, not really—for what she'd heard. He must care something for her feelings to try and appease her.

Colin looked up at her. "What's wrong?"

She blinked at him.

"You're somewhere else."

"We should get back to the search. I'd rather Lord Jasper didn't walk in on me with my skirts tossed up around my waist."

He looked at her for a long moment, and she almost told him she didn't care. She almost told him not to stop and pulled him back for a kiss. She had waited so long for him to hold her like this, touch her like this, want her like this. But she didn't speak, and she saw as he clenched his jaw that he was summoning his resolve.

"You have a point," he said. He pulled back and helped her to her feet. She tried to right Brown's livery, but it seemed hopeless. When she adjusted the bodice, trying to put it back in place, she glanced at Colin, who quickly looked away. "I'll just go back to my desk."

"I'll go back to my drawers." She bent to lift the pile of papers she'd been reading and then remembered something her father had mentioned one night at a dinner party. She hadn't really been paying attention until she heard Battersea's name. It was something about insurance. He had collected a large settlement from his insurance agent. Something about lost goods on the *Ranger*. She had not realized at the time, but now she wondered if the *Ranger* might not be a ship. Leaving her piles of documents where they were, she rose and went to the drawer with the files for R. She sorted through them, but there was no file for *Ranger* where it should have been.

Perhaps she had not heard correctly. Idly, she continued thumbing through the files, trying to remember the conversation. She was almost to the bottom of the drawer when she saw *RA*.

Daphne held her breath. RA should not be filed so far away from the top of the pile. She lifted the other files out and stared down at a filed labeled *RANGER*.

Perhaps she'd been paying more attention than she thought.

Daphne sank to the floor, not caring if she didn't look ladylike, and opened the file. She perused the cargo log. It detailed crates of spices, wines, silks, and other fabrics bound for Canada. There were other goods as well—muskets, gun powder, books—but the majority of the cargo appeared to be luxury items. There was nothing unusual about that. Canada was a vast unchartered land situated across an entire ocean. They would have to import spices and silks and probably exported furs and timber.

Feeling a bit disheartened, she paged listlessly through course charts and names and salaries of the various captain and crew.

"Find anything?" Colin asked.

She looked up to find him watching her. "I don't think so. I remembered my father discussing lost goods on a ship called *Ranger*. I thought Battersea owned it, and I've found the file here. But everything looks in order."

Colin's green eyes narrowed. "That does sound familiar. Something about an insurance settlement. It must have been substantial if it was in the papers."

She looked back at the documents she'd set aside. "Did the ship sink? Why would he receive an insurance settlement?"

"Shall I take a look?"

"Yes." She patted the floor beside her. "It will take me at least another quarter hour to go through this. If you take part, we can do it in half the time."

He crossed the room and sat beside her. She handed him a stack of loose papers and took the captain's log for herself. She'd already begun it and found it rather tedious, but she could finish it if Colin looked at the other materials.

The captain wrote daily of the wind and the weather and the course corrections. There was apparently an issue with one sailor on board, and he had been confined to the brig for drunkenness. That was the extent of the excitement. She turned the page and found the log had skipped several days.

"This is odd."

Colin glanced up at her. "What is?"

"These pages are missing from the log. It's"—she looked at the dates and flipped back and forth—"about a week's worth of annotations."

"I will look through these, but the papers I have pertain to the insurance settlement."

Daphne leaned close and studied the papers Colin held between them. "Five thousand pounds for silks?"

"And another three thousand for the other fabrics. I haven't read all the documents, but it appears the *Ranger* was set upon by privateers who boarded and took the silks, muslins and laces, and gunpowder."

She met Colin's gaze. "Not the muskets?"

His brows lifted. "That was my thought as well. Even if a pirate had plenty of weapons, they could always use more. And muskets are more valuable than gunpowder."

"Is there an explanation?"

He turned the pages and pointed to a section about a quarter of the way down one piece of parchment. "It says that the crew were alerted to the presence of the other ship and fought the pirates before they could load the muskets on their ship. Apparently, the pirates boarded under cover of darkness and when the crew was short one man on watch."

Daphne nodded. "There was a crew member in the brig for drunkenness."

Colin looked up at her, his gaze meeting hers. Daphne was uncomfortably aware of how close they were. She could feel the heat of his body seeping into hers. "So the story is plausible," Colin said.

Daphne watched his lips move. She couldn't help thinking what nice lips he had. They were always so soft and teasing when he kissed her.

"Daphne?"

"Hmm?" She looked back at his eyes.

"I said the story is plausible. At least the insurance company thought so."

"Right." She had to avoid looking at his lips. Instead she looked back at the documents he held. "But I'm still curious about those missing pages of the log." Perhaps looking at his hands was not better than his lips. He had long, straight fingers with rounded tips and blunt nails. He'd touched her in the most private of places with those fingers. He seemed to know how to work magic with them.

"Is there anything in the log about the attack?"

"I'll see." Daphne blew out a breath she hadn't realized she'd been holding, glad for something to do besides look at Colin. Being close to him was distracting. But even when she didn't look at him, when she kept her focus on the pages of the log as she leafed through it, she inhaled his scent with every breath she took. It was a mixture of soap and something musky he must have used to shave. Or perhaps it was in his soap. It smelled clean and woodsy, and she wanted to bury her nose in his neck and inhale more deeply. And then she was imagining burying her face against his neck, brushing her lips against the skin there, darting her tongue out to taste his flesh.

"Are you even reading those pages?" he asked.

She stopped, realizing she had just been turning pages without reading a word. "No, I...I'm distracted." She chanced a look at his face, which wore an expression of amusement.

"By what?"

She looked away. "Nothing. I'll look again." She turned back to the last page of the log she remembered reading.

"Daphne."

She jumped at the quiet way he said her name.

"What?"

"Am *I* distracting you?"

She cleared her throat which seemed rather tight with him so close. "It might have been better when you were over there." She pointed to the desk.

"Why?" Oh, he was enjoying this. She could hear the amusement in his voice.

"Because then I couldn't smell you."

"What?"

They both froze as Lord Jasper's footfalls sounded rapidly on the stairs. He paused at the doorway. "Lights out. Someone is coming."

Thirteen

"What do you mean, someone is coming?" Daphne asked, fear clutching her chest and squeezing tightly.

"I think it might be the Watch. There's two of them."

Colin rose and shuttered the lamp on the desk and then Daphne did the same to the one beside her. The room was thrust into darkness, and she could just discern Lord Jasper's shape in the door frame.

"Stay in here," he said. "I'll close the door. You lock it and keep quiet and still."

"Where will you be?" Colin asked.

"There are a dozen places to hide on the ground floor. If they suspect someone is here, I don't think they'll come upstairs, but I'll stop them before they reach you." He closed the door. Daphne didn't hear him walk away, but Colin made his way carefully to the door and locked it.

"How will he stop them?" Daphne asked.

"It's better not to ask him too many questions," Colin murmured. "He won't answer, and if he does, you might not like what he says."

"That sounds ominous." And then she ceased whispering and listened because she heard the sound of a man's voice coming closer. Lord Jasper had been correct. There were men approaching. She couldn't make out what they were saying, but they were definitely nearing the shipping offices.

What if they were Battersea's employees or Battersea himself? She shivered and Colin, who had returned to sitting beside her, put an arm around her shoulders and pulled her against him. "There," he said, whispering in her ear. "Now you can smell me better."

She elbowed him in the ribs, and he groaned. "Watch my ribs."

She'd forgotten he'd bruised them. "Sorry, but you are incorrigible."

"True enough. And now that you're close, I can smell your perfume. What is it? It smells pink."

"What does pink smell like?" she whispered.

"Sweet and a little tart"—he sniffed again—"and pretty."

She laughed quietly. "I am hardly sweet."

"And you're much more than pretty." His lips grazed her neck, nuzzling the sensitive flesh there. She let out a shaky breath as the lips she'd been admiring earlier made her entire body come alive. It felt as though tiny little fires licked their way up her skin from the tips of her toes to her weak knees to her inner thighs and higher.

But she also couldn't quite get the image she'd had of her own lips on his skin out of her mind. She turned toward him, careful to make no sound, as it seemed the Watch had paused outside the building and were smoking and talking. She could hear their low voices as she ran her hands up Colin's shirt.

"What are you doing?" he whispered.

"I want to kiss you." She pushed the papers off his lap, not caring if she made a mess of the *Ranger* file, and climbed over his legs to straddle his thighs. It was an extremely unladylike position, but it was too dark for him to see much more than her shadow. Colin didn't seem to mind her unladylike behavior, though. He pulled her closer to him, so their bodies were flush.

"That's better," he said.

"Much." She found his collar with her hand and pushed it open. His clothing was coarse as would befit a sailor, and he wore a loose neck cloth she easily pushed out of the way. She unfastened two buttons, parting his shirt at the throat. She could hear that his breath had sped up, but he hadn't stopped or questioned her.

Daphne leaned forward to press her lips against the bare skin of his neck just where his collarbone met his shoulder. She inhaled, and there was that clean, masculine scent again. She pressed her lips against the flesh there then moved them slightly higher until she could feel his rapidly beating pulse. She licked it and he made a quiet groan.

"You taste as good as you smell," she whispered. His hands came up to rest on her waist as she bent to nuzzle his neck again. She traced a path to his earlobe and nipped at it lightly. His hands tightened. It seemed that particular action had the same effect on him as it did on her.

She explored further, finally reaching his jaw and tracing the rough stubble to his mouth. He was waiting for her, his mouth warm and ready as he opened for her, kissing her back. She could feel the desire in the way he held her, kissed her. It made her dizzy. Their tongues met, and she rocked against him, suddenly aware of the hard bulge between them.

"Is that?" she asked then stopped because she didn't know what to call it.

"My cock?" he whispered against her lips. "I'm hard for you."

"That's what happened on our wedding night when you…" She didn't want to remember the pain, though she knew he had tried to be gentle.

"It happens to me every time I touch you." His hands ran up and down her back. "Every time I kiss you. You don't seem to understand how much I want you."

"I want you too," she said. She wanted him desperately. Her body was on fire for him, and she didn't care that they were in Battersea's office or that there were men standing below or that he didn't love her. She was a woman who wanted a man, who wanted her husband.

Her hand came between them, tracing the length and hardness of him, but when she started to loose the fall of his trousers, he stopped her. "Not here and now," he said. "I made a poor job of it the first time. I'm not following that by taking you on the hard floor of this bastard's office."

She licked his neck again. "But I want you, Colin. I've hardly been able to read a word since you sat beside me. I want your hands on me."

"I think that can be arranged." And she felt his hands slide under her skirts to the skin of her thigh just above her garters. Oh, yes. She knew what he would do to her now. She leaned back, giving him access, as he traced a slow path to where her body throbbed.

"You're becoming a wanton," he murmured.

"I can't help it." She inhaled sharply as his hand grazed her core. "The things you do to me."

His fingers teased and enticed. "Do you know what I plan to do to you tomorrow night? In our bed?"

"No—*Oh*." She moaned.

"Shh."

She nodded, clamping her lips shut but allowing her hips to move against his talented fingers.

"Do you want me to tell you?"

"*Please*."

"I'll undress you. Slowly and in the lamplight. I want to see every inch of you." He dipped a finger inside her, and her body clamped tight to it as she rocked against his palm, which pressed hard to the place she most needed his touch.

"I want to kiss every inch of you," he whispered. "Especially here." His thumb moved in a circle and she made a small whimper.

"Colin, *please*," she begged. She was so close to the pleasure she knew he could bring her, but it seemed when she came close, he pulled back, teasing her, making her wait.

"And when I have you naked and sated, your body flush with pleasure, that's when I'll take you."

"How?" she asked, his voice, his words making her heart pound in time to the throbbing of her body.

"I'll part your legs and slide my cock inside you. Like this." His finger slid in and out of her. "So slowly. Filling you. Making you cry out in pleasure. You won't have to be quiet like you do tonight."

She almost sobbed with need. "I want you now," she murmured.

"You want pleasure. Then take it." He pressed his thumb against her, and she moved against it until the pleasure crescendoed and crashed over her. Colin put a hand over her mouth, but she bit her lip to stay quiet. When the swirling ecstasy subsided, she collapsed against him, limp and used, and smiling.

He kissed her cheek, and in that moment, she wanted to believe he cared for her. At least a little.

***

Colin held Daphne close, liking the feel of her soft, warm body pressed to his. He worried he was becoming too used to having her close, to touching her body, to holding her. But then again, he was an adult male. He had needs he had put aside for years, and once he'd had her, he wouldn't think of her so much. He wouldn't have to worry he was beginning to feel too much for her.

He hadn't expected to feel anything more than attraction and affection for her. She'd always been beautiful and vivacious. He'd liked her. He just hadn't wanted to marry her. But then he hadn't wanted to marry anyone at twenty-two years of age. He'd wanted freedom and adventure and to see the world.

Now he'd had all of that and more, and even before the Duchess of Warcliffe had come to him, demanding he intervene with her daughter, he had been thinking it was time to mend the relationship with his wife.

His wife. Daphne—who was smart and resourceful, brave and passionate, independent and loyal. And yes, a bit reckless. But she'd taken responsibility for her mistakes with Battersea. She didn't expect anyone else to fix her problems, and she wasn't too proud to accept help either.

He liked her.

He remembered her as being pouty and needy in her pink with dozens of bows. But now he saw that she had been as unsure of things between them as he had been. She had probably been scared and hopeful.

He'd let her down. He had not been what she needed. Colin pulled her closer and vowed not to let her down again. And didn't that strike fear into his heart? He doubted he could be what she needed, but he wanted to try. Maybe she wouldn't demand he crack open his chest and expose his heart as he feared. Maybe she was willing to take pleasure and affection and leave it there.

And who the hell was he fooling?

Daphne gave a sated sigh and pulled back from him. "I don't hear the voices any longer. Do you think they've moved on?"

He didn't hear them either, which meant they probably had. Jasper would be back in a moment to give the all-clear. As though he'd summoned the bounty hunter, he heard Jasper's quiet footsteps on the stairs. The fact that he heard Jasper at all meant the man was giving him notice of his approach. Colin helped Daphne to her feet and rose himself. His cock protested being ignored yet once more, but Colin managed to cool his ardor by imagining Pugsly's ugly little face.

"Colin?" Jasper tapped on the door.

"Are they gone?" Colin asked, voice low. He crossed the room to open the door. Jasper hadn't lit his lantern again.

"I think so. I didn't want to take any chances. You can light the lantern in here. There are no windows."

Colin moved to the place he'd left the lamp, and fumbled about until he managed to light it again. He turned to look at Jasper and Daphne, who stood on opposite sides of the room. Jasper looked as he always did in his dark cloak and mask, but it was difficult to get used to seeing Daphne in servants' livery. Her hair was disheveled and her cheeks pink, but she looked less debauched than he'd feared.

"Made any progress?" Jasper asked.

"We have, actually," Colin said, and told Jasper what they'd found and what they had not found—the missing pages of the log book.

"Is Battersea the sort of man who might try and cheat the insurance firm?" Jasper asked.

"Most definitely," Daphne answered. "You don't believe his account of pirates?"

Jasper shrugged. "I find it questionable. The British Navy has made piracy all but obsolete. There are still small bands of smugglers operating on the coasts, but it's rare in this day and age to see an attack like the one described."

"And an attack that claimed only gunpowder and silks," Colin added. "I don't believe that, even pressed for time, the pirates wouldn't have taken the muskets. Those missing log pages are the key."

"Then we find them. Why don't I read the rest of the log? Surely the captain will mention the attack. You two search for the missing pages." Jasper held out a gloved hand and Daphne gave him the log.

"If Battersea were smart, he would have burned those log pages," she said.

"He very likely did," Colin agreed. "But we have to be as certain as possible they're not here. I'll start on this side and you start on that."

It was an impossible task, he thought as he opened one drawer after another and looked through folders and stacks of documents. He could put his hands on the pages and not realize they were the ones he sought. He didn't have enough time to search thoroughly. That would have taken days, and they had only a few more hours.

The lamp burned on and the three of them worked in silence until finally Jasper closed the log and set it on the desk with a thud. "That was interesting."

"Why is that?" Daphne asked, sliding a drawer open and poking her head in to peer in the back.

"There's no mention of the pirate attack until the end of the log. The account is on loose parchment stuck into the back. It's the same writing and purports to be the missing pages, but there's no evidence the pages were ripped out."

Colin strolled over to take a look. "You think the captain was told to fabricate an account later?"

"It's a possibility. Battersea might have paid him to lie."

"But why?" Daphne asked. "What really happened to the silk and gunpowder if pirates didn't steal it?"

"We need to find the missing pages to know that."

She straightened and leaned back against the file drawers. "I don't think we'll ever find them. We've been searching for hours. They're probably ashes."

"I don't think so," Colin said, going to back to where he'd left off earlier. "If the captain was bribed to give a false account, Battersea would have kept the evidence of the captain's lie in case the man ever had a change of heart. Battersea could see him sent to prison for falsifying an insurance claim."

Daphne gave him a weary look. "So we keep searching."

"Wishing you had stayed behind now?" Colin asked, sliding a drawer open.

"Then you wouldn't have thought to look for the *Ranger*," she said. "You needed me." She turned and opened her own drawer.

"True," Colin admitted. "Though it's likely the *Ranger* is not the first time he's been part of a swindle. I think we would have found something sooner or later."

Daphne scowled at him before huffing and going back to her search. Jasper gave Colin a bewildered look and Colin just shook his head. Jasper had a point that she had overreacted, but Colin knew he still had a few things to learn about women.

Jasper joined the search and the three worked in silence for what felt like hours. Colin's back hurt and his eyes stung when he closed them for a moment with exhaustion and strain. He opened one more drawer, determined that if he found nothing in it, they would have to admit defeat and leave the docks before too many people were about. Just then Daphne sank to her knees.

Colin abandoned his drawer and went to her. "Are you not feeling well?"

"I feel…perfect," she said, lifting several papers aloft. "I found them."

"Are you sure?" Jasper asked. Daphne cut a look at him, and Jasper held up his hands in defense. "Let me rephrase. What do they say?"

She spread the papers on the floor and Colin brought the lantern close so they could all read. She rearranged them to the order she wanted then pointed to the one to the farthest left, near Jasper. "It's the same handwriting and you can see it's been torn from a binding."

Jasper opened the captain's log and compared the last entry before the missing pages to the first one on the floor. "The dates coincide."

The three of them leaned close, reading the first page, with Daphne turning it when all three indicated they had finished the front. The proceeded to read all five or six pages that way and then Colin sat back.

"He's bloody well crafty. Even if his insurers suspected something was amiss in his tale, they wouldn't have come to this conclusion," Colin said.

"I don't understand," Daphne said. "The captain wrote that the silks and gunpowder were damaged by a water leak. Couldn't Battersea collect damaged goods insurance, or whatever it might be called?"

"It's possible, but he wouldn't receive the full amount of the value of the goods," Jasper said. "Only a fraction. And he couldn't sell the goods, although there might still be some who would buy the silk at an extensive mark down. But if he claims the good were taken, a total loss—"

"He is paid their full value," Daphne said.

"And if the crew sells what can be salvaged then that's an extra profit." Colin rose and paced away. "The captain must be in on it. Initially, he gave a truthful account, but when he returned, Battersea somehow persuaded him to lie."

"It's possible the captain was paid off, but I'll be damned if we have time to go through and find a bank draft," Jasper said.

"We don't need the draft to damn Battersea," Daphne said. "We need the captain."

Colin and Jasper exchanged a look then both looked at Daphne.

"What did I say?" she asked.

"You just gave us our next step." He hated to admit it, but she had been invaluable tonight. She was clever and so much more than the Society miss he'd thought her to be for all those years.

Jasper held up a hand. "Not I. My wife will wonder where I've been, and I have card swindlers to deal with. You'll have to find the captain on your own."

Colin was the one who scowled now. "I can't take her to search for a ship's captain alone. I'll have my throat slit."

"Why?" Daphne asked. Colin didn't bother to point out that she would be a prize for any number of criminal men.

"Take Duncan," Jasper said. "He's big enough and has nothing to do but squire prospective brides about. As for that, he usually scares them away within a quarter hour."

"No," Daphne said at the same time Colin said, "Good idea."

"No! I'll owe him a favor, and my friends will never forgive me if I introduce their daughters to a man like him."

"I think you have bigger problems than Society's opinion of Duncan Murray," Colin said.

"Oh, very well! When do we go?"

Colin smiled. She did not even hesitate, though she must have understood the danger. He understood it all too well, and a part of him was already panicking at the thought of anything happening to her. But then the woman was practically fearless. It was difficult not to find himself feeling more than he liked to admit for this woman and wondering how he would ever go back to life without her. Daphne was still waiting for an answer, so Colin considered. "I'll see what I can find out about the man—Captain Gladwell—whether he's in London or on a ship right now."

Daphne's face fell. "I hadn't thought of that."

"If he's in London, we pay him a visit tomorrow evening. I can call for you after four."

She shook her head. "You won't need to call for me. We're moving into our house tomorrow or have you forgotten?"

He had forgotten. And that meant he couldn't spend all day gathering information on a merchant captain. Colin had to move in with his wife.

And he thought he'd been panicking before.

Fourteen

When the duchess had arrived home and peeked in her daughter's bed chamber, Brown had managed to convince Her Grace Daphne was sleeping soundly and should not be disturbed. And even though Daphne didn't actually arrive back at the Warcliffe town house until almost four in the morning, no one but her maid seemed aware she had been out all night. Brown reported no suspicious activity had been remarked upon. So if Battersea had come for her, he had been stealthy about it. Before she'd gone to bed, she peered out her curtains into the gray morning. She saw no one there, but her skin prickled with awareness.

She might not see him, but he would come for her.

Daphne fell into a fitful sleep until about noon, when her mother woke her and asked if she felt well enough to relocate to the new town house or if they should put it off for another day.

"Absolutely not, Mama," Daphne said. "I feel much better." She worried for her parents' safety with Battersea prowling about. The sooner she was away, the safer they would be.

"You look a little pale and tired." The duchess cupped her face.

"Nothing some tea and toast will not cure." Daphne smiled brightly until her mother left and Brown came in to dress her. "Is everything packed and ready?" Daphne asked as Brown shook out a pale pink muslin with small green sprigs of flowers on the material. There were pretty green bows on the cuff of the sleeves.

"Yes, my lady."

When the dress was over her head, Daphne helped smooth it down. "Is the staff in residence?"

"I believe they were to arrive several hours ago, my lady. Turn this way, my lady."

"Good. Then go ahead over there now and rest for a few hours. I won't need you until this afternoon when I have to change."

Brown paused in her efforts to pin the dress into place and caught Daphne's gaze in the mirror. "Are you certain, my lady?"

"That's the least I can do to thank you for keeping my mother at bay last night."

Brown went back to her task. "I didn't like lying to Her Grace, but you are my mistress, my lady."

Daphne turned and put her hand on Brown's arm. "Thank you for your loyalty."

Brown smiled. She was not a pretty woman as she usually wore a sour expression, but she smiled now and looked rather attractive. Daphne turned her back to the mirror and peered over her shoulder. "Am I all laced and tied and pinned?"

"You are, my lady."

"Then I'm off to my last breakfast with my parents."

The rest of the day was a blur of directing servants to place this here and that there, making certain she met the new staff and that they knew what she expected, and taking inventory of silver, plates, linens, and other household items. She saw Colin in passing and asked for his opinion a time or two, but later when she asked about him, she was told he was out. She hoped that meant he had located Captain Gladwell.

Without Colin in the house, she was easily startled. The clang of pots or the heavy thud of furnishings being moved made her jump, even if it was difficult to believe Battersea would come here in the broad daylight. He probably did not even know she had moved town houses yet, but she did not feel safe without Colin close by. She might not be able to trust he would never abandon her again, but she knew he would keep her safe until Battersea was no longer a threat.

After that, she supposed they would go back to living separate lives as so many peers did. He could go to his family estate in the country or travel on the Continent. She would go to country house parties. They would occasionally meet up in Town and sleep under the same roof. She would see him more than she had in the past, but he would use the frequent physical distance to keep her emotionally at bay. He would become a stranger to her again.

At about half past five Daphne collapsed in a chair in the parlor and closed her eyes. It was a bright, cheery room in the day. But now that the shadows were creeping in, she could not help but remember this was the room where Colin had announced, *I'm not in love with her.*

And then he'd spent the rest of the evening doing and saying things that thoroughly confused her on that point. Her stomach growled, and she wondered if she should give some instruction about supper. She had not wanted the staff to prepare a meal if Colin arrived in a hurry to be off to confront Captain Gladwell.

"Has no one fed you?" a voice asked.

Daphne jumped and searched the room for Colin. She found him seated near the window, his body in shadow, and she thanked God it was not Battersea. It took a moment for her to force air into her tight chest.

"How long have you been there?" she asked.

"An hour or so."

She put a hand to her pounding heart. "You startled me. I didn't even know you were there."

"I'm rather good at blending in."

She rose. "Don't do it with me. I like to see you."

"Good." He stood and the room seemed to grow smaller. "Shall we fetch you some supper and see about having a word with Captain Gladwell?"

"You found him?"

"Not exactly, but I have it on good authority that he is here in London. I made a few inquiries this morning and have an idea where to look for him."

"Do you know where he lives?"

"I know the general area. I thought we might stop in at a few taverns and if we spot him, we can follow him home. The area is not respectable but not dangerous, either."

"How will we know what he looks like?"

"I'll tell you what I know on the way." He looked her up and down. "Are you wearing that?"

"No. I should have changed an hour or so ago. This is a day dress."

"Put on something less…pink." He leaned closer to her. "I liked you in black last night."

Daphne felt a curl of pleasure uncoil in her belly. "I'll see what my maid can find."

Colin locked eyes with her then finally stepped back. "Don't be long."

With Brown's help, she changed into another mourning dress in a matter of minutes. Colin waited for her at the bottom of the steps, her gray cloak over his arm. He waved the butler away and put it around her shoulders himself, his fingers brushing the bare skin of her collarbone. Was it too scandalous to admit she wanted to forget Captain Gladwell and Battersea tonight and just go to bed?

"You don't have to go," Colin said quietly.

"No." She would not be left alone again or shirk her responsibility. "*You* don't have to go. This was my mistake, and I will rectify it."

He led her out of the house, hailed a hackney cab, and directed it to an area not far from the river. "What about the Scotsman?" she asked when they were underway. "Is he meeting us?"

Colin shook his head. "He had a prior commitment. A ball, if you can believe it."

Daphne sorted through her mental inventory of invitations. "The Ridgeton ball?" Doubtful. "Or was it the Lansdown ball?"

Colin gave her a dubious look. "I didn't ask. I told him to make room on his social calendar for us tomorrow."

"And what if we find the captain tonight?"

"We either follow him and find out where he lives and what he does, or, if he seems relatively harmless, we confront him. Just don't cause any problems. I can't fight and protect you at the same time."

"I don't cause problems."

He huffed out a disbelieving breath. "You do nothing but cause problems. Just stay close to me. A tavern isn't one of your garden parties. Some men see any woman in a tavern as fair game."

Daphne wouldn't admit it, but it sounded a little exciting to her. Not that she wanted to be any man's fair game, but she had done nothing for years except go to Society entertainments. The most exciting thing that happened at one of those was a debutante found kissing a man on the terrace or a lady whose assets were exposed when she tripped and fell over.

A dark tavern filled with bawdy wenches flirting with patrons who were not gentlemen seemed rather exciting.

Colin rapped on the roof of the hackney, drawing Daphne out of her imaginings. She looked out the window and saw a rather ordinary street lined with closed shops and yellow lights spilling out of taverns. A few men walked along the street, which was not yet dark enough to require a lantern, and a few women hurried by as well.

When they'd exited the coach and Colin had paid the jarvey, he pointed across the street. "We'll start there," Colin said, indicating a tavern with a picture of a tall ship on the sign hanging above the door.

"The Clipper," Daphne read. "It seems a likely tavern for a sea captain."

"Possibly, but more importantly, I've heard the food here is better than some of the other establishments. So we start here."

Daphne followed him into the dark interior and was sorely disappointed. There was one woman listlessly wiping a table and a few men older than her father sitting at tables and eating what looked like soup. The publican, a stocky brown-skinned man with close-cropped wiry black hair, nodded to them as soon as they walked in. "I don't know anything," he said.

Daphne opened her mouth to reply, but Colin took her hand and squeezed it.

"We came to eat, not talk," Colin answered.

"Sure you did." The man looked Daphne over. "I see her sort in here every day. All the ladies of the court come in to dine."

Colin ignored him and led Daphne to a small table. It looked clean and when she traced a gloved hand over the surface, it didn't come away sticky. The tavern wench came over and leaned a bony hip on the table. "Don't mind Isaac," she said. "You came to the right place for dinner. Our cook is the best. Pinched him from the palace, we did."

"Really?" Daphne asked.

The wench smiled at her. "Sure and if you believe that I have some jewelry to sell you."

Colin put his hand over Daphne's. "Two plates of whatever the cook has made and two cups of ale."

The wench sauntered off. Daphne snatched her hand away from Colin's. "I wouldn't have bought any jewelry from her." She looked about the room again. "I've never been to a place like this. I've eaten in a tavern, of course, but my father always secures a private room." Her gaze met those of the men across the room, who had been silent since she'd arrived and were making no pretense about watching her. "I can see why."

"They've never seen anyone who looks like you walk in here. They're curious, but harmless."

The wench set two mugs on the table. "The food will be ready shortly."

Colin sipped his ale and Daphne followed. She didn't drink ale often, but she liked it when she did, and this was quite good. All the activities of the day had made her thirsty and her cup was soon empty. Colin raised a brow then signaled for another.

"Now they can go home and tell their wives that a duke's daughter drinks ale just like any other woman."

Colin smiled. "That wasn't what I meant when I said they haven't seen anyone like you."

She was feeling warm from the ale and a bit lightheaded as she'd had nothing but toast all day. "Is this the part where you tell me I'm beautiful?"

His mouth quirked up. "I've already told you that."

"Have you? I don't remember."

He leaned across the table. "You're beautiful, Daphne."

Before he could lean back, she grasped his wrists. "So are you, Colin."

"Perhaps that's enough ale until the food arrives."

"I'm just telling the truth. I've always thought you were beautiful. You have those green eyes." She studied his eyes now, so pretty and vivid. They were deep enough to hold so many secrets.

"A lot of people have green eyes." He reached for her ale and she scooted it closer to herself, out of his range.

"Not like yours. Not that light green fringed with those black lashes. Women would kill for lashes like that. *I* would kill for lashes like that."

She might have been mistaken, but she thought his cheeks reddened. He cleared his throat. "I had no idea my eyelashes were so coveted."

"Don't go around fluttering them now," she teased.

"I make no promises."

She stared at him. "Look at you. Teasing and talking like an actual person."

"As opposed to?"

She shrugged and sipped her ale. "You are always so serious and stoic. I admit I was a bit afraid of you when we were younger. A bit afraid and completely smitten." His face registered shock and she realized what she'd said. "Did I say that out loud?" she asked.

"The part about being smitten with me?"

"I did." She finished her ale and raised her hand for another. He caught and lowered it.

"I think you'd better slow down."

"I don't know. Perhaps I should drink more. I should have told you how I felt a long time ago," she said.

He paled slightly.

"Oh, but I forget that you don't like to talk about feelings. You don't want to hear how I was half in love with you for years."

"Oh, God." He looked slightly ill.

Daphne continued, ignoring his obvious discomfort. "You don't want to know how I begged my mother to arrange for me to marry you. How she didn't think it was a good match, but between your mother and me pressing her, she finally acquiesced. I was a fool." She was still a fool. Hadn't he announced last night he did not love her? But she wanted him to know. She didn't want to look back and wish she'd told him how she felt, especially when the threat of Battersea might mean any moment now might be her last.

Colin stared at her, his eyes a darker shade of green now. "You *wanted* to marry me?" He sounded as though he were choking.

"That's what I'm saying. I loved you."

"Stop saying that."

"Why? It's the truth. I wanted to be your wife. Well, until I actually *was* your wife."

She didn't know what Colin would have said next because the tavern wench returned and set two bowls of thick stew on the table along with a loaf of warm bread.

She eyed Daphne's mug. "More ale?"

Colin drained his. "Two, please."

The wench nodded and sauntered off. Colin didn't take his gaze from Daphne. She peered critically at the food before them. "This actually looks good." She dipped a spoon into the stew and tasted it. "Not bad."

"I hesitate to mention this again, but did you say—" He seemed to reconsider the question. "Did you mean to imply that before we married, you—you—"

"Loved you? Yes." She ate another bite of stew while he gaped at her. "But then what did I know about love? I thought we would ride away from the church in a carriage and live happily ever after. Instead you went to war and I…I suppose I stayed behind and waited for you."

The server returned with the ale and Colin took his and drank deeply.

"You really had no idea, did you?" She reached for her ale, but he took it out of her hands.

"No more. I won't survive any more confessions."

"It wasn't meant to be a secret. I planned to tell you on our wedding night. Remember I asked you about your secrets? That was mine." She hadn't thought it would surprise him, though. To her, it had been so obvious.

"I thought you didn't want the marriage any more than I did."

Daphne set her spoon on the table. She wasn't hungry any longer, and she was glad he had taken the ale, though it was still within reach. Her stomach had turned sour. "The truth is—"

"Oh, God. No more truths."

"—that I knew you didn't want to marry me. I thought you'd change your mind. I thought I'd be such a good wife that you wouldn't be able to help falling in love with me. Obviously"—she gestured to the tavern—"my plan did not succeed." Because the truth was that Colin FitzRoy would never love her. He would never be hers. He was with her for the moment, but that wouldn't last. Even now, he wanted to escape her.

As if to prove her point, he said, "I think I should take you home."

Perhaps because she was feeling spiteful, she said, "You mean, *we* should go home. Together."

His brow lowered in confusion then his eyes went wide. Clearly, he had forgotten they lived together now. He couldn't escape her quite so easily. The knowledge gave her little comfort. He'd find an escape soon enough.

"But Colin, we can't leave now. We haven't found Captain Gladwell."

The serving wench happened to be passing by, and she doubled back. "You're looking for Captain Gladwell?"

"Yes," Daphne said, her hopes rising. Obviously, this woman knew Gladwell. She shot a quick glance at Colin to see if he was as thrilled as she. His face told her nothing, though. He sipped the ale—*her* ale—but his expression was carefully schooled.

"We're looking for a ship to transport some cargo," Colin said. "We were told Gladwell can be trusted."

"What are you—" Daphne broke off at the narrowing of Colin's eyes. She pressed her lips together. She could play at deception. She'd practically been raised on it.

The server looked over her shoulder at the publican, who was busy moving wine casks behind the bar. She moved closer to Daphne and lowered her voice. "He was already in here tonight. He left less than a quarter hour before you come in."

"Damn it," Colin said. "Do you know where he lives? Perhaps we can speak to him there?"

"I don't know, but he usually walks home along the water. I live that way, and if I leave when he does, he walks me home. He's a kind old man. Walks with a bit of a limp and carries a cane, so I have to walk slowly."

Colin rose. "Thank you." He pressed a coin into her hand. The server looked down at it and her eyes widened. "This is more than your dinner, sir. I'll fetch change."

Colin held his hand out to Daphne. "Keep the change." He dragged Daphne out of the Clipper as the server called her thanks.

***

Daphne did not move quickly, and Colin finally turned to her in exasperation. "If we hurry, we might still catch him."

"My hat is falling off," she complained. "I need to secure—"

He grasped the hat ribbons, yanked them loose, and handed her the hat. "Problem solved."

"Really!" But she moved more quickly, and he no longer had to drag her behind him. He wanted to move quickly, to leave the tavern where she'd confessed so much to him behind. He hadn't been able to breathe in there.

Daphne *loved* him. She had *always* loved him. How had he not known that? Or had he known but refused to admit it because he did not know how to deal with a woman who cared for him and whom he had feelings for as well?

Yes, he had feelings for her. He could admit it, if only to himself. She wasn't the girl he remembered, but a woman who was clever and brave and funny and desirable. The problem was that none of this mattered. He couldn't allow himself to feel anything for her. It was worse than having been mocked as a young man for having feelings; it was that he knew what it was to have loved and lost.

He'd loved his mother. He was her youngest, so she'd spent more time with him than her other children and he'd felt close to her. When she'd died, it was like a part of him died as well. He'd spiraled into a dark well of sadness and despair. He'd wanted to curl up there and die, but his father hadn't allowed it. In the end, it had taken every last ounce of strength Colin possessed to crawl out of that black place. Daphne wanted him to love her, but the part of him that loved was gone, and he was too much of a coward to resuscitate it. Colin could not bear to feel the pain of loss again.

They reached the waterfront a few minutes later and Colin looked down as far as he could see in one direction then the other. He saw no one but mudlarks in the shallows and whores leaning against buildings. No older men with canes in either direction.

"I should have asked her which way," Colin said. "But we can come back tomorrow."

Daphne pointed to the mudlarks. "What are those boys doing?"

He should have known she would not be so easy to manage. He had not exaggerated when he said she caused trouble. "Looking for anything of value in the river to sell or pawn," he answered.

She grasped Colin's arm. "Give them some money."

He sighed, knowing a few coins wouldn't help the children beyond today or tomorrow. "Lads, come here and I'll give you a penny."

A couple of the boys looked at him, then looked at another boy, the tallest, seemingly for approval.

"What do we have to do for it?" the taller boy asked.

"Nothing," Daphne answered. "Just take it and get something to eat."

The leader shook his head. "We don't take no charity."

Colin shook his head. "It's not charity. I want a bit of information."

The leader seemed to consider then waded out of the water and approached them, two or three of the others following. All were barefoot and wore trousers with the legs rolled up. A couple of them were soaked to the skin as they'd obviously dived underwater to search for hidden treasures.

"What kind of information?" the leader asked, hands on his hips. He was thin as a rail with hollows under his eyes. His hands were red and raw and his clothing was patched and threadbare.

"We're looking for Captain Gladwell," Colin said. "Can you show us where he lives?"

The leader looked at the other boys. They were smaller but similarly dressed, their clothing hanging off their thin bodies. Colin caught the slight shake of the leader's head and the other boys' barely perceptible nods. "We don't know a Captain Gladwell," the leader said. "Now we'd best get back to work before it's full dark."

"Wait!" Daphne called after them. "He walks along the waterway nightly. He has a limp!"

"It's no good." Colin put a hand on her arm. "They think he's in some sort of trouble and will protect him. We'll have to come back tomorrow and wait for him."

Daphne sighed. "This could go on for days. I can't hide from the earl forever."

He heard the note of fear in her voice. "I'm with you," he said, looking her in the eye to show her she was safe with him. Colin put his hand at her back and guided her back the way they'd come. The area was relatively quiet at this time of evening. Once true dark fell the taverns would fill up. But in the shadowy dusk, he and Daphne saw few other people. "Battersea won't try anything with me beside you."

"He'll find a way to abduct me when you're not with me, and I'll never be seen again." She shivered and Colin pulled her close, feeling strangely protective.

"I won't allow that to happen."

She smiled at him. "Be careful. I might begin to think you care."

"I…" Colin didn't know what to reply. He couldn't retort that he didn't care. He *did* care. She was his wife and of course he would protect her, but he didn't think she wanted such a standard response. He knew what she wanted, and he couldn't give it. Not to her or to himself. In the end, he remained silent.

Perhaps that's why he heard the footsteps behind them. He turned to look and saw nothing but the fog that had been steadily rolling in from the river. It was thicker now, and he could barely see the shapes of the mudlarks in the distance.

He moved forward again and a moment later heard the steps again. "Someone is following us," he whispered to Daphne.

Of course, she spun around and peered hard at the fog. "Who is there?" she asked.

Colin winced. He shouldn't have said anything to her.

"Someone who can 'elp you," replied a small voice.

"Why, it's just a child," Daphne said.

"I may be little," the voice said, "but I know something you don't. Something about Captain Gladwell."

"Come out of the fog," Colin said, "and we'll talk."

There was a long moment of silence and then the voice said, "Just so you know, I let you 'ear me. Try anything and I'll disappear, and you'll never see me again."

"I have no doubt you know your way about much better than either of we do. We don't want to hurt you. We just want to know where the captain lives."

Slowly a small figure began to emerge from the fog. The child looked like an unearthly spirit with the mist swirling about his coat and trousers. "Blunt first. Then information." The child held out his hand.

"How do we know you won't just run off after we pay you?" Daphne asked.

The urchin put his hands on his hips. "I give you my word, that's 'ow."

"Fine," Colin said. "But come out of the fog so we can see you and speak without shouting."

The child seemed to consider then pointed to an alley between two shops. "We can talk there and not be disturbed. I'll go first."

Colin knew if he was volunteering to go first, there must be a way out the back. He held back until the child had entered the dark alley. When he started forward, Daphne hesitated. "I don't like the looks of it."

Colin couldn't argue. If the child was hoping to trap him, it was the perfect arrangement. Who knew what or who might be waiting in the alley? He bent and reached into his boot for his weapon, a long knife with a wickedly sharp blade. "If there's any trouble, get behind me," he said.

They entered the alley and were momentarily blinded when a lamp shown on their faces. "Now give me the blunt," the urchin said.

Squinting, Colin tossed him a penny. The child caught it one-handed. "That's it?"

"There's more when you tell us what we want to know. Lower the lamp and tell us where Gladwell lives."

The lamp wavered then the light slid down. Daphne gasped as they both got a look at the child. "But you're a girl," Daphne said.

Colin had been thinking the same thing, but he was wise enough not to say it.

The girl sneered. "No, *you're* a girl. I'm a female, much as I 'ate to admit it."

"But you're dressed like a boy," Daphne pointed out.

The child pointed to Daphne's dress. "And 'ow would I climb over a wall or through a window wearing skirts? Now, do you want to talk fashion or do you want to know about Gladwell?"

Daphne opened her mouth, but Colin spoke first. "Tell us where Gladwell lives."

The girl shook her head. "Oh, no. I'm no snitch."

Daphne let out a huff of air. "Then why did you follow us? You're wasting our time."

"Because I can get a message to the captain. Maybe tell 'im you'll meet 'im 'ere tomorrow."

"Fine," Colin agreed. "Tell him to meet us at the The Clipper at six tomorrow. We just want to talk. Give him our names—Mr. FitzRoy and Lady Daphne."

The girl nodded, her large brown eyes shrewd. "That's a lot to remember."

Colin flipped her a shilling. "Will that help you retain everything?"

"If you're asking if this is enough, I think one more shilling will guarantee I get the message perfect."

"What's your name?" Colin asked.

The girl put her free hand on her hip. "Why?"

"I like to know who's fleecing me."

A ghost of a smile crossed her pale face. " 'Arley."

"That's not a name," Daphne argued.

The girl shrugged. "That's what everyone calls me. I think it's cuz I'm 'arley around."

"It's *hardly* around." Daphne corrected. "Not *'arley* or *harley*."

"What do your parents call you?" Colin asked.

"Don't 'ave parents," Harley said. "It's just me, and I like it that way."

"I see. Well, give that information to the captain for us." He tossed her another shilling. "And if you ever decide you don't like it on your own, come find me, Colin FitzRoy. I have a friend who runs an orphanage, a good one, and he can help you."

"What's the name?"

"The Sunnybrooke Home for Boys."

"Will he take her in?" Daphne asked. "She's a…female."

"He'll take her. Ask around about it, Harley. Then come and find me."

"I'll think about it. Until tomorrow, gov!"

The lamp went out and Daphne and Colin were cast into darkness. Colin figured they were probably alone too.

He led Daphne out of the alley and down the street where there were more pedestrians and he might be able to hail a hackney.

"I certainly think you overpaid," Daphne said.

Colin laughed. "First you want me to give out money, now I overpaid.

"Two shillings to deliver a message?" She shook her head. "It's highway robbery."

"It's worth it if the captain meets us tomorrow."

"I think we should eat at The Clipper again. The food was delicious. I could eat another bowl. All of this searching is exhausting. I don't think it's even eight o'clock, and I'm ready for bed."

Colin was ready for bed too, and if he had his way, neither would be sleeping any time soon.

Fifteen

Daphne lay back in the bath Brown had drawn for her and closed her eyes. When her maid had told her Mr. FitzRoy ordered a bathing tub for their room, she had expected something small where she sat with her knees to her chin. But this was luxurious. Her knees were still bent, but she had enough room to lie back and rest her head on the lip of the copper tub. She'd washed as soon as she'd submerged in the water, and now she just wanted to soak. It seemed quite decadent, and with the tub so close to the fire, she was warm and cozy and growing sleepy.

"Don't fall asleep in there," a male voice said from behind her.

Daphne turned her head. Brown slipped out the door just as Colin entered. She was a bit startled to see him. She'd never been naked with a man in the room before, but if she was being honest, she would admit she had been hoping he would come to their bed chamber sooner rather than later. If her time with him was to be limited, she had better make the most of it. No, he didn't love her, but she knew one way to elicit an emotional response from him. She just had to be brave enough to follow through with it.

She gave him a lazy smile that belied the pounding of her heart. "What else should I do with no one and nothing to entertain me?"

He moved closer, his eyes staying on her face. He certainly had self-control. "I might have some entertainment in mind," he said.

Now her belly fluttered. He wanted to take her to bed. Finally, she would have the wedding night she should have had all those years ago. She gripped the sides of the tub with her hands, warning herself not to hope for too much. He would leave again, and she couldn't allow her heart to become too attached. It wouldn't survive another break from Colin FitzRoy's disinterest.

But he did not look disinterested now.

"I should dry off." She pushed herself up, standing in the tub. "Hand me my towel, will you?"

She saw the instant he lost his self-control. A muscle in his jaw clenched, and then his gaze swept down and over her body. She had the urge to cover herself, but she stood with her hands at her sides, letting him look. She wasn't particularly modest, but the way he looked at her made her feel hot and prickly all over.

"I'm dripping wet," she said.

"I can see that," he murmured.

"Hand me my towel."

He blinked at her as though he didn't understand the language she spoke.

She pointed to the chair near him where her towel had been draped. "My towel."

"Oh." He lifted it and moved toward her. Finally, his gaze rose back to her face.

"Have you never seen a naked woman before?" she asked.

"Not like you."

The statement pleased her inordinately. She lifted the towel to her wet hair and wrung the water out. Taking her time, she lowered the towel to dry her body. Finally, she offered Colin her hand and stepped out of the tub. Giving him a view of her backside, she walked to her robe, which was near the fire in the hearth. "I like the tub you purchased," she said.

"So do I."

She pulled the robe on, cinched it, then sat in the chair near the fire so her hair could dry. Her brush had been placed on the small table near the fire and she lifted it and ran it through her hair. "Do you think that little girl—Harley—will actually give Captain Gladwell our message?"

He blinked as though taking a moment to comprehend her. "Yes. If nothing else, she'll want to warn him someone is looking for him. I doubt we'll see her again. Children like her have often been in and out of orphanages and prefer their freedom."

Daphne glanced at him over her shoulder, surprised he had moved closer and was standing beside the chair. She moved to the floor to be nearer to the fire as the room was drafty. The carpet was soft, and she tucked her legs under her as she sank into it. "Can't we make her go? It isn't safe for a child out on the street."

"She'll only run away." He knelt behind her. "Let me help with that." He held out a hand for her brush, and when she offered it to him, he ran it through her hair. Somehow it felt different when he brushed her hair. It felt…erotic.

"It was my plan to seduce you tonight," she murmured.

"We can seduce each other."

She shook her head and looked over her shoulder at him. "You're always in control. I want you to lose control." She didn't say she wanted to arouse his passions, his emotions, but that was part of it. Somehow she knew if he was ever to love her, first she had to find a way to break through the barrier he'd put between them. Perhaps if he cared for her, she could risk trusting him with her heart again.

"I'm a soldier. I've been trained to remain calm and controlled."

She turned to face him, placing her hands lightly on his knees. "There's no battle here, Colin." Her hands slid upward, and he dropped the brush and caught her wrists before she could touch him where she wanted.

"Slow down."

"Why? I've been waiting seven years. That's slow enough."

"We have all night." His voice was raspy and his eyes dark.

"Then indulge my curiosity," she said. He narrowed his eyes. "Take off your clothes." It was a dare, pure and simple.

He shook his head. She'd known he would make some sort of protest. He so clearly did not want to be vulnerable with her. He didn't want to be exposed. But she wouldn't take him any other way. Not anymore. This was her only chance. *Their* only chance.

"I took my clothes off. Your turn."

"You were in the bath."

She glanced at the tub. "The water is still warm. I don't mind waiting." When he still hesitated, she said, "At least take off your coat."

Finally, he didn't argue. He removed the coat and laid it over the chair, sitting cross-legged before her. "Come here," he said, indicating his lap.

"First your waistcoat. I don't want to get it wet."

He scowled but unfastened it and removed it. It too was folded and placed on the chair.

"Your valet must love you."

"He's trained me well. Come here."

She cocked her head. "What about your cravat?"

"What about it?"

It was proving more difficult to make him drop his mask than she had anticipated, but she would not give up yet.

"Let's make a deal," she said. "I untie my robe." She indicated the knot at her waist. You untie your cravat."

His gaze dipped to that knot and then slid to her breasts. Her robe, pink silk, did little to hide her body, but she thought her offer might just tempt him.

"Fine." He reached for the cravat and she reached for the robe's knot. He untied his neckcloth, and she slowly pulled the knot of her robe. The material of his neckcloth fell in a tumble down the front of his shirt just as she released the tie of her robe. The garment gaped but didn't fall open.

"Now, come here," he said, the tone of his voice brooking no argument. Holding the sides of the robe together, Daphne scooted closer. "Closer," he said.

Her knees were touching his crossed legs. "I can't come any closer."

"Yes, you can." He hauled her up and onto his legs so that her own legs straddled him. Her robe fell open, and she gasped at how exposed she was. He pulled her even closer, the heat of his hard erection pressing against her sex.

"I want to touch you," he said, nuzzling her neck with his mouth.

"Where?" she teased. "Here?" She pointed to her collarbone. He kissed her there. "Or here?" She moved the fabric of her robe aside to reveal her shoulder. It fell open so her breast, with its hard, pink nipple, was also visible. Her hand trailed down to cup her flesh. "Or here?"

His hands landed on her waist, the heat of him seemingly warmer than the fire at their backs. He slid up her ribs to cup her breasts, his thumbs rubbing over her hard buds. She moaned quietly, arching back when he lowered his mouth to suckle her.

"I should have known your nipples would be pink. Pink like your—"

She pulled his mouth back to her flesh, writhing as he teased and laved. Then her own hands went to work, unfastening the buttons of his shirt and dipping to the waist of his trousers to pull the tails out. When her own hands touched the bare skin under his shirt, he jerked.

"You don't like that?" she asked.

"I don't know," he said.

She pushed the fabric higher. "I want to see you. I want to press my body against yours."

"Take it off," he said, apparently deciding not to argue. He unfastened his cuffs and she slid the shirt up and over his head.

Her breath caught in her throat. He was magnificent. His chest was broad and strong with a light dusting of dark hair. She touched one of his nipples, a light brown color, and he let out a breath. She bent to kiss his collarbone, his shoulder, then trailed her tongue to his nipple and sucked it.

"Daphne." His voice was hoarse and gravelly.

She looked up at him. "You don't like it?"

"I don't know."

"Perhaps we should experiment more so you can give more definitive answers." Her hands slid down to his taut belly, but he grasped her wrists when she reached his waistband.

"Too fast?" she asked. "Or you don't know if you like that?"

"I know one thing I like." His hands landed on her thighs, and he slid upward, making light trails toward her core.

"I like this too," she murmured, pressing her breasts to his bare chest. "I want you to touch me." His hand brushed over her sex. "There."

She moved against his hand, her breasts tingling from the friction of skin on skin. His finger dipped inside her, and she clenched around it, bucked her hips. "It hurt the first time you were inside me," she said. "Will it hurt this time?"

"I don't think so. I know something about how to make you ready now."

"Then what are we waiting for?" Her hand slid down his chest again and this time he didn't stop her at his belly. She found the fall of his trousers, unfastened them, and felt the hard heat of him spring forward. Her fingers slid over him, stroking him as he stroked that bud that gave her so much pleasure.

"Take me in your hand," he said, his voice almost a growl. "Wrap your fingers around me." She obeyed, and when he moved, she understood what to do. She slid her hand up and down the length of him. He was wide and thick and so hard.

"Let me taste you," she said.

His eyes closed, and when he opened them they were so vivid green she couldn't look away.

"Was that the wrong thing to say?"

"That's not something wives do."

"Some do. Where do you think I heard about it?"

"Wc had better talk later about your friends," he said then groaned as she moved her hand up and down his length again. "I don't have the control for you to do that tonight. Next time."

"What now then?" she asked.

"Lie down." He took her robe, which had pooled behind her, and spread it on the carpet. She moved to lie on it, and he stood, removing his boots, stockings, and finally his trousers. She studied his body as raptly as he'd studied hers. She'd seen sculptures and paintings in museums, but they couldn't convey how warm he was or his clean, woodsy scent or even the way his muscles moved when he turned to lay his trousers on the chair. That gave her a lovely view of his buttocks, which were paler than the rest of him but firm and round.

He turned back to her, and she spread her legs. She knew she was probably shocking him with her less-than-wifely ways, but she wasn't a virgin and she still felt too much like one. She wanted this. She wanted him inside her, making her feel the way he had the last few days.

She was rewarded for her boldness when his eyes lost their controlled coolness and heated. His hands clenched at his sides, and he licked his lips. He wanted her. Desire was an emotion, and she would take it.

"What do you call that? A cock?"

Surprise made his mouth open and close and then his cheeks turned pink. "More words your friends taught you?"

"You taught me, wicked man. Have you forgotten already?"

"I shouldn't have told you that word."

"Then I couldn't say this—I want your cock inside me."

He closed his eyes. "God, Daphne. You're killing me."

"Come here then." She opened her arms and he went to her, kissing her mouth and lowering his body until it pressed against hers in all the best places. Her hands scraped down his back until she cupped his backside and squeezed.

He laughed. "You're shameless."

"I haven't even begun."

"Neither have I." His mouth dipped to her neck and then his tongue trailed down her sternum until he circled that place between her breasts. His hands fondled her as his mouth continued its path. Somehow he tickled her belly while making her writhe in anticipation at the same time. His hand slid to her hips and then her thighs, opening her legs wider. "Still want my cock?"

"Yes, but first your mouth." He paused at her sex, looked at her, breathed warm air over her. She moaned and rocked toward him. "Colin, *please*."

He bent forward and touched his tongue to her entrance then dipped inside. She groaned and clenched, knowing she was too loud and not caring. When he slid his tongue up toward that most sensitive place, her breath increased until she was panting. Her fingers dug in the carpet, looking for purchase, until finally—thank God finally—he flicked his tongue over her. She let out a small scream and lifted her hips. He paused, looked at her.

"More," she begged. She would have been humiliated if this had been anyone else, and if she couldn't see how much he liked her response. He was breathing almost as fast as she was. His flushed face and his bright eyes just made her desire hotter. She loved him. She didn't want to love him, but she couldn't seem to make herself stop. Even after all the years and all the pain and loneliness, it was Colin she wanted.

It was Colin she had always wanted.

"More," he agreed and flicked that tiny bud again.

"Oh, *yes.*"

His tongue was driving her mad, the way he laved and scraped and left her wanting more. Finally, when she was all but out of breath and whispering *please, please, please* he gave her what she wanted. Stars seemed to dance in front of her eyes as pleasure so sharp and bright washed over her. She lifted her hips, giving herself to it. Colin took hold of her hips, held her steady, and entered her.

"Oh, yes!" she cried. *This.* This was what she had wanted. He filled her, and she couldn't get enough of him. She couldn't stop moving, pressing up against him to take more of him. And when he slid deeper inside her, rocked against her, she made incoherent sounds of pleasure. She never wanted this to end. The pleasure only deepened and intensified as he moved within her. And every time he buried himself deep, pressing against that tender bud, she saw stars all over again.

Her legs wrapped tight around him, taking him deeper. It was slightly uncomfortable but satisfying too.

And then she looked up and into his face. His eyes were so green she could hardly believe they were real. He met her gaze with an intensity she recognized in herself. She knew the pleasure he felt because she felt it too. She locked eyes with him, and he didn't look away. Daphne's heart pounded with the dual emotions of fear and elation she felt in that moment. She'd never been so vulnerable. She'd never been so close to Colin—to anyone. Although feelings and emotions raged inside her, she latched onto his face and his eyes. He had always been a calming presence in her life. Her family and her life was a wild whirlwind, but when Colin was there, she felt suddenly at peace. Her father's bellowing, her brothers' roughhousing, the threat of Battersea—it all faded when Colin looked at her.

Everything in the room faded for her now. She still felt the silk robe underneath her back, the heat of the fire, the friction of his body against hers, but it was as though the person who felt those things was someone else, and the true person was the one she could see reflected in his eyes.

"Daphne," he said, his voice sounding pained. She'd never heard him sound like that.

"Yes," she answered, encouraging, moving with him, wanting him to find his peak. Then something in his eyes changed. The wall there dropped away, and there was naked need in his expression. He needed to climax, yes, but there was more. He needed her. He needed to be loved, and he was so frightened to admit that.

Almost as soon as she saw it, it was gone. He was closed off from her again. "Colin." She put her hands on the side of his face, wanting that intimacy back. Wanting to reassure him that he was safe with her. But he kissed her, breaking eye contact, and then moving within her in such a way so that all rational thought was lost. He cried out when he climaxed, and it was the most beautiful sound she'd ever heard. And then he collapsed, lying his head on her bare shoulder, and catching his breath.

Finally, when she was beginning to doze, he moved away, lifted her, and carried her to the bed. She hadn't been carried like this since she was a small child, and it felt so sweet and made her feel cherished and loved. He tucked her under the sheets, and she waited for him to join her so she could wrap her arms around him and lay her head on his chest. She'd seen her mother do that to her father once when she was very young. One of her brothers had been very sick and both of her parents had been by his side for the better part of two days and nights. When her brother finally showed signs of improvement, her parents had gone to the duchess's room and lay on her bed, both fully clothed. Her father had put his arm around her mother, who had rested her cheek on his chest.

It was an image she'd never forgotten and one she had thought of often both before and after her marriage.

But Colin didn't come to bed. Finally, she rose on her elbows and looked about the room, expecting to see him banking the fire or washing at the basin. But the room was empty but for her.

He'd left her alone.

As usual.

Sixteen

Colin's hands shook and his skin felt clammy. He'd retreated to the small chamber nearby, suitable for valet or lady's maid, locked the door, and sat on the cot in his dressing robe, trying to calm himself. What the hell was wrong with him? He'd done what any number of men in London were doing tonight. He'd done what he'd been wanting to do for longer than he could remember.

He'd enjoyed it—and maybe that was the problem. He'd thought it would be more like the first time, except Daphne would get some pleasure out of it this time. He hadn't been prepared for the way he'd felt. Emotions had welled up inside him faster than he could tamp them back down. He hadn't realized that being with her like that would be such an intimate experience. And he hadn't realized, until he was buried deep inside her and she was looking at him with adoration—no, it was love; he could admit it since she already had—that he didn't know what to do with her feelings.

He could have accepted them as a gift. She'd surely intended them that way, but it didn't seem right when he had nothing to give in return.

And that was when the truly shocking realization hit him. He cared for her, deeply. It was far more than the sort of husbandly affection one should have for one's wife. It was more than wanting to keep her safe or wanting to make sure she was satisfied. It was something that made his entire chest ache. And she'd seen it. He knew she'd seen the moment he'd realized it, and her seeing it had made it real. Her seeing the depth of his emotions terrified him because if he really cared for her, if he—dare he say it—loved her, she could hurt him. What if she died like his mother? What if she rejected his love, cut him down and made him bleed?

He'd struggled to recover himself and then had his composure completely ripped apart again by the most amazing orgasm he'd ever experienced. He didn't have much experience, truth be told, but he hadn't expected it to feel like that.

And even now, while his hands trembled and his chest fought to expand, he wanted to go to her. He wanted to hold her and tell her she had never done anything to displease him. That he hadn't left, he hadn't stayed away, because of her. It was never because of her.

But he didn't trust himself now. He didn't know how he would feel or react the more time he spent with her. He needed to go back to keeping his distance from her. The greater the distance between them, the quicker his feelings would fade. He wouldn't need her quite so much or want her quite so desperately. It was better for him to sleep in this small chamber, not beside her. Colin blew out the lamp and made himself as comfortable as he could on the cot. He closed his eyes and saw Daphne's face then heard the sound of his mother's rattling cough in his memory.

When Colin rose early the next morning, he remembered the dreams of his mother. He wasn't an idiot. He knew what they meant. When his mother had died, he'd completed the process of closing himself to any and all feeling. He'd numbed himself because the pain had simply hurt him too much.

He remembered hearing her coughing and coughing and coughing, and it seemed with every fit that wracked her body, some of his love for her drained away.

He did also realize that just because he'd loved and lost the only person he'd deeply and completely loved didn't mean that he'd lose someone else he loved like that. If he allowed himself to love Daphne, it would not cause her to become ill and die. But as logical as he could be about it, there was still a risk. And Colin had long ago decided he wouldn't risk his heart again. Many men were married to women they treated with fondness and respect. One didn't have to love one's wife to have a happy marriage. He could make this work and keep Daphne happy without giving her every piece of him. Both of their hearts would be much safer, less prone to breaking, with an arrangement like that. After all, he didn't want to break her heart any more than he wanted to risk his own.

He went back to the master bed chamber and found his valet waiting. It was barely ten, early for a lady like Daphne to rise, but the chamber appeared otherwise empty. "Where is Lady Daphne?" he asked.

Jacobs straightened the sleeve of the coat he'd laid out. "I believe she went down to break her fast, sir. Are you ready to dress?

So much for climbing into bed with her so she wouldn't know he hadn't been there all night.

"Yes. I'll dress and join her. Make it quick, Jacobs."

"Oh, good. We are in a hurry."

Jacobs did dress him quickly. Colin wasn't one to fuss over his attire and poor Jacobs was rarely called upon to use his creative talents. "Sir, do you remember when you asked me to loiter about the Earl of Battersea's town house?"

Colin turned his head sharply to look at Jacobs who tsked at him and started straightening the coat of his shoulder all over again. "You learned something interesting?"

"Initially, no. I found what I'd expected. He treats his servants abominably. More than one maid has left his service with a bellyful."

"But then?" Colin prodded as Jacobs tied his cravat.

"Then his staff mentioned that men often came to the earl. Men with particular tastes. The earl seemed to enjoy the challenge of finding a woman to meet the man's requirements, if you will."

Colin shook his head and Jacobs gave him such a severe frown, he stilled. "So he's a pimp?"

"I don't think these women were necessarily willing. That might be part of the challenge."

Colin felt his lip lift in disgust. "So he's abducting virgins and providing them to men for amusement."

Jacobs nodded. "If what the staff told me is true, it would seem so."

Colin let out a breath. "You do know the problem with this information, Jacobs?"

"Yes, sir. The word of a servant will not hold up against the word of an earl."

"Exactly. We'd have to catch him, which would be practically impossible. Fortunately, Battersea is a man of many crimes, and I have another I might be able to pin to him yet."

"I do wish you luck, sir. Your cravat is adequate if you are still in a hurry. If not, I could do a much more attractive knot—"

"This is fine." He strode out of the room and down the stairs to the dining room. The doors were open, and the scent of tea and toast and Daphne floated out to him. Though it wasn't an appropriate topic for a lady, he was eager to tell her what he'd learned. "Daphne, I've learned of more nefarious doings on the Battersea's part. What's the matter?"

She merely looked at him, her blue eyes icy, her pink-clad, bow-lined shoulders straight as she deliberately set her tea cup on the saucer. "Why, nothing at all is wrong. What would ever give you that impression, husband?"

He knew better than to answer that question. He'd grown up with three sisters and knew what it meant when the room cooled three degrees after he walked in. Had he done something—

Ah, yes. Of course, he had.

Colin glanced at the footman, standing in the corner, pretending he hadn't heard a thing. He hadn't thought to ask where their servants came from. He'd supposed he would have to hire them, but when he'd arrived, the house had been fully staffed. The Duke of Warcliffe's doing? Did that mean the servants reported to his father-in-law?

"What's your name?" Colin asked the servant.

"James, sir."

"James, you're excused."

"Excused, sir?" The footman's eyes widened. "Have I done something wrong, sir?"

"No, you're not being let go. You're being told to go down to the kitchen. Or up to your room. Or anywhere that is not here."

"Yes, sir." James walked briskly through the servants' door, and Colin took a seat opposite Daphne.

"You should have sent him away after he'd poured your tea," she observed.

"I can pour my own tea," he said.

She nibbled her toast. "It seems you are quite good at doing things on your own."

"Daphne, are you angry about last night?"

She gave him a withering look. "Angry?" She pretended to consider. "Let's see." She held up a finger. "First, I reveal my most intimate feelings to you over dinner. Second, we return home after a rather harrowing evening, and we share possibly the most astonishing experience I have ever had."

Colin winced, knowing where this was headed.

"Third, you carry me to bed and when I reach for you, you're gone. Without even a good-bye. You might have simply left money on the dresser."

Colin recoiled as if slapped. "You go too far."

"Do I? That is how I felt. And I know it's partly my fault. I knew you didn't care about me and—"

"I do."

She closed her mouth and stared at him.

"I do care about you. I left because I…" He didn't know how to say it. How was he to tell her he'd been frightened, shaken, overwhelmed by what he'd been feeling? She was staring at him, waiting. And he didn't know how to tell her. How to explain he was doing what was best for both of them?

The silence dragged on, and she sighed. Finally, she rose. "I have correspondence to attend to and am at home today."

Colin wanted to groan. If she was at home that meant hordes of callers would descend on them. Everyone would want to see the new house and perhaps catch a glimpse of the ever-absent husband. Colin watched her glide out of the dining room and then did what any man of courage and mettle would do.

He fled.

***

The afternoon seemed to drag on as she chatted with one lady after another on the prescribed topics of the weather, fashion, and one's general health. Lady Isabella and Lady Pavenley bemoaned the fact that they hadn't seen Daphne at the most recent Society functions. They giggled and hinted that Mr. FitzRoy was keeping her too busy in their new bed chamber. More than one caller also mentioned that the Earl of Battersea had inquired after her. Apparently, he'd mentioned calling on her in her new town house. Daphne understood the threat. Battersea was coming for her. Daphne smiled and hid her pain and fear by focusing on her embroidery until finally, at long last, it was too late for morning calls.

Brown informed her Madame Renauld had sent the dress she'd ordered, and they took it out of the wrapping. Brown gasped with pleasure. "My lady, it is beautiful."

Daphne stared at the dark blue dress, which was unadorned, and wondered. "It seems a bit plain," she said.

"The color will make your eyes look even bluer than usual. It is a very good choice."

"Yes, well, I'd rather it was pink, but Mr. FitzRoy and I have a meeting tonight, and I think a darker color would be more apropos."

Brown frowned. "I hope it is nothing dangerous, my lady."

"Of course not. Help me dress. He will be home shortly."

Colin kept her waiting so long that she began to fear he would go meet Captain Gladwell without her. Finally, he returned home and looked quite surprised to see her in the foyer, waiting.

"We shouldn't keep the captain waiting," she said, while their butler helped her don her gray cloak. She had never thought she would wear it this often.

"No, we shouldn't. Your dress—"

She looked down at the blue fabric before her cloak covered it. "What of it?"

"It's not pink."

"I ordered it from my modiste the other day. It just so happens I have need of darker dresses lately."

"Yes." His gaze swept over her, and she tried to ignore the heat that followed where his gaze touched. "It's very nice."

She gave a nod of acceptance. Odd, as she could not remember him ever having complimented one of her pink dresses before. A half hour later they were back at The Clipper. The same publican scowled at them when they entered, but this time he jerked his head toward a table in the corner where a white-haired man sat with what looked like a glass of sherry before him.

"Let me talk," Colin said quietly. As they approached, the man stood, and Daphne noticed a cane leaning against the wall behind him.

"Captain Gladwell?" Colin asked.

The man nodded. "That's me. You must be Mr. FitzRoy and Lady Daphne. We don't see your kind in here very often," he said, nodding at Daphne. She offered her gloved hand, and he bowed over it. "Please sit, and tell me to what I owe the honor of this visit."

Colin and Daphne sat in chairs across from the captain. A serving girl, not the same one from yesterday but a younger one who seemed rather hurried, approached and asked if they would like something to eat or drink. Daphne opened her mouth to say yes to both, but Colin waved his hand. "No, we're fine."

"Thank you, Barbara." Captain Gladwell smiled at the girl.

She was gone again in a moment.

"We understand you were captain for a ship called the *Ranger*."

The captain stiffened. "I was. What of it?"

"We're interested in that ship and its owner, the Earl of Battersea."

"I can tell you it's a sound ship. I've sailed it many times. It's not the only ship I've sailed. I had a long career in His Majesty's Navy. Now I hire out my services. I don't know much about the owners. Their kind don't deign to talk to me." He drank the rest of his sherry. "Is that all?"

Daphne felt her heart sink. This was looking to be a complete waste of time. They'd been wrong in thinking Battersea ever directed the captain to alter his log or lie to the insurance company.

"Not yet," Colin said, motioning for the captain to remain seated. "So you never spoke to the earl? You never discussed a voyage to Canada, one where gunpowder and silks were damaged by water?"

The captain looked at Daphne then back at Colin. "Why do you want to know? Do you work for the insurers?"

"No," Colin said.

The captain rose. "Then I have nothing else to say on the matter." He reached for his walking stick. Daphne stared at him. He obviously did not want to share what he knew about the *Ranger* and Battersea, but if he walked away, she had no other option to rid herself of Battersea. She jumped to her feet, scooted around the table, and put her hand on the captain's arm.

"Sir, I know you don't know me, but I promise you can trust me when I say my husband and I mean you no ill will. I am here out of desperation. I find myself in an...uncomfortable position with the earl. It is largely my fault. I acknowledge that, but the earl has not behaved like a gentleman. Thus, I've been forced to take matters into my own hands."

The captain's expression softened. "I am sorry to hear that. We all make mistakes from time to time."

"And we must all face the consequences of those mistakes. The earl has consequences to face as well. Please, sit down. Look at these papers." She glanced at Colin, hoping he was not angry she had taken over. But he was nodding his encouragement.

The captain allowed her to lead him back to his chair and then stared at his own log entries when she removed them from her reticule and laid them on the table.

"How did you get these?" he asked.

Daphne raised a brow. "A lady cannot reveal *all* her secrets, sir." She pointed to the entries. "These are the entries made on the days when the earl claimed pirates attacked his ship. You note the attack at the end of the log. But here, on these pages, you only mention a water leak that damaged the goods. You say nothing of pirates."

The captain looked up at her. "Those pages were supposed to be destroyed."

"Is that what the earl told you? But, of course, he kept them," she said gently. "That way he could blackmail you later, if need be."

The captain sat back. "What do you want from me?" His gaze traveled to Daphne then Colin.

"We want the truth," Colin said. "Did pirates attack the *Ranger*?"

The captain smiled and shook his head. "I haven't had a problem with pirates in thirty years. There might be some in the Mediterranean and a few hanging on near Barbados or Jamaica, but the heyday of pirates attacking ships on the shipping lanes of the Atlantic is long gone."

"Then why did you write in the log that your ship—I'm sorry," Daphne corrected, "the earl's ship was attacked by pirates?"

"I think, my lady, you already know the answer to that. Money. It always comes down to money. He would receive more compensation if his ship was attacked and he lost the goods completely than if he claimed the truth. And we did sell what we could, at a reduced price, of course."

"So the earl was paid for the goods and compensated for them by the insurers." Colin pointed to the log entries. "This is illegal. You know that?"

"I know it, and I don't like it. But it's his word against mine. He's an earl and I'm just a lowly captain. I said what he wanted me to say, wrote what he wanted me to write." He looked up at Daphne, pity in his eyes. "I am sorry you are on the wrong side of him, my lady. He has a reputation for brutality when dealing with enemies."

"I'm well aware, sir."

"Will you stand against him now?" Colin asked. "You wouldn't be standing alone. Lady Daphne is the daughter of a duke, and my father is a viscount. We'll support you."

The captain looked long and hard at his empty sherry glass. "I want to help, but I can't. The earl is too powerful. I have a wife and grandchildren to support. My only son died a few years ago, and his widow relies on me. I can't risk their well-being or my income."

Daphne sank into her chair, feeling tears prick her eyes. She was doomed. This had been her last chance.

"What if we can bring him down on another charge?" Colin asked. Daphne stared at her husband, wondering what he had in mind now. Wondering if she really wanted to know.

"If he's already been tainted and weakened, would you come forward then?"

"What's the other charge?"

"Nothing to do with you, but being that he's a peer, we may need more than one charge to force him to face any real punishment."

The captain looked at both of them. "Yes. If you can bring him down, I'll tell my story. I'll stand with you." He rose. "Now, I should get home before it's too late. If you do what you say, young Harley knows where to find me."

When he was gone, Daphne turned to Colin. "So how will we bring Battersea down? I thought the *Ranger* was our only chance."

Colin shook his head. "Order a drink, and I'll tell you the story Jacobs told me."

Seventeen

At home Colin paced the bed chamber. Daphne had been thrilled at the second avenue of possibility for bringing Battersea to justice. But if he was to catch the earl luring innocent girls to a secret house or abducting them and transporting them to the countryside, it would take time and effort. Colin didn't mind the effort. Who knew what other interesting tidbits about Battersea might turn up if he began to follow the man?

The problem was the time. Battersea must know where Daphne was now, and she was no longer safe. Colin couldn't very well spend his time following the earl if his wife was in danger. Nor could he lock her up indefinitely. Battersea would find a way to get in, and she was not the sort to be content surrounded by the same four walls for long.

He looked over at her now. She was sitting at her dressing table, applying some sort of cream to her face. When he'd come in, her maid had been taking down her hair and brushing it. The sight of that loose silvery blond hair trailing down her back made his hands itch. He wished he could tell the maid to leave and take Daphne's hair down himself.

Instead, he'd retreated to the dressing room until the maid had departed. And he hadn't yet touched Daphne or even spoken to her. He didn't know if she wanted him to touch her after the way he'd behaved after their lovemaking last night.

"I still don't understand why we can't just ask his staff to testify against him," Daphne said, her voice breaking the relative quiet in the room.

Colin looked at her and their eyes met in the mirror above her table. He was glad to have a reason to look at her. "The word of a footman or groom will not hold up against that of an earl." She should know that.

"But what if we asked three or four to testify? Certainly, no judge would think that many men and women lied."

She was grasping now, and he knew she only did so because she was desperate. "I want him caught too," he said, moving behind her. "But if we misstep and alert him to our plans, he'll only cover his tracks. We need to catch him *in flagrante delicto*, so to speak. Then the word of his staff and Captain Gladwell will hold more weight."

The faint scent of roses drifted to his nose, and he wondered if the cream was scented with rose.

"What if I made a complaint against him?"

"What complaint?" Colin asked. "He's done nothing to you, and all that you suspect is based on rumor."

"It was hardly rumor to the baroness he killed!"

Colin placed his hands on Daphne's shoulders. She wore her pale pink robe, and her shoulders felt slight and cold under the silk. "I won't allow anything to happen to you."

Her eyes closed and her shoulders relaxed slightly. "I really thought the captain would help us. I'm so tired of being frightened and jumping at every sound. I feel as though I'll never be able to walk down the street or ride in the park without looking over my shoulder."

"Then I'll just have to entertain you inside for the present."

Her eyes opened, and they were dark when she met his in the glass. "How do you propose to do that?"

He hadn't meant to say it. He'd just wanted to say something to comfort her. He hadn't even meant it in a sexual way, but he was certainly thinking along those lines now.

He bent, brushed her hair off her shoulders, and kissed the delicate skin behind her ear. "Would you allow me to take you to bed?"

She made a sound like a low purr and shivered in his arms. "Will you run away as soon as you've had me?"

The idea of staying, of risking caring more for her, needing her, tied his belly in knots. But he couldn't quite put the necessary distance between them yet. He still wanted her too much. "I promise I'll stay this time. Just let me kiss you."

She stood and pushed the chair back, forcing him to take a step backward. "And what if I want to kiss you?" she asked.

His brow rose. She had never been a woman who was afraid to say what she wanted. Daughters of dukes were known for getting their way. But he hadn't expected her forwardness to make him so hot and eager. "I have no objection."

She stepped close to him, looking at up at him until he could hardly hold himself back from kissing her. Finally, she brought one of her soft hands to his face and brushed her fingers over his lips. "You have such skilled lips," she murmured. "I'm rather fond of your lips." Her eyes met his. "And your tongue."

He reached out and took her in his arms, pulling her hard against him. Her body quivered with anticipation. He loved how responsive she was to him, how much she wanted him. She didn't try to hide her desire or act demurely. She knew what she wanted. "If you don't kiss me soon, wife, I'll be forced to take matters into my own hands."

"Don't get me started on your hands," she said, wrapping her arms around his neck and brushing her lips over his. A thrill of arousal zinged through him, waking his body from head to foot. Every single muscle and hair and fiber of his being was aware of the feel of her mouth on his, her hands in his hair, her breasts pushed against his chest. She kissed him more firmly, opening her mouth slightly then rocking against his burgeoning erection. He groaned as he went rock hard. How had he existed for so many years without her? His hands swept over her body, touching every inch of her, unable to get enough.

"You are wearing too many clothes," she said, stepping back.

"I was about to say the same to you."

She shrugged. "You first." And then when he didn't move to undress, she circled him, her hand trailing along his buttocks. "Don't make me wait, Colin."

She moved to the bed and lay back, propping herself on her elbows to watch him. He wanted to go to her there, spread her legs, and take her with her chemise and robe around her hips. Instead, he slipped off his coat. No woman had ever watched him undress before and no one had ever watched him as intently as she did. Every article he removed—his waistcoat, his neckcloth, his boots—caused some sort of reaction from her, be it a sound of pleasure or a nod of approval.

Finally, he wore only his trousers and his shirt. He reached for the placket of the trousers, and she shook her head. "The shirt first. Draw it over your head." She illustrated by pulling her robe and chemise up over her knees. "Slowly."

His eyes remained on hers as he pulled the tails free and lifted the shirt up, revealing his chest. When he'd dropped it on the floor and looked back at her, her legs were slightly open, revealing the pink of her sex. Colin couldn't seem to look away until she said. "Now the trousers."

"What about you?" He felt slightly vulnerable standing before her with her gaze so hot on his body. He could almost forget it when he glanced at her with her legs slightly parted, giving him a view of what waited.

"I promise I'll take everything off once you do," she said.

He didn't move.

"You want a gesture of goodwill?"

"Please," he said, his voice rough.

She loosened the belt at her waist and sat. The robe slid down one shoulder, giving him a view of her bare skin and the hint of her round breast under her thin chemise. Her hand went to the bow between her breasts and she toyed with it for a moment before pulling it slowly free. The bodice of the chemise gaped open and she allowed it to slip over one pale breast until it caught on her protruding nipple. "Take off your trousers," she said again, and he didn't hesitate. She licked her lips when his cock sprang free. But before he could join her on the bed, she rose and walked to him. The chemise slipped further down, revealing her pink nipple, jutting slightly upward. She sank to her knees before him, and he wanted to tell her she did not have to do this. Wives did not do this sort of thing. Instead, he slipped her robe off her shoulders as well as the other sleeve of her chemise so both breasts were revealed when her tongue darted out to lick from him from root to tip. He gripped her shoulders and tried to remain on his feet as she licked back down. Her hands came up to slide along his thighs then between them as she cupped his testicles.

"'What a piece of work is a man,'" she quoted.

He almost laughed. "Shakespeare now?"

"Why not? I'll teach you to laugh at me." She closed her mouth over his tip, her warmth enveloping him and making him dizzy with want. Then she sucked slightly, and he jumped in her hand. She pulled back. "You like that."

"I like everything about you."

"Lie down on the bed."

He narrowed his eyes. "What do you have planned? It will be easier for me to use my mouth and tongue on you if you are the one to lie down."

"Do you want to argue or do you want me to take my clothing off?"

He went to the bed and lay down, turning to face her with his head resting on his elbows. When she had his attention, she gave him her back and allowed her garments to slide, quite slowly, down her straight back, over her round bottom, and to drop past her shapely legs and pool on the carpet. She turned to look at him, giving him a view of one slightly upturned breast.

"Come here," he said, his voice low. She turned slowly and walked toward him, hips swaying. He wanted to touch her, smell her, bury himself deep inside her. But when he reached for her, she caught his hand and brushed it over a nipple. Then she climbed onto the bed and over him, straddling him about the waist.

She bent and kissed him, and he didn't wait to see how she wanted it. He was in no mood for slow and soft. He took her mouth, and she met his passion with her own, their tongues tangling as their breathing sped up. He filled his hands with her flesh—hips, thighs, breasts—then reached between her legs and felt the hot wetness there.

"Yes," she said against his lips. He stroked her, and she moved against his hand, her bottom nudging his erection. He began to flip her over, but she shook her head. "I want you like this."

"And what do you know about this position?"

"I have a good imagination and—as I've said before— ladies *do* talk." She lifted her bottom and his cock was enveloped in her heat as her sex slid over him. Her fingers locked with his as she slowly took him inside her. When he was buried halfway, she paused and looked down at him, her eyes glazed with pleasure. "I don't think I can take more."

"Am I hurting you?"

"No."

"Go slowly."

She pushed up, lifting herself up and then down, driving him to madness but taking more of him each time. Her cheeks were pink and her chest heaving as she rode him, and when she took him completely, she cried out in delight and ecstasy. He tried to move inside her, but she clenched her knees around him. "My turn," she said and began to rock against him. He tried to think of anything but the way her breasts jiggled and her hips swiveled and her sex gripped him tightly. He tried not to watch her, but it was impossible to look away, especially when she cupped her own breasts and squeezed her nipples. He was buried deep then and she rocked quickly.

He was completely spellbound, and when her gaze, hazy with passion, locked with his, he didn't look away. He let her see his desire and his need. He couldn't stop her from seeing his love. Her eyes reflected it back to him.

"Colin," she breathed, her voice with wonder. Her mouth opened in an O, and he felt her muscles tighten, release, then tighten again and she said *yes, yes, yes* on an exhale.

The feel of her orgasm and her muscles clenching around him drove him over the edge. He gripped her hips to hold on as he came, hard but slow so that it seemed as though the orgasm went on and on. When he could breathe again, he realized she'd collapsed on top of him, her skin slick with perspiration and hot with arousal. The scent of their mingled bodies lingered in the air, and he was still inside her. He trailed his hand up her back and then down over her bottom. His chest felt heavy, not from her weight, but from emotions he did not want to examine too closely. He wanted to say something—not *I love you*; God, not that—something that would let her know this—*she*—meant something to him. That what she'd seen in his eyes was true and real.

He opened his mouth and remembered the words of his first love: *you're just a silly little boy.*

Daphne wouldn't say that. He knew it, but his chest tightened now when he thought of opening himself to her. His cheek stung with the memory of his grandfather's slap.

Stop sniveling and act like a man.

He needed air. He needed space.

"I have an idea," Daphne said. That gave Colin pause.

"I rather like your ideas," he admitted. Give him fifteen minutes, and he would be ready to push her on her knees. He could escape afterward.

"I know you are thinking of running away." She pushed up, propped her head on her hand, and looked down at him.

"I don't run away."

"Well, your heart began to pound just now and your whole body tensed. I supposed I had better speak now before you…disappear."

He could hardly be annoyed with her. She was so lovely, looking down at him with her hair falling over one pink cheek and her lips soft and moist and ready to kiss.

Anticipating the direction of his thoughts, she put a finger over his lips. "You said we need to catch Battersea in the act—*in flagrante delicto*, you said."

"It can be done, but it will take time."

"What if I served as a lure? If he abducts me, we could catch him more quickly."

Colin's heart squeezed so tightly he could not breathe. He pushed up and away and threw his legs over the side of the bed. He had to gulp in air like a fish out of water.

"No," he managed in a strangled voice.

"Why?" she asked. "It's the answer to all our problems."

"No!" He stood and walked away, ignoring his nudity. "No. The point is to keep you out of his path. I won't deliberately put you in it." He turned to face her. "He's dangerous, Daphne. If anything went wrong—if I couldn't get to you—"

Her blue eyes were wide as she sat among the tousled sheets and stared at him. "You really *do* care about me."

"What does that have to do with anything?"

But her eyes were bright as though she had just been blessed with divine inspiration. "It has everything to do with—well, everything. I didn't understand before. You act as though you care for me and yet you won't admit it. You can't seem to wait to escape me—"

"Daphne, this isn't—"

"I see why now. You're scared something will happen to me. You are as scared of losing me as I am of losing you!"

"I'm a man." He picked his trousers up from the floor and shoved one leg into them. "I'm not scared."

She gave him a dubious look. "We've both been hurt before, Colin, but we can't keep expecting the worst. I have to trust you, and you have to give me a chance."

He fastened the placket of his trousers and looked for his shirt. He had to end this conversation. He wasn't ready to talk about his feelings or his fears. "Why don't we focus on the real problem—Battersea. The idea of you acting as bait is ludicrous, and the answer is no." He tossed his shirt over his head and shoved his arms through the sleeves.

"Where are you going? Stay and talk to me." She slid out of bed, and he had to make an effort not to look at her lovely body.

"I'll be back," he said, gathering his coat, boots, and waistcoat in one arm.

"Do you really plan to run from me forever?" She put her hands on her hips and stared at him defiantly.

"I have a meeting at my club. I'll be back after that." He couldn't quite stop his gaze from sliding over her.

With the image of her—naked, hands on her hips, in the center of their bedchamber—etched in his mind, he pulled on the rest of his clothing as he strode downstairs, gave the servants orders not to admit anyone and to lock all doors and windows, then walked out of the house.

As soon as he was on the street, he bent and gulped for air. His chest hurt as his heart pounded it from the inside like a hammer. Did she not understand that he could not lose her? Why would she even suggest putting herself in harm's way? If he lost her, if anything happened to her—

Colin closed his eyes. He could not go through the pain of loss like that again. And look at him! He was doubled over on the street at just the thought of losing Daphne. *This* was why he'd stayed away. *This* was why he'd refused to let himself feel too much for her.

But damn it all to hell! She'd broken through his wall, kicked a hole in his defenses, and now she just wanted to stick a bellows in the opening and fan the fire.

Colin finally caught his breath and began to walk, aimlessly at first, and then in the direction of the Draven Club.

He shouldn't have left her. He'd promised he wouldn't. This wasn't just about him anymore. He'd hurt her in the past, and he would hurt her again if he continued rebuffing her attempts to get close to him. She loved him. That was no small thing. She wanted him to tell her he lo—that he cared for her. But if he said it, if he allowed himself to feel it, there was no going back. He would be committing to a real marriage. There would be no living separate lives and meeting once every Season in London. He would give himself to her wholly—she would accept nothing less—and that meant living every day with the fear she would be hit by a carriage or contract some horrible disease or die in childbirth.

"Colin! There you are. Colin!"

Colin snapped out of his thoughts and turned toward the sound of the voice. It was his father's voice, he realized now. His father's coach glided toward the side of the street, splashing through puddles Colin only now noticed. It must have rained while he'd been with Daphne.

"Sir," he said, approaching his father's lowered window. He peered inside and saw the viscount with Pugsly on his lap. "What are you doing out this late and alone?"

"The steward has called me back to the country. Agricultural crisis, you know." His gaze traveled over Colin. "Are you well? You're looking a bit ragged."

Colin well knew it, but he hadn't bothered with trying to button his waistcoat or tie a cravat. "Is there something I can do to help?"

The viscount waved his hand. "No, no. Tenant dispute. I can handle it. I went to your club, but the man at the door said you were not in. I was just on my way to your town house.

John Coachman says he knows where it is, though I haven't been invited yet."

Colin refrained from rolling his eyes. He'd had more on his mind than entertaining. "What do you need from me, sir?"

"I need you to take Pugsly for a few days. You know he does not enjoy long carriage rides, and with all the children in the town house, he has not been himself. Louisa suggested your home might be more peaceful at the moment."

Colin could hardly refuse. His father spoke the truth that the elderly dog did not like children or long carriage rides. More than once he'd been forced to replace boots after Pugsly had cast up his accounts on a trip to the country.

Colin held out his arms. "Of course, I will take him."

The viscount handed the dog through the window to Colin. Pugsly licked his face.

"Shall we take his personal items to your town house?" the viscount asked. Colin remembered he had instructed the butler not to admit anyone.

"I'll take them." He held out his hand and the viscount gave him a box, which Colin tucked under his arm.

"Feed him twice a day and walk him three times, at least," the viscount instructed.

"I know, sir. He'll be in good hands. When do you leave for the country?"

"At first light tomorrow. I want to be there by dinner."

"Safe travels, sir."

"Yes, and when I return, I want to see your house and that lovely wife of yours. Remember what I told you about marriage and Lady Daphne?"

"I remember, sir."

"Good." He sat back and rapped on the roof of the coach. "Take good care of Pugsly."

A few minutes later, Colin handed Pugsly and his box of personal effects to Porter as soon as the Master of the House opened the door to the Draven Club.

"Thank you, sir." Porter looked at the dog squirming in his arms. "What shall I do with it?"

"It's a him, and his name is Pugsly. Put him in the parlor with a fire. He'll be content there for the present." He started up the stairs. "Don't let me forget him, Porter."

"No, sir."

Colin knew he wouldn't find any of the married members of the Survivors at the Draven Club this late, but he hoped Duncan and Stratford had foregone the balls tonight, and he was fortunate enough to find them in the card room. They were not playing, but Stratford had built a tower out of cards and Duncan was giving him advice to keep it from falling.

Stratford glanced at Colin when he entered then stepped away from the card tower. "What happened to you? You look like you just came from bed."

Colin took a seat next to Duncan. "More or less."

"Lucky bastard," Duncan muttered.

"Still no prospects for a wife?" Colin asked.

"Nae yet."

"Rowden has a match tonight. You should come with us," Stratford said, stepping close to the tower again and holding a card just above two cards, like a roof.

"Steady," Duncan advised. "Take yer time now."

Colin waited until the card had been placed before speaking again. "I'd rather not see my friend have his nose bloodied."

"The odds are he'll bloody the other man's nose," Duncan said.

"I have a more pressing problem."

"What's that?" Stratford asked, bending to study the card tower.

"The Earl of Battersea." He went on to summarize the situation with Battersea and Daphne, pausing on occasion while Stratford carefully placed a card.

"The solution seems simple enough to me," Stratford said after placing a card very high and watching as the entire tower teetered.

"Aye," Duncan agreed. "Ye are the Pretender, are ye no?"

"Exactly," Stratford said, tapping the card in his hand. "Why wait for a man to approach Battersea and ask him to find a woman? You do it."

"In disguise, ken?" Duncan added.

"It's really very simple." Stratford, who was known for strategy then laid out a scheme that made Colin's head spin. It was simple and would catch Battersea in the very act.

"That's brilliant," Colin said. "Are you certain it will work?"

"Not a doubt in my mind." Stratford placed the last card on the tower and with a *whoosh* the entire tower toppled into a stack of cards. Colin hoped the fall wasn't a bad omen.

Eighteen

Daphne was almost asleep when the door to the bed chamber opened. She was facing the door and opened her eyes, surprised to see Colin enter, holding a candle. She debated pretending to sleep, but he was looking at her and had already seen her eyes were open.

"Did I wake you?" he asked.

"No. I couldn't sleep."

He approached the bed, set the candle on the table beside her, and then sat. The bed dipped, and she slid closer to him. She had donned a white nightgown with pink ribbons on the bodice, and she saw his eyes briefly lower to the ribbons then back to her face.

"I shouldn't have walked out like I did," he said. Her brows rose. Was this an apology of sorts? "I should have stayed and talked to you. I'll do better next time."

She wanted to believe him. But she wasn't certain she could trust him. And wasn't that ever the problem between them? He had never been there when she'd needed him. She couldn't trust him to be there in the future. But she needed him now. She had no choice but to count on him in this moment.

"I do have a plan," he said. "If you're not too tired, I'd like to tell you about it."

Daphne pushed herself up. "I'm not tired at all." From somewhere downstairs a dog barked, and she knitted her brows. "Was that a dog?"

"Pugsly. I'll explain later. I would like your opinion of the plan. It involves you as well."

Her breath caught at that statement. Not only did he want her opinion, he had included her in the plan. Finally, he seemed to understand that she needed to be part of the solution with Battersea.

"Murray and Fortescue reminded me that I know something about disguises. We can use that skill against Battersea."

"How?" she asked.

"I will dress as a wealthy Frenchman and approach Battersea at the theater tomorrow night. I will say that I am a man with particular tastes, and that I know he is a man who caters to those tastes."

"Are there really such men?" she asked.

"Unfortunately, there are. And if a man or woman has enough money, he or she can usually acquire whatever he or she desires."

He took her hand, and she looked down at their linked fingers. He rarely initiated such casual affection.

"I will tell him I want him to bring me you—not you specifically, but I will describe a woman who looks exactly like you, who is the daughter of a peer, and so on. If the information Jacobs gave me is correct, Battersea has a residence where he brings women—willing or not—just for these purposes. Battersea will tell me when and where to meet him, and we'll know where to keep watch. I'll push him to have the woman—you—in two nights' time. He'll probably argue it can't be done, but I'll offer him an obscene amount of money, and he'll agree."

Daphne squeezed his hand. "And then do I go out walking alone so he can abduct me?"

He gave her a horrified look before seeming to reach for patience. "No. You are never to even think about doing such a thing. You will attend a Society function. We'll look through your invitations and accept one to a ball. I don't care whose ball, but we make it known you will attend. This, of course, is the part of the plan I cannot control. Battersea will do one of two things. He will try to kidnap you from the ball, in which case I will catch him and expose him, and with Gladwell's added accusations, he will be done for."

"Or?" she asked.

"Or he will see it's not possible to take you from the ball and find another woman who will meet the Frenchman's needs. Mr. Murray and Mr. Fortescue have agreed to wait at Battersea's secret lair to catch him with that woman or, on the off chance that the earl is successful in abducting you—which he won't be"—he clenched her hand—"they will rescue you."

"And then we'll have him."

"Yes."

She went through the whole thing in her mind again. She could see no obvious flaws. There were things left to chance, she supposed. Battersea might tell the Frenchman he had no interest in helping him. Or something might go wrong, and Battersea might succeed in abducting her. He would certainly take advantage of that opportunity. But Colin had said he would not allow her to be taken, and if she were abducted, his friends would be there waiting to rescue her—provided she hadn't already rescued herself.

"It's a good plan," she said. "Very good."

"Stratford has a knack for making them, so I let him have his way with it. It was a bit more complicated, but I simplified it for all our sakes."

"And so tomorrow night you go to the theater as Monsieur…?"

"I haven't decided on a name yet."

Her free hand reached out and slid down the lapel of his coat. "You have time. Right now, you should come to bed."

His brow rose. "With you?"

She would not ask him again. She did have some pride. "Wherever."

She saw his throat work as he swallowed. "I want to stay with you."

She pushed hard to tamp down the hope that threatened to bubble up. "I'd like that too. I was thinking of you before you came in." She released his hand and fingered one of the bows between her breasts. She might not have him with her much longer, but she could make the most of the time she had. Slowly, she began to loosen the bow.

"Stop," he said.

She paused. "Why?"

"I want to do it."

She allowed her fingers to linger on the bow, fingering the silky ribbon. He stood, stripped off his coat and stepped out of his boots. He started back toward the bed, but she shook her head. "Your shirt and trousers too." She did not want him to have any excuse to leave her.

He pulled the shirt over his head, revealing his broad shoulders and taut stomach, burnished gold by the firelight. Then he stepped out of his trousers. He was already swollen and hard for her. Her heart leapt in anticipation when he knelt on the bed then braced himself over her. She was not used to the feel of a man's body against hers. He nudged her lips open with his, and she forgot to think as his mouth took hers, leaving her breathless and aroused.

Bracing himself on his elbows, his fingers brushed hers out of the way, and he took hold of the pink ribbon. It looked so small and fragile in his hands. He pulled at the ends, freeing it, and revealing a small V of her skin. His hand skated down to the next ribbon. He wrapped the ends around his finger then pulled it free. Her nightgown opened wider, revealing the curve of her breasts. There were two more ribbons tied in delicate bows. He lowered his mouth, kissed the V between her breasts and took the next ribbon between his teeth.

Daphne groaned at the heat of the desire that swept through her. She wanted that mouth on her. All over her. Clenching the ribbon delicately between his teeth, he loosened it. The garment opened wider, almost revealing her fully. One of his hands traced her bare skin from neck to the top of her abdomen and then he took the last bow in his hands. Slowly he untied it, and her gown fell open, leaving her bare from the waist up.

"Beautiful," he murmured, kissing his way back up her abdomen then detouring to lavish first one breast then the other with attention. Daphne's hands clenched in his hair as she moaned and arched for him. At some point, he shoved her nightgown off, and her skin slid against his. She couldn't get enough of the feel of his hard body moving against hers. His hand dipped between her legs and stroked her. Her hips bucked and she moaned her approval. When two fingers entered her, she gasped in pleasure. He touched and fondled, kissed and caressed until she could not breathe, could not think, could do nothing but feel.

When she climaxed, she called his name and bit his shoulder. He chuckled, took her waist in his hands and rolled her onto her stomach. "Little vixen. You're dangerous."

"Don't stop touching me," she murmured as he lifted her hips and wedged them open with his knee. It was strange to have him behind her like this, to be open to him. It felt even stranger when he entered her. He felt large, and the pressure was different. He rocked into her slowly, making her moan and push back to take more of him. His hands moved over her hips, then her breasts, then down to her still sensitive sex.

His movements were slow and steady and so were his fingers as they stroked and teased. She hadn't thought she could climax again. She was already heavy and her body still tingled, but as he rocked into her and his fingers played over her tight bud, desire began to swell.

His mouth was on her back, his teeth scraping over her skin lightly. She moaned his name as well as other demands she did not think a lady should know about much less voice. He whispered encouragement as he pushed deeper into her, the sensation mixing pleasure and pain. And then he removed his fingers, licked them, and placed them back on that nub of nerves, and she spiraled into oblivion.

He thrust harder into her, his shout matching her cries of pleasure. "Colin, I love you," she heard herself say. She hadn't been able to stop it. He hadn't stopped thrusting and his own cry had sounded ragged in her ears. She prayed he hadn't heard. Her knees weak, she collapsed, and he rolled off her and gathered her to him.

"That was..." She tried to catch her breath. She tried to think of words to describe what they'd shared. He kissed her temple and pulled her close.

"I know. Sleep now."

She knew it was his way of avoiding any talk of emotions, but she was too tired to argue. She closed her eyes and slept.

***

Colin woke when the maid came in to tend to the fire in the early hours of the morning. The girl kept her gaze away from the bed, and Colin thought that was probably a good thing as he and Daphne were both still naked and tangled up in the bed sheets. Sleeping with her kept him warmer than he was used to, and he'd thrown off the covers. He pulled them back now in case the maid looked over. He tried to go back to sleep when the maid finished and scurried back out, but it was difficult with Daphne's round bottom pressed against his thighs. He wanted her again, which unnerved him. Shouldn't he be tiring of her by now? Instead his mind continued to think of new ways to have her or about how much he'd like to try what they'd done all over again.

He supposed he was making up for all the years living as a celibate. He'd certainly woken up many mornings in the past wishing he had a woman beside him. The difference was that having the real woman was not without complications. She'd told him she loved him at the tavern. That had been alarming but somewhat abstract. At some point in the past, she'd loved him. But he'd heard her say it last night, and it wasn't at all abstract or in the past. The admission had startled him and also pleased him. He'd come even harder after she'd said it, and he hadn't wanted to think too closely as to why that should be.

But had she meant the declaration or had she simply said it in the throes of passion? Or perhaps she'd said it because she couldn't stop herself in that moment. He had pretended he hadn't heard, but what was he supposed to say or do if— no, when—she said it again?

You've said that already would probably anger her.

She'd have a similar reaction to *I know*.

Thank you didn't seem quite right.

He rather liked *Good. Keep that to yourself from now on,* but he doubted she would oblige.

Why couldn't she just love him silently? Why did she have to say it? And why couldn't he say it in return? It didn't have to mean anything. It was just words. But he'd never said it to anyone. And if he said it to her, he knew he would mean it. He did…feel that way—some strong way, at any rate—for her. Hadn't he shown her that? Why was there a need to say the words? And if he said those words, would not more words be required in the future? When did he fall in love with her? What did he love about her? What did he love most?

Colin wanted to tear his hair out at even the idea of such conversations. He could kiss her. That would shut her up, but that would not work forever.

She sighed and rolled over, one of her legs sliding over his hip. Colin glanced down at her face, and she had a small smile on her lips. "I could feel you were awake," she murmured, her eyes half closed. His cock had indeed been awake. It was always awake in her presence, it seemed.

"And now you're awake," he said as she rocked against him. She was warm and wet and ready for him.

"Whatever shall we do?"

"We'll think of something." And he kissed her.

***

Several hours later, they'd been forced by propriety out of bed. Daphne had spent the day reading and attending to correspondence, and Colin had just about perfected his disguise. He'd shown her several incarnations, and he'd realized she had a good eye for details. As any master of disguise knew, the details made all the difference. She'd pointed out a Frenchman would style his hair more artfully with a bit of volume on top and tousled curls falling over the forehead. Jacobs had been all but ecstatic when Colin had told him to use the pomade in order to achieve the look.

She'd nodded when Colin showed her the end result but frowned at his cravat, sliding a hand over Pugsly's fur in concentration. The dog had made himself at home in her lap. "A Frenchman at the theater would wear a more elaborate knot."

He'd frowned. "Are you and Jacobs collaborating?"

"How so?" she'd asked.

He'd marched back to his dressing room and gave Jacobs the good news. A bit of clay and cosmetics lengthened his nose slightly and the same cosmetics applied skillfully thinned his lips. He was still studying the result in the looking glass when Pugsly erupted into barks.

"It appears we have a guard dog," Jacobs said.

"Go see who it is," Colin ordered. He did not want to be seen in his disguise by one of Daphne's friends or family members. The last thing he needed was to have one of them call him FitzRoy when he was speaking to Battersea.

His valet let out an annoyed breath at the order. After all, it was not in his job description to answer doors, but he returned shortly with a bemused smile. "It is a street urchin, sir. Apparently, she has come to see you."

"Why would a street urchin want to see me?"

"I cannot claim to know, sir, but it appears Lady Daphne knows her. She keeps calling the creature *Harley*."

Colin swore under his breath and marched down the stairs. When he entered the parlor, Daphne was just finishing handing Harley a cup of what he presumed was tea. The child looked even smaller and dirtier in the late afternoon light. She must have smelled of something Pugsly found interesting as he was assiduously sniffing her foot.

"Oh, Mr. FitzRoy," Daphne said. "Look who has come to call."

Harley scrunched her nose at him. "'E don't look like your Mr. FitzRoy."

"Doesn't he?" Daphne said in that way all young ladies of breeding did when they wanted to avoid answering a question. She sat in the chair beside the girl, her pink dress with bows trailing at an angle over one breast quite at odds with the dark, simple garb the child wore.

"No, 'e don't." Harley scrutinized him. "But it were dark the other night."

"If you don't mind me asking, Miss Harley, how did you find us?" Colin asked.

She shrugged. "You said if I were interested in that orphanage to come find you. I found you."

Society ladies were obviously not the only ones capable of avoiding questions.

"Yes, but how?" he pressed.

Her shoulders hunched up to her ears, which were all but hidden by the cap she wore. Surely the butler had attempted to take the cap, but she must have refused. "I'm good at finding people. I found Captain Gladwell, didn't I? Told 'im to meet you at The Clipper."

Colin considered. "You did, but we are some distance from your jurisdiction."

Her eyes went wide. "Wot's that mean?"

"It means you are far from home," Daphne said, her voice soothing.

"Well, that ain't my fault." Harley sipped her tea, looked down at it in surprise and sipped it again. "Yer the ones who live all the way over 'ere. Wot's in this tea then?"

"Do you like it?" Daphne asked with a smile.

"It tastes…I don't know."

"Sweet?" Daphne offered. "I added a little sugar."

Harley drank more.

Colin checked his pocket watch. He still had hours before anyone but the actors arrived at the theater. He had time to pay Neil and the boys at The Sunnybrooke Home for Boys a visit. "You said you want to go to the orphanage," Colin said to Harley. "Are you ready now?"

"Don't rush me, gov. I want to finish this so-called tea."

Daphne covered her mouth with her hand to hide a smile. "Do you have time to take her, Mr. FitzRoy?"

"If we go now. I'll have one of the servants call for a hackney and have the jarvey wait and bring me back. I should return within a couple of hours."

"I'll go as well," Daphne announced. "I'd like to see the orphanage and Lady Juliana. I knew her a little before her marriage."

Lady Juliana was Neil's wife. As the daughter of an earl she had been a benefactress of the orphanage and then apparently simply taken over the day-to-day operations. Colin didn't know how Neil did it, but if any man could handle a bevy of orphans, Neil was that man. He'd certainly kept Draven's troop in line.

But Colin didn't have time for social calls this evening. He had a mission. He'd take Harley to Neil, convince the man to allow a girl into his all-boys orphanage, and then finish his preparations for the theater.

"Not tonight," he told Daphne. "There isn't time."

She nodded. "I probably shouldn't call at this hour unannounced."

Colin knew she was tired of staying home. For a woman who had been used to enjoying all the Season had to offer, her life had been severely curtailed. She seemed to be taking it well, but like a spirited mare, she was beginning to strain against the bridle. "This will be over soon," he told her. She smiled brightly, almost convincing him. He looked at Harley again. "Finished?" he asked.

She drained the last of her tea. "I'm ready." She stood and tromped heavily to the door of the parlor, acting more like she was off to prison than a clean bed and a roof over her head.

Daphne rose. "I'll come visit you soon, Harley," she said.

"You don't 'ave to do that."

"I want to. And don't worry. Lady Juliana and Mr. Wraxall are kind people." At least she knew Lady Juliana was kind, but if it soothed Harley, she'd say the same about Mr. Wraxall. "They will treat you well."

Harley scuffed at the floor with her bare foot. "Let's go then."

Colin escorted her into the foyer and gave the butler his instructions. Colin almost went back to the parlor to kiss Daphne farewell but decided that was far too sentimental. Instead, he squared his shoulders and rushed to the hackney, keeping his hat low over his face.

Nineteen

Colin gave the jarvey the address and settled across from Harley. The low light slanted into the carriage before he closed the curtains, not wanting to be seen. Flickering lamps illuminated the child's wan face. They rode in silence for a few moments, Colin parting the curtains and peering out when the conveyance paused. The jarvey called down that a lorry had overturned and there would be a slight delay. Harley seemed to sink down further into her seat. Colin sighed impatiently.

"Yer lady is kind," Harley said a few minutes later.

"I suppose she is," Colin answered, peering through the curtains again.

"She gave me sugar in me tea. Not every lady would do that." When Colin didn't respond, she added, "And she let me sit on the chair."

"That is the purpose of chairs," he replied drily, though he knew what she meant. She was dirty and her clothing stained. Many ladies wouldn't so much as admit her into their houses not to mention allow her to sit on their expensively upholstered furnishings.

Several more minutes of silence followed. Colin looked out the curtains frequently and Harley sighed, shifted, and muttered to herself.

"Change your mind about the orphanage?" Colin asked when the conveyance finally began to move again.

"Not exactly," she said.

"What does that mean?"

The expression on her small face was the embodiment of guilt. "It means I think I made a mistake, is all."

Colin felt a small frisson of alarm course through him. "What sort of mistake?"

"The kind you won't like. The kind I can't take back."

Colin resisted the urge to demand she tell him immediately. Instead, he kept his voice level. "What is it you've done?"

"I didn't really know you when I did it," she said, seeming to explain without having yet identified the crime. "I didn't know yer lady was so kind."

"What have you done?" Colin now demanded, fear rising in him like hot air.

"And the blunt 'e offered was too good to pass up. I should 'ave known it was too good."

Fear began to claw at Colin's chest, raking his heart and lungs with hot talons. "Who paid you?" He resisted the urge to grab her and shake her. "What were you paid to do?"

"I don't know 'is name, gov. But 'e was a nob like you. He gave me a 'ole pound to get you out of the 'ouse and 'er alone. He said 'e'd give me another once I did it."

Colin rapped on the roof of the hackney. "Turn around," he ordered. "Now!"

"But, sir!"

"Turn around!" Colin yelled.

"Yes, sir."

The hackney swerved and turned, and for a moment both Colin and Harley had to hold onto the seats to steady themselves.

"I'm sorry," Harley said when the carriage was steady again. "I didn't—"

"I don't want to hear your apologies," he snapped. "Can you tell me what he looked like? The man who paid you."

She shook her head. "It were dark, but 'e had a voice like yours. All clipped and proper like."

The fear had sunk itself deep into his flesh now. Colin could hardly breathe. "If anything happens to her…" He didn't know what to say. He didn't know how to finish. What would he do if something happened to Daphne? This was

Colin's worst fear realized. It was as though he'd expected this and could hardly be surprised it had come to fruition. He'd known something would happen to her. He'd known he couldn't allow himself to fall in love with her.

But now he knew something else as well. It didn't matter that he'd tried to wall his heart off or keep his feelings bottled away. He felt the pain and fear anyway. And now he worried he would regret never telling her how he felt. He'd regret not having told her he loved her. Because he did. Colin loved Daphne.

The carriage moved too slowly. Colin could wait no longer. He rapped on the roof again and called for the driver to stop. When he did, he leapt out and tossed him a handful of coins.

"What you about, gov'?" Harley called.

He didn't answer. He simply began to run. By the time he reached the town house, his chest felt as though a knife had been plunged into it and his false nose was melting off. He tossed it aside and stormed into the house, calling for the butler. The man was already rushing toward him. "Sir! We did not expect you back so—"

"Where is she?" Colin panted.

"Lady Daphne?" the butler asked. "I-I'm not sure. In the parlor?"

Colin gestured to the open door of the empty parlor. "Wrong. Where is she?" he yelled.

"Perhaps she retired to her chamber, sir?"

"No," said a voice coming down from the stairs. It was Brown, Lady Daphne's maid. "She's not in her chamber. She came up to fetch her gloves as she wanted to take that dog out."

Colin glanced at the table near the door where Pugsly's leash had been left. It was not there. He rushed back to the door, fumbling to open it.

"She said she would only walk him in front of the house, but she's been out for some time, and I was coming to check on her," Brown said.

Colin could hardly hear the maid over the pounding of his heart. He threw the door open and all but flew down the steps, looking right and left for Daphne. The street was empty except for a few men hurrying on their way. No sign of Pugsly or Daphne.

Correction. No sign of Daphne. Harley was racing up the walk with Pugsly in her arms. The dog's leash trailed on the stones below her bare feet.

"I found 'im on the corner," she said. "He barked at me when I ran past, and I thought, that looks like 'Er Ladyship's dog."

"Show me," Colin said, taking the dog and handing him to the butler. "Show me where you found him."

She led him to an unremarkable corner. Some bushes stood nearby and a small patch of grass that had probably appealed to the pug. Colin stared down the street then at the ground for any sign of Daphne. But if she'd been there, she hadn't dropped anything or left any evidence. He'd come this same way Harley had but hadn't noticed Pugsly. His gaze trailed again to the bushes. If Pugsly had been scared, he might have crouched beneath them. It was growing dark now, so Colin signaled for the butler to bring the lantern. "Shine it over near those bushes," he instructed then bent and peered inside.

A splash of pink caught his eye, and he reached through the branches and plucked out a small pink bow. It was one of those that had adorned Daphne's dress today. She'd been here. He studied the bow's frayed edges—she'd struggled enough that one of her bows had been ripped off.

It was all the evidence Colin needed. He was too late, and the pain and regret crashed over him. Steeling himself, he bore the onslaught then pushed it away. He was good at that, and he needed to think now, not feel.

"Get my horse ready and send for Lord Jasper," Colin ordered. "Tell him to meet me at Battersea's town house."

***

When Battersea pulled the hood off her head, Daphne blinked at the sudden brightness. As soon as she could keep her eyes open, she tried to take in as much of her surroundings as she could. She was in a place unfamiliar to her, a room with old-fashioned paper on the walls. She sat at a scarred and dusty table in a chair that felt wobbly and uneven. The place smelled of slightly damp carpet and onions. No fire had been lit, and she was cold, but she shivered from fear.

Battersea stood before her, smiling.

She couldn't speak. He'd gagged her with a strip of linen right after his men had grabbed and bound her hands. She'd bit him, but he'd still managed to secure the cloth. Then he'd pulled the hood over her head.

There was no sign of his men now. She'd assumed they were his men, but they'd not worn his livery. Perhaps he'd simply hired them to help abduct her. But she'd known his carriage when it had appeared on the street. His family crest was on the door. So surely his coachman knew what the earl had done. Surely, someone would help her.

But one more glance about the room did not give her any confidence she would receive aid at all soon, if ever. She had no idea where she was, and perhaps the only other person who knew she was here was the coachman. She could imagine Battersea paid the man well to keep his mouth shut. She'd have to use her wits and save herself. She tried moving her hands, but they were bound securely in her lap. Still, it could have been worse. They hadn't been in the carriage long enough to leave Town, so at least she was still in London.

Somewhere in London.

"You led me on a merry chase," Battersea said, still smiling.

Daphne glared up at him, which only seemed to amuse him further.

"Such lovely blue eyes but filled with such hatred. This is your fault, you know," he said, moving behind her. She had to turn her head to watch him. "If you'd only paid me what you owed."

She tried to retort that she had paid him, but she couldn't move her mouth around the cloth. Battersea reached around and yanked the cloth down about her chin.

"What was that?"

Daphne didn't waste her chance. "Help me! Help!" she screamed.

He chuckled. "Go right ahead and scream. No one will hear you, and if they do, they won't come to your aid. People keep to themselves in this part of the city."

He put his hands on her shoulders and Daphne tried to dislodge them. "Don't touch me."

"If you would simply relax, I think we will both enjoy this much more."

"Get your hands off me!" she yelled. "I paid you."

"Oh, come now, my lady. I think we both know this isn't about the blunt."

No, it had never been about the gambling debt. She could see now that even if she had somehow won that night at cards, he'd still have found a way to come for her. "What you're doing is kidnapping and rape," she said.

"We'll see," he said, sliding his hands down her back and making her skin crawl. "You might find you enjoy it."

"You might find yourself a eunuch."

He chuckled. "Perhaps we should have a drink first. We have plenty of time. We'll spend the night here and then travel to a friend's country house. My friends there will be so pleased when I show them the present I've brought."

To Daphne's relief, he released her and walked to the other side of the room. It had been dark in that corner, but he carried the lamp with him, illuminating a bed with a brass headboard and ropes tied to it. He lifted a bottle of wine sitting on the table beside it and two glasses, carrying them back to the table.

"You see," he said, setting the wine on the table. "This place has all the comforts of home." He poured two glasses then took a small vial from his waistcoat pocket and allowed a few drops to fall into one of the glasses. He pushed that one toward her.

"What is that?" she asked, nodding at the vial.

He smiled again, his thin lips stretching over his taut face. "Something to help you relax."

Daphne eyed the glass warily. She wouldn't drink it voluntarily, but she was also under no illusion that he wouldn't force it down her throat if it came to that. Her gaze drifted to the wine bottle, still half-full. It was within reach, barely.

"My husband will kill you for this," she said.

He shrugged. "I am not so easy to kill. And if he tries, I have every right to defend myself. Perhaps I will kill both of you before the Season is over. Although, if you prove especially entertaining, we may keep you for a while." He smiled again, his eyes going dark with what she assumed was anticipation of pleasure. Daphne lunged for the wine bottle, grasped it with her bound hands and threw it, barely missing Battersea's head. It crashed against the wall behind him, red wine running down the tattered hanging papers.

Battersea stared at the wine and then rounded on her. "Look what you've done." His hand flashed and she felt the hot slap across her cheek. She sat stunned for a moment as he walked to the broken bottle and began to pick up the pieces. "No gratitude," he muttered.

Daphne blinked and forced herself to concentrate. She ignored the pain in her face and moved slowly, lifting the drugged wine and changing its place with the clean glass. Her gaze fastened on Battersea while he worked, but he didn't look back at her. When he finally did, she was sitting back, looking as though she hadn't moved. He tossed the broken glass in the rubbish bin then went to the table and drank from the glass with drugged wine, his work having made him thirsty. Daphne had to fight not to smile. That was until he set the glass down.

She held her breath, afraid he would taste whatever it was he had put in the wine and know what she'd done. Instead, he lifted the clean glass and stepped toward her. "But you haven't been drinking," he said, his voice deceptively calm. "Time to have a drink."

"I don't want a drink," she said, afraid if she gave in too easily, he would suspect.

"Come now, Lady Daphne. Don't make me force this down your throat. I want no more violent outbursts from you.

Have a sip. It will calm you." He offered the cup, bringing it to her mouth. She allowed him to pour a measure into her mouth and watched him smile in triumph. "That wasn't so bad, was it? Now another." She opened her mouth again, and he poured more down her throat.

He reached for his own glass, careful not to mix the two, and sipped again. Daphne watched him intently. How long would it take for the drug to have an effect?

"Isn't this nice?" he said. He sipped his wine again then sat in the chair opposite her.

"Give me my glass," she said. "I'll drink it."

His brows rose with suspicion. "How do I know you won't throw it across the room?"

"To what end?" she said, trying to sound defeated. "You've already given me half. I feel myself drifting already." She had no idea if that was the effect of the drug, but it was as good a guess as any.

He pushed her glass across the table, and she took it between her hands, bound at the wrist.

"A toast," he said, lifting his glass. She lifted her own. "To tonight." He clinked their glasses together and drank. She drank as well, watching him over the rim of her glass. His eyes closed briefly then opened again. His brows seemed to lower as if in question, but before he could wonder at his sudden tiredness, she yawned.

"I need to lie down," she said. "I'm so weary."

"I'll take you to the bed." He rose, stumbled, and shook his head to clear it.

Daphne still said nothing, but now Battersea lifted his glass and sniffed it. He had only a little wine left at the bottom, and he stared at it. Then his dark eyes rose to hers. "What have you done?" he asked.

She widened her eyes in innocence. "Me?"

"What have you—?" He sat quite suddenly on the floor, tried to rise, and toppled over. This was her chance. Daphne rose and grasped the lantern. Where was the door that would lead out of this place? She ran toward the door, narrowly avoiding Battersea's hand when he reached out to grasp her ankle.

"What have you done?" he called, his words slurred.

Daphne yanked the door open and ran into a dark corridor. At the end of it was a steep staircase. This was the way she'd come up. She remembered stumbling over her skirts as he'd pushed her up and up. Now, she ran down the steps, opened the door at the bottom, then paused to peer out. What if Battersea's coachman waited for his master outside?

But there was no coach outside. Nothing and no one except darkness and a low rolling fog.

She stepped out of the house and onto the street. And then she began to run.

Twenty

Colin had railed at every single one of Battersea's servants until some of the maids were weeping and a few of the male servants looked ready for a fight. "Where is she?" he demanded for what might have been the fiftieth time that evening. "Where?"

"Sir," Battersea's butler said, his voice calm and ingratiating. "As we have told you, we do not know. His Lordship went to the theater. There is no lady here."

"He has her," Colin said, marching past the servants who'd lined up to stare at him. "Tell me where she is."

"FitzRoy," came a voice from the doorway. Colin spun to see Jasper standing there. Several women gasped at his masked face and dark clothing. "He wouldn't bring her here. We're wasting time."

"Where is she then?" Harley demanded, coming up behind Jasper. "We don't 'ave no clues save 'er poor bow."

Jasper cut the girl a glance and then addressed the staff again. "We're sorry to trouble you. FitzRoy, with me."

Colin didn't want to leave. He wanted answers, but he also knew when he had lost. Daphne wasn't at Battersea's town house, and if the servants knew where she was, they weren't saying. He followed Jasper out of the town house and stood on the front walk beside him. Behind them, the butler closed the door and locked it.

"Where's my horse? I need to go after her."

Jasper grasped his shoulder. "Riding off without a destination in mind will only waste time."

"He *has* her, Jasper!"

"I know," Jasper said quietly. "But you must allow me to handle this. You are too emotionally involved to think clearly."

Colin blinked at him. He had never been accused of being emotionally involved in anything before. But Jasper was right. His mind was completely scrambled. He was being led by his emotions, and that wouldn't help Daphne. And he had to find her. He couldn't lose her now. Not when he'd finally accepted that he loved her.

"We *will* find her," Jasper said, his tone reassuring. "We just need to make a few inquiries."

"I can 'elp with that," Harley volunteered. "I'm good at making inquiries." She said the word like *ink-rees*.

Jasper looked at Colin. "Who the devil is this? She followed me all the way here."

"Just an urchin I thought to bring to Neil."

"Oy! I ain't just an urchin. I know things. After all, it were me the nob paid to trick you into leaving 'Er Ladyship."

Jasper put a hand on Colin's shoulder just as he surged forward. "This might not be the best time to remind him of that," Jasper told Harley. "Still, you might prove helpful."

"How?" Colin asked.

"Where did Battersea approach you?" Jasper asked Harley.

"Wot's that mean?"

"Where did he talk to you about tricking my friend?"

"Oh, that were outside The Clipper. See, the nob 'ad 'is man watching that one"—he pointed to Colin—"and 'Er Ladyship. Following them about and reporting back."

Colin would have grabbed Harley and shook her if Jasper hadn't still been holding his shoulder. "Steady," Jasper said.

"It might have been helpful to mention something of this before," Colin said through clenched teeth.

"You didn't ask me before."

Colin took a calming breath. "I don't see how we can trust her."

"Oy! You can trust me. I didn't know 'Er Ladyship before. I want to 'elp 'er now."

"Better late than never," Jasper muttered. "But that doesn't help us discover where the earl might have taken Lady Daphne."

"Maybe 'e knows," Harley said, pointing to the corner of Battersea's town house.

"Who?" Colin asked, seeing no one.

"I saw him," Jasper said. "I think he wants us to follow him away from the eyes of those in the house."

"Who?" Colin asked again. But he followed Jasper along the gate and around the corner.

"Him." Jasper pointed to a liveried servant who beckoned them further along the lane until the row of town houses obscured Battersea's.

"Well?" Jasper asked when the servant paused. The lad was young, probably no older than sixteen, and Colin's hopes fell. He doubted this servant had the seniority to know anything of importance in Battersea's household.

"You can't tell anyone I spoke to you," the servant said in a hushed voice.

"Do we look like we're snitches?" Harley demanded, her hands perched indignantly on her hips.

The servant gave her a wary glance. "I'm talking to the gentlemen, not you, scamp."

"Oy! I ain't no scamp!" Harley demanded.

"Cease your racket or I will cease it for you," Colin snapped. Harley closed her mouth.

"I couldn't say anything in front of Rudolph," the lad said, his voice still low. "He's loyal to the earl, but I've seen some things I don't like. I'm looking for other employment. I haven't secured it yet, so I don't want to be seen talking to you."

Jasper nodded. "If what you say proves helpful, I'll make sure you receive an excellent reference. What's your name?"

"Jeremy Donnelly, my lord."

"Mr. Donnelly, do you mind telling us what you saw?" Colin asked.

Jeremy glanced toward Battersea's town house again. "Comings and goings I didn't like. A few of the maids were ill-used. I've seen that before. But there were one time…" He trailed off.

"Go ahead."

Jeremy dragged his eyes from the direction of the town house. "You said you were looking for a lady. I promise you she's not at the town house. The earl doesn't bring them to his residence anymore. At first, we thought maybe he'd reformed himself, but then Oliver—he's Battersea's tiger—told us about a house the earl keeps. It's in St. Giles. Oliver was on duty when the earl told the coachman to take him there. Oliver watched him go inside and then the coachman told him he could go get a pint because it would be awhile." Jeremy looked over his shoulder.

"Go on," Jasper said.

"There's a pub nearby. It's called the White Hart or the White Stag. I can't remember. The coachman went there, but Oliver waited by the coach. He didn't like to leave the horses. And he said…" He lowered his voice so much that Colin had to lean in to hear. He was so close to the lad he could smell the starch of his livery and the lad's fear. "He said he heard a woman crying and pleading. When Battersea came out later, he didn't bring her with him, but he told the coachman to send someone to clean it up. That's what Oliver told me he said—*send someone to clean it up*."

"That's it," Colin said. "Let's go."

Jasper held up a hand.

"Anything else we should know?"

"Just be careful. Oliver told a few of us what he saw and said he was going to tell the magistrate. I never saw Oliver again."

"Thank you," Jasper said. "We'll see your bravery in this matter is rewarded." He turned on his heel and walked back to his horse, Colin right behind him with Harley running to keep up.

"Do you know the place?" Colin asked Harley as he mounted his horse.

"I know the White 'art. It's a bad area."

Colin blanched. If Harley thought it was a bad area, then it was no place for Daphne. "Do you think you'll know the house?"

"I 'ave friends out that way. They'll know."

"Take her with us," Jasper said, turning his horse toward St. Giles. Reluctantly, Colin held his hand down to Harley.

"You want me to get on that beast?" The girl shook her head. "I'll find me own way."

"Suit yourself." Colin had no more time to waste. He followed Jasper into the rapidly falling dusk.

***

Daphne ran toward people, lights, and sound. She heard voices further up the street and headed that way. But she didn't take heed of the people she passed. Children called out to her and women in doorways eyed her with hollow eyes. Daphne ran past them all. It was rapidly growing dark, and the women and children would retreat inside. That left the men, and she could feel their eyes crawl along her body as she ran past.

Up ahead she saw the lights of a pub. She couldn't see the name, but she could smell the scents of ale and wine and hear the sound of men's voices. Surely someone there would help her. She put her head down and forced herself to hurry, not to look back to see if Battersea was following. She ran headlong into a large figure, only checking her stride when she had all but slammed into him. He caught her about her arms, and she looked up into the face of a man close to her own age but with eyes that seemed much older.

"Well, what 'ave we 'ere, lads?"

"Release me."

"Oh, did you 'ear that me fellows? 'Er Majesty said, *release me.*" He mimicked her voice, making her sound young and silly.

Daphne struggled out of his grip. "Move out of my way." But she could see now it would not be so easy. The man was not alone. He had three friends with him, and they all looked at her as though they were starving and she a four-course meal. "I said, move out of my way," she said, her brain frantically trying to come up with a way out of this mess.

"These are our streets," the leader—the man she'd bumped into and who stood far too close for comfort—told her. "I think we'd better 'elp you find yer way. Right lads?"

He looked down at her and smiled, his teeth yellow and brown. She could smell him, no matter how shallowly she tried to breathe. He smelled of garlic and the stench of unwashed bodies.

Daphne took a step back and immediately realized her mistake. Retreat would invite pursuit. And these men wanted nothing more than a lively chase. "If you touch me, you will regret it," she warned.

"Ooh. I'm trembling in me boots," one of the other men said, and they all laughed.

Daphne turned and ran. If it was a mistake, so be it. She had no other choices. She heard the laughter close behind her as the men chased her. The street, which had been full of people mere minutes before, was now all but empty. She heard the distant sound of hoofbeats, the horse and cart's progress obscured by the quickly falling darkness, and wondered if she could cross the street before it ran her over. If she could time it right, then the men would have to wait for it to pass before pursuing her. Daphne took her chance, running into the street when she saw the outline of a horse.

The beast reared up and she ducked her head, hoping the blow was swift and painless.

But no blow came, and she heard her name called. Strong arms grabbed her, and she fought them. Those men had caught her after all.

"Daphne, it's me. I have you."

She opened her eyes. Colin was before her, and coming up right behind him, leading another horse by the halter, was the masked Lord Jasper.

"Colin," she sobbed. "I have to run."

Colin grasped her face in his hands. "If you're worried about that group of ruffians, they've tucked tail and run. For the moment."

Daphne's legs gave way and she sank against Colin who lifted her into his arms and cradled her close.

"Where are you hurt? What did he do to you?"

"I'm not hurt," she sobbed. "I don't know why I'm crying."

He carried her to the side of the street, set her down, removed his coat and draped it over her shoulders. "You're in shock." He pulled her close. "You're shivering and your skin is like ice."

"You're shivering too," she said, her teeth chattering. She couldn't seem to get close enough to him. She wanted to bury her nose in his chest and inhale his scent. She never wanted his arms to release her.

"I'm in shock as well. I thought—" His voice broke, and Daphne looked up at his face in alarm. His expression was one of anguish and fear. She'd never seen so much emotion on his face before.

"I'm not hurt," she reassured him, forgetting about herself.

"I almost lost you."

"No." She cupped his face with her hands. "You'll never lose me."

"I've been such an idiot, Daphne. I didn't want to tell you I loved you." He closed his eyes. "Even now my chest hurts when I think it, when I say it. All these years I've been afraid to feel the way I felt when I lost my mother. And then when I started to have feelings for you, I was afraid you'd think me silly or lovestruck."

Daphne's ears were ringing with his words. She wasn't entirely certain she was awake at this moment. But this couldn't be a dream. In a dream, she wouldn't be sitting on a dirty stoop in the rookeries, shaking with cold while Colin confessed his love for her. "You love me?" she asked.

"I love you," he said, his voice catching slightly.

Daphne threaded her hands into his hair, wanting this to be real. Wanting this moment to never end.

"I think I loved you the first time I saw you in one of your ridiculous pink gowns with thirty-seven bows."

She laughed, the sound a bit hysterical as tears sprang to her eyes.

He cupped her cheek. "I think I fell in love with you when you told me you were on your way to St. James to gamble. It was the most outrageous idea I had ever heard, but you made me believe you could do it."

"It was a foolish idea. Thank God you talked me out of it."

He kissed the tear on her cheek and murmured, "I know I fell in love when you first kissed me."

"I still have you beat." She smiled up at him. "I fell in love with you years ago."

"I told you I'm an idiot. All this time I didn't want to love you because I was afraid I'd lose you. But tonight I realized I could lose you anyway and then you'd never know how I felt. And we'd never have this"—he kissed her lightly—"time together."

"You told me now." She kissed him back, pulling him close. He was hers. She still couldn't quite believe it, but she was beginning to hope.

Somewhere nearby a man cleared his throat. "This is quite touching, but perhaps we should move off the street before those ruffians return with friends."

Daphne felt her cheeks heat. Colin helped her to her feet, tucking her close to his side.

"I hesitate to upset you again, my lady," Jasper said, "but where is the Earl of Battersea?"

She pointed back the way she'd come. "He has a house. That's where he took me. He tried to drug me with something he'd put in wine, but I switched the cups and drugged him. I don't know how long it will last."

"Then we'd better hurry," Jasper said. "Show me the house, and I'll fetch the magistrate."

Daphne took a shaky breath. She could do this. She could walk back, show Colin and Lord Jasper where the house stood. Battersea couldn't touch her now. Colin wouldn't let him. *She* wouldn't let him.

She stood, with Colin's help. He put his hand on her back. "I'm here," he said. "I won't leave you."

Daphne looked at him, seeing in his eyes that he meant every word. She nodded and took a deep breath, starting back the way she'd come. Her legs felt like jelly, and she needed Colin's support. Then a child skipped into view.

"Found it!" Harley announced.

"Where the devil did you come from?" Colin asked.

"The nob's house. I told you I 'ave friends 'ere. They showed me where it was. I went inside too. The nob is sleeping like a baby." She gave Daphne a look of appreciation. "What did you do to 'im, Yer Ladyship?"

"He did it to himself," Daphne answered, relieved she wouldn't have to go back to the house after all. She leaned into Colin, allowing him to support her.

"Do something useful and fetch the magistrate," Jasper told Harley.

She gaped at him. "Wot you want 'im for? I ain't going near 'im, not even for ten quid."

"Never mind. I'll fetch him," Jasper said. He mounted his horse and rode away.

"I'd better go too," Harley said.

"The offer is still open," Colin called after her. "I'll take you to the orphanage."

"Naw, gov'. I like me freedom."

Daphne leaned her head on Colin's shoulder. "When this is done, we have to find her."

"I knew you would say that."

She stiffened suddenly. "I just remembered I lost Pugsly. He escaped when Battersea's man grabbed me."

"He's safe at home," Colin said. "I doubt my father will ever ask us to keep Pugsly again, though."

"Well, I won't tell if you won't."

Colin smiled. "Loyal to the end, I see. You never gave up on me, did you?" He pulled her close, looking down into her face. She forgot they were in the open, out on the street, when he held her like this.

"I gave up on you thousands of times, but as many times as I tried to stop loving you, I couldn't."

"Thank God for that." He touched his forehead to hers. "It won't be easy for you to trust me, to believe I won't run off again."

"There may be times it won't be easy for you to stay. Times when you'll want to run off." She gave him a teasing look.

"From you? Never."

She swatted him.

"But in all seriousness, you can trust that I love you, Daphne. And I'll spend every day for the rest of our lives proving that to you."

"You don't have to do that."

"There's nothing I'd like better." And he kissed her.

Twenty-One

"I cannot believe she had the nerve to show her face here," Lady Pavenley said in a not so quiet whisper.

"She should be hiding her face in shame," Lady Isabella agreed.

Daphne stepped out from the potted plant separating her from her former friends. It was the first ball she'd attended in a fortnight, and Colin had gone to fetch her a glass of champagne. Obviously, the gossip had been raging in her absence.

"Enjoying your evening?" she asked Lady Pavenley and Lady Isabella.

They both stiffened.

"I did hear you, in case you were wondering. But I don't see why I should be ashamed." She plucked at one of the pale blue bows adorning her sapphire blue dress. "It's not my fault Battersea abducted me. And if he hadn't, the information about the other women he took to that house and abused would not have come to light. Nor would Captain Gladwell have testified about the insurance fraud the earl perpetrated." Daphne looked at her nails. "I do believe the Lords might just find the earl guilty of his crimes. And when that happens, my husband has promised to host a grand ball. I'll tell him to take your names off the guest list."

"Lady Daphne," Lady Pavenley said, her tone placating. "I'm afraid you misunderstood."

"No, I think you did," Daphne said. "I never liked you— either of you—and I should have told you long before. Now, if you'll excuse me, I promised Mr. Murray a dance."

"The Scotsman!" Lady Isabella exclaimed. "He's practically feral."

"Then I don't suppose you want an introduction. I promised to introduce him to the *ton*. By the time I am through, he will be the most sought-after gentleman in London."

"I'd like to see that," Lady Pavenley sneered.

Daphne would like to see it too. She'd never really exerted her social power before. Now was as good a time as any. If she'd been sweet and kind, she would have said it was because poor Mr. Murray needed a wife. The truth was he'd become a daily fixture in her dining room, and the cook was complaining at how much he ate. It was time to send him back to Scotland, time to have Colin all to herself.

Because Colin was hers now. He trusted her with his heart, and she was learning to trust him with hers.

***

Daphne danced with Mr. Murray and then with Colin not once, but twice. He'd tried to convince her to leave after their first dance, pointing out that dancing with one's own husband was exceedingly gauche. But Daphne retorted that as the daughter of a duke and the wife of a war hero, she was in no danger of censure. Finally, sometime after midnight, Colin convinced his wife to leave the ball and go home with him. He didn't care for dancing, but he had to admit, Daphne was an exceptional dancer. And she had looked too beautiful to resist. Her new blue gown made her skin luminous, and her eyes shone brighter than ever. The dress showed far too much of her body, but then that was the current style. And he certainly liked how easy the current style made undressing his wife. Currently, she stood before him in a chemise, stockings, and nothing else.

"I don't think I'll go to many more events this Season," she told him, sipping her wine before putting it on the table and moving to unfasten his cravat. "I've had enough excitement and gossip for a while."

Colin raised a brow. He had no doubt she would change her mind about staying home when the next invitation arrived, but for the moment, he had her all to himself. She dragged his neck cloth free and unfastened his collar.

"I introduced Mr. Murray to half a dozen young ladies tonight. Certainly, I have done my duty."

"You have been most generous," he said, his voice low and heated. "Even Duncan was surprised when you agreed to help him."

"I have my reasons," she said. "I like having you all to myself." One sleeve of her chemise had fallen off her shoulder, revealing most of her lovely round breast, and Colin was suddenly quite impatient to have his hands on her. He pulled her close and kissed her. Daphne kissed him back, laughing. "I'm still undressing you."

"Later," he said, kissing her again. "I'm impatient to touch you."

"And what about me? I want to touch you."

"Later," he said again, pushing her back against the bed and tugging her chemise down about her waist.

Later, when they were both naked and flushed, and she lay warm and curled against him, he leaned close, heart pounding, and whispered in her ear. "I love you, Daphne."

For just a moment, a bubble of panic rose up and threatened to choke him, and then she murmured. "I love you too, Colin." And she snuggled closer and sighed. He sighed too, his body relaxing and his heart full.

When he'd hired young Jeremy Donnelly at Colin's suggestion, the Duke of Mayne had remarked that he saw a change in Colin. Neil Wraxall said the same when he'd introduced Harley to him, though they hadn't yet convinced her to leave her life on the streets behind. Colin was beginning to see it too. He smiled more. He laughed easily. He didn't push his emotions away as often.

And tonight, he let them wash over him like Daphne's scent. He thought he might just recognize the emotion he felt at the moment—pure, unadulterated joy.

About Shana Galen

Shana Galen is three-time Rita award nominee and the bestselling author of passionate Regency romps. "The road to happily-ever-after is intense, conflicted, suspenseful and fun," and *RT Bookreviews* calls her books "lighthearted yet poignant, humorous yet touching." She taught English at the middle and high school level off and on for eleven years. Most of those years were spent working in Houston's inner city. Now she writes full time, surrounded by three cats and one spoiled dog. She's happily married and has a daughter who is most definitely a romance heroine in the making.

Would you like exclusive content, book news, and a chance to win early copies of Shana's books? Sign up for monthly emails at her website for exclusive news and giveaways

Keep reading for an excerpt from The Highlander's Excellent Adventure, on sale September 8, 2020!

Ines

"She is an unmarried young lady," her brother-in-law said. "It's absolutely out of the question."

Ines narrowed her eyes in annoyance, even though neither Benedict Draven nor her sister, Catarina, could see her. She was eavesdropping. Again. She hadn't meant to—not this time. She'd been passing by the drawing room and heard her name. She'd promised herself she wouldn't eavesdrop on her sister and brother-in-law. They were married and deserved their privacy. But that promise did not apply in case of emergency. And this obviously qualified as an emergency as their discussion pertained to her future.

"We cannot keep her here, under lock and key, forever," Catarina said calmly. "She is young and wants some independence. It is not as though she is one of your fine Society ladies. She is a lacemaker."

"She's part of my family now, and I won't have her living alone above the shop. Even if I thought it was safe, you know her temperament."

Ines bristled but restrained herself from interjecting as that would only prove Draven's point.

"I was a bit wild at her age too," Catarina said, a smile in her voice. "If you remember."

Draven made a sound of dismissal. "That was war, and you were desperate."

"Yes, desperate to escape an arranged marriage to a cruel old man."

Ines nodded her head—she'd been facing a similar fate at one time. She'd run away with Catarina when, at the tender age of fourteen, their father had tried to marry her to one of his friends. She didn't like to think of how close she'd come to being trapped forever. Of course, when she'd escaped, she'd thought she was embarking on an exhilarating adventure. The reality was hours of detailed work in the back of a shop with other lacemakers. Her only excitement had been attending mass on Sundays. Ines ran a finger over a rough piece of paint on the wall and scratched at it as Draven spoke again.

"Why don't we see how things progress with Mr. Podmore?"

Podmore. Ines almost retched aloud. Mr. Podmore must be the most tedious person in London, if not the whole of England. Probably the entire world. He was forever going on about carriages. He was a successful cartwright, and his conveyances were known for their sturdiness and reliability. He'd once spoken for a quarter hour, uninterrupted, on the importance of wheel spokes. Ines had almost fallen asleep. She would never allow herself to be pushed into a marriage with a man like Podmore. She wanted passion, excitement…danger.

"I am afraid the interest there is all on one side," Catarina said. "But perhaps if they pursue an enjoyable activity together, it might help. I will suggest a ride in the park when he arrives today."

Ines started. Podmore was to call on her today? *Caramba!* She had to escape before he arrived or she might be trapped with him for hours, and she simply could not listen to another monologue on wheel spokes.

Ines stepped back and bumped into someone. She spun around and stared into the face of Ward, Draven's butler. He was only a little taller than she. His head was bald, but a shadow of stubble darkened his cheeks. "Ward!" she hissed. "What are you doing there?"

It was a ridiculous question. Ward was everywhere. One never knew when or where he would turn up.

The butler raised a brow. "I might ask you the same question, Miss Neves."

She blew out a breath. This was why she wanted to live above the shop. There was no privacy here. Her color rose as she realized how hypocritical that thought was considering she was the one eavesdropping.

On the other hand, Ward was eavesdropping as well... Ines straightened her shoulders. "I will pretend I did not see you, if you pretend you did not see me."

"Happily, miss."

Ines started for the front door, but Ward cleared his throat. She turned back. "What is it now?"

"Mr. Murray will arrive and knock on the door any moment. I suggest you exit another way."

Ines had no idea how Ward always knew who was coming and who was going and when they would appear, but she was too stunned by the mention of Duncan Murray to say anything.

The image of the Scotsman immediately flashed into her mind. All she had was his image as she had never been introduced to him. Ines had only glimpsed him through cracks in doorways. But those quick peeks had shown her quite enough to arouse her interest. He was tall, oh so wonderfully tall, and big and strong. She liked big men, men who had to turn to the side to fit their shoulders through the door and duck under the lintel to avoid banging their head. Mr. Murray had thick arms and legs—she'd seen his legs because he often wore a kilt. They were muscled and covered by brown hair. He had quite a lot of hair. The hair on his head was long enough to pull back in a queue, which was how he wore it when he visited. But she imagined untying the piece of leather securing his hair and running her hands through the freed locks. Then maybe he'd kiss her with those lips that always seemed to give everyone a mocking half smile. She'd feel the bristle of his two days' worth of stubble.

She didn't need to have met him to know he was a man of passion, excitement, and danger.

"Are you well, Miss Neves?" Ward asked.

Ines realized she'd been standing still, staring off into space. "Yes, why?" she asked quickly.

"Your face has gone red and your breathing has quickened."

"I am thirsty," she said, putting her hands to her hot cheeks. "I think I shall go to the kitchens and ask for a cup of tea." She walked away as rapidly as she could, certain Ward had known exactly what was causing her cheeks to color.

Once in the kitchen, she didn't see the cook, and she set about heating water to make her own cup of tea. She didn't really want any tea, but she needed something to do while she calmed her thoughts.

She had to hide somewhere until Podmore had gone. But if she left, she would miss the chance to spy on Mr. Murray's arrival. She would have to sneak around because Benedict always met with the Scot in private. Ines had once overheard—very well, *listened in*—when Catarina told Draven that Murray was wild and would be a bad influence on Ines. Benedict had said that of course he was. That was why the troop had called him the Lunatic. A description like that only made Duncan Murray more intriguing.

She *had* to find a way to meet him one day.

Ines heard a carriage stop outside the house and groaned aloud. Today would not be that day, obviously. Murray always came on a horse. Podmore always came in a carriage. He had several—a gig, a curricle, a barouche. She knew all about them. She had to escape now or she'd be forced to spend the afternoon with him, and it was such a lovely afternoon—warm and sunny and far too pretty to spend with dull Mr. Podmore. If she could avoid him today, she would be spared his company for the next few days as tomorrow her family was to travel to the country for the wedding of the sister of the Duke of Mayne.

Ines left the cup of tea brewing on the table, wiped her hands on the apron, and crossed the room to the courtyard door. She opened it, peeked out, and when she didn't see any of the servants about, stepped outside and closed the door behind her. Sheets and table linens hung on a line to dry and a half-painted chair had been abandoned in a corner. She could hide here for a little while, but a few sheets would not provide much cover. She had to find somewhere Catarina wouldn't think to look.

She heard a coachman speak to the horses out on the street, and an idea came to her. She would hide in Podmore's carriage. No one would look for her there. She could hide inside until Podmore came back, then slip out the opposite side when he returned. She would miss his visit completely.

Pleased with her plan, Ines opened the courtyard gate, slipped outside, and went around the side of the house, where she spotted the carriage. It didn't look exactly like the one Podmore had showed her last time. It wasn't as shiny and didn't have gold accents. This was much plainer, though she was certain he could make it sound like the most amazing carriage ever constructed.

The coachman had left his box and was speaking with a deliveryman nearby. His absence made Ines's task easier. She walked to the door of the coach, careful to stay low so the coachman would not see her through the windows. But even that was not a worry as the coach's curtains were closed. She opened one door, slipped inside, and closed it again. In the darkness, she couldn't help but smile at her own cunning.

She sat back, prepared to wait until she heard Podmore returning. The squabs were comfortable but not as luxurious as she'd anticipated. Where was the velvet Podmore insisted upon? Perhaps he had realized that velvet seats in summer were far too warm. The heat in the closed space was already making her uncomfortable and sleepy.

A few minutes passed, and then a few more, and she heard the coachman climb back on his box. The coach started moving a few minutes later, which was to be expected. They were looking for her inside the house, and Podmore would not want his horses to stand for too long.

Ines was rather used to riding in coaches now, though she had never even seen a coach in the tiny village where she'd grown up. But even after having ridden in coaches dozens of times the past five years, she still enjoyed the feeling of being carried by a momentum not her own. She closed her heavy eyes and waited for the horses to come to a stop outside Draven's house again. She should probably hop out as soon as the coach stopped. Podmore would have given up on her by now and might be waiting for his coach to carry him home. She would exit on the street and try to sneak back into the house via the courtyard.

Catarina would scold her, but Ines was not sorry. She had told her sister she did not care for Mr. Podmore and that she did not wish to marry any man that she didn't love. She wanted a man who could offer passion, excitement, and—Catarina usually cut her off by then. Her sister treated Ines's pronouncement the same way she treated Ines's requests to move to the little room above the lace shop: with a big sigh. Her older sister seemed to forget that when she had been only a little older than Ines, she had run off on her own and tried to find a husband to save her from the marriage her father had arranged. Not long after, Catarina had swooped in the night before Ines was to be married and offered to take Ines with her to Spain. Ines had agreed, eager to escape a life she hadn't wanted. But now, when Ines craved a little freedom of her own, Catarina still treated her like the girl of only fourteen.

The way Catarina babied her infuriated Ines, but emotional scenes did not sway Catarina. They'd grown up with a violent father who often screamed and yelled for hours. That was before he used his fists. Catarina was not impressed if Ines yelled or stamped her foot or even if she cried. Ines was not ashamed to admit she'd tried all three tactics. Now she would have to think of something else. Perhaps if she took on more responsibility at the lace shop. She could prove that she could be trusted with greater obligations. She pondered that idea for a little while.

She must have fallen asleep because when she jerked awake, she was surprised to find her muscles stiff, as though she had been in the same position for some time. Then she noticed the heat of the day had faded and the noise of London, a noise she had become so accustomed to, had quieted. At the same time, she realized the carriage was still moving. Why was it still moving? Wouldn't the coachman have just made a circle or two and returned to her home to collect Podmore? Ines snatched open the curtains closest to her and stared out into a field dotted with sheep. She opened the curtains on the other side, heart pounding, and stared at a small cottage.

This was not London.

This was not Podmore's coach.

Buy now!

Printed in the USA
CPSIA information can be obtained
at www.ICGtesting.com
CBHW071625010724
10952CB00032B/312